OKSANA,
BEHAVE!   A NOVEL

MARIA
KUZNETSOVA

SPI
EGE
L&G
RAU

SPIEGEL & GRAU
NEW YORK

Published in the United States by Spiegel & Grau,
an imprint of Random House, a division of
Penguin Random House LLC, New York.

SPIEGEL & GRAU and colophon is a
registered trademark of
Penguin Random House LLC.

The following chapters appear, in different form,
in literary journals: "I Pledge Allegiance to the Butterfly"
in *McSweeney's Quarterly Concern*, "Light Year" in
Kenyon Review Online, and "The Yalta Conference"
in *The Southern Review.*

LIBRARY OF CONGRESS CATALOGING-IN-PUBLICATION DATA
Names: Kuznetsova, Maria, author.
Title: Oksana, behave!: a novel / by Maria Kuznetsova.
Description: New York: Spiegel & Grau, [2019]
Identifiers: LCCN 2018021375| ISBN 9780525511878 | ISBN
9780525511885 (ebook)
Subjects: LCSH: Russian Americans—Fiction
Classification: LCC PS3611.U985 O46 2019 | DDC 813/.6—dc23
LC record available at https://lccn.loc.gov/2018021375

Printed in the United States of America on acid-free paper

spiegelandgrau.com
randomhousebooks.com

9 8 7 6 5 4 3 2 1

First Edition

Book design by Elizabeth A. D. Eno

To my parents

You never reach any truth without making fourteen mistakes and very likely a hundred and fourteen.

—Fyodor Dostoyevsky, *Crime and Punishment*

CONTENTS

OKSANA,
BEHAVE!

1992, KIEV, UKRAINE

After I asked what America would be like, my grand-mother sighed philosophically and released a mouth-ful of smoke out the passenger window. "America, Ukraine, it's all the same in the end," Baba said, as her brother, Boris, drove us to the station. "We just need a change, that's all. Some things will be better in America, and some will be worse," she declared, taking another drag on her cigarette. "But think of all the men!"

I was only seven, so this wasn't much of a selling point. Mama and Papa were quiet on either side of me in the back seat, offering no consolation or clarification. For the last few months, they had stayed up late whispering about leaving Kiev, and during the day, they left to say goodbye to friends until it was our turn to go, when their remain-ing friends came over to say goodbye to us. I didn't really know why we were leaving. All I knew was that we were at the start of a long journey that would end in a place called Florida, a land of beaches and theme parks. And now we were speeding by the Dnieper River and the rolling hills and maple trees I couldn't imagine living without, even on this gray November day.

"When will we be back?" I said.

"Never," Mama answered.

"Very soon, darling," Papa said.

"In a while, foolish child," said Baba, "when our hearts are healed and hungry for this place once more."

"Will our hearts be healed by New Year's?" I asked. I had been looking forward to my school's New Year's party, where the teachers let me run around without punishing me, and where I could steal a few tangerines and chocolates when they weren't looking.

"Do not be sad, Oksana," Papa said, though he seemed quite sad himself. "Kiev is in your soul. You can return there anytime you want." He tapped my heart for emphasis.

"Dearest God I don't believe in," Mama said, shaking her head. "What did I do to deserve such a silly child? Who cares about Kiev, darling? You have your family with you, lucky fool. Everything you need is right here."

Baba pointed her cigarette at me. "You know what your problem is?" she said.

"Having an annoying family?" I asked.

"You ask too many questions. What's there to know, little idiot? You are born, you have some laughs and a rendezvous or two, and then you fall into the void. Just try to enjoy the ride, darling," she added before turning away.

I didn't see it at the time, but everyone's conduct during the rest of the drive captured their distinct approaches to life. There was Papa watching the Dnieper flow by, with longing and misty eyes. Mama with her hands on her lap, looking forward and wishing we'd hurry up already. Baba fluffing her bright-red hair and scoping out the romantic prospects on the street. Her brother, Boris, driving with a smirk, not caring about the lipstick on his collar, the high heel in his back seat, or about staying behind.

And then there was me, always in the dark, not knowing that this was the last day all of us would ever spend in Kiev together or that Florida would just be the first stop in a series of places I would try to call home—stomping and howling, desperate for someone to tell me what would happen next.

I PLEDGE ALLEGIANCE
TO THE BUTTERFLY

We had been living in Gainesville, Florida, for a year when Officer Friendly told my third-grade class that you could call 911 from home and the cops would show up right away. Nobody else seemed as stunned by his revelation as I was, but that was no surprise. I had been released from ESL at the start of my second school year in America, and there were a lot of things I was slow to learn.

Like, for example, why people called me "Rod." I thought it was because I was Russian or just scrawny, but one day Billy Spencer sang, "Have I told you lately that I love you . . ." at me and I figured out it was Rod for Rod Stewart because I had a bit of a mullet. Mama chopped it off, but the name stuck. The only people who used my real name were my teacher—Mrs. Thomas—and my ESL friend, Raluca, or I should say ex-friend, because she moved back to Romania over the summer without telling me. I tried not to take it personally.

Cassandra called me "Okey Dokey," which was definitely closer to Oksana than "Rod." We only talked after class, when we walked to the lobby so she could get picked up by her mom and I could cross the street to meet my grandmother behind the clump of palm trees where I made her wait.

But the day after the officer's visit, Baba was flirting with Mr. Trevors, the crossing guard, by the front entrance, dangerously on display. Kids swarmed around like the ants in our kitchen, looking for their buses or parents or just their friends to walk home with, and nobody seemed to notice her. Baba squeezed the crossing guard's arm, her fiery hair flying in all directions, her purple dress flailing about her high-heeled veiny legs.

Cassandra spotted her and said, "Yuck. Your mom is even older than my mom."

"That's my grandma."

"Oh," she said, disappointed. "How old is she anyway?"

I knew my parents were thirty-one, but I had no idea how old Baba was. "No clue. Eighty, ninety, something like that," I said. No one at school had spotted her before, and it made me twitch. I said, "You really think if I call the cops they'll come?"

Her eyes grew wide. "Yes, yes," she said. "Call the cops!"

"What do I say?"

She rubbed her hands together. "Say, 'Help! My grandma is trying to kill me!'"

"All right," I said. As Baba caressed Mr. Trevors's arms and then his STOP sign, it sounded like the truth.

"Okeydokey, Okey Dokey. I'm flying away," Cassandra said, flapping her hands like wings, which had to do with her saying the Pledge of Allegiance to the butterfly instead of the flag every morning, a ritual that baffled and intrigued me. She flew off to her mom, a silver-haired lady who waited for her in a Jeep, merciful enough to never step out and embarrass her.

But Baba had no mercy for me. I approached her with my head down, incognito. Thankfully she had taken a step away from her prospect.

Mr. Trevors was a nice bald war veteran. He lifted a hand at us and said, "Have a nice day, Sveta! Have a nice day, Rod—I mean Oksana!"

Baba winked and strutted away. She leaned toward me and said, "Such biceps!"

"A cop came to class," I told her. "He was nice."

"Some are," she said. Then she told a boring story about one summer in Odessa in 1957 when a police officer named Bobik wrote a song about her legs.

The sun baked us along Main Street, also known as Prostitute Street. It was covered in broken glass and only had a couple of palms for shade. It ran along the Pick'n Save, where Baba took me to get a doll once a month, Dick's Adult Video, and a gas station with an inflatable alligator in front of it. Lizards scattered at our feet. There were always a few kingdoms on the ground, little deflated balloons. Men put them over their things to have sex with the prostitutes.

I never saw actual prostitutes there, but sometimes men would honk or slow down and shout at Baba and she didn't know why. Mama and Papa said not to tell her, because she needed the attention since her daughter had just died, her husband had kicked it a while back, her father had been purged, her morning work at the lab was unpaid, the Soviet Union had just collapsed, she had to share a room with me, her family had been gutted by fascism, the world was cruel and unwelcoming, et cetera.

She got one honk and tittered. "Your grandma still has it all, doesn't she?"

"Are you eighty or ninety?"

She laughed. "Eighty or ninety what, dear child?" She realized what I meant and pretended to choke me. "Fifty-five years young. Hardly old at all, infinite imbecile!" She walked a few steps ahead of me the rest of the way.

When we got home, I knew Mama was napping, because it was quiet. If the TV was on, then she was applying for accountant jobs or trying to learn English or silently weeping or calling her best friend, Valentina, who lived in a place called New Jersey. Everyone my parents knew back in Ukraine was in New Jersey now, except Mama's mom, who had stayed in Kiev because "her mind was too troubled," but we were in Florida because that was where Papa found a job as a physicist for the university. It didn't seem like such a great job to me, because he also had to deliver pizza for Dino's.

I went to the room I shared with Baba, while she smoked on the patio. The carpet was brown and crawling with cicadas, and the walls displayed a photo of Baryshnikov framed in a heart and her dead daughter's painting of the Dnieper, a dark-blue river with a white sandy beach on its far side, a place where I had loved to swim. Our beds were separated by a nightstand with a sad photo and letters from Baba's suitors from Kiev on it; if she was in a good mood, she'd read me choice passages before she wrote back with a demented smile on her face. If she was not in a good mood, then she would bring a glass of cognac into the room after dinner and stare at the river painting until she decided to turn the lights off. My only possessions were the pile of dolls by my bed and the tower of *Sweet Valley High* and *Boxcar Children* books Mama brought me from the library.

Baba's cigarette smoke wafted through the window. I had to act fast before I lost my nerve. I took a breath and put my hand on the receiver and pictured Officer Friendly in his blue uniform. He was tall and handsome and he had a mustache and winked at me when I said, "You'll really be there if I need help?" I imagined Cassandra clapping her hands and dialed.

"Nine-one-one, what's your emergency?" said a lady's voice.

"Um," I said. "I just wanted to see if this worked?"

"Honey, is there an adult I can talk to?"

"Nobody here speaks English," I said, hanging up. I had done it! My heart pounded wildly. Then the phone rang again and I picked it up.

"May I please speak to your mother or father?"

I hung up again. It rang a third time, and I heard Mama grab it. She used her careful English voice, which was nothing like her Russian voice; she seemed nice in English.

"Oksana Ivanovna Konnikova," she called. I approached her with my best angel face. Her skin was paler than usual, making her dark eyes and hair look even more striking. She was tragically beautiful and her eyes were filled with desperate rage. I was tan, sandy haired, and hideous. "Tell this lady nothing is wrong here," Mama said. She shoved the phone in my direction and it looked like a weapon, like a rocket launcher from *Doom*. Outside, Baba crushed her cigarette with her heel, and as she opened the sliding glass door and entered the apartment, she looked menacing too. I screamed wildly.

"Help!" I cried. "My grandmother is trying to kill me! Help!"

I wept and choked and ran out to the back porch and past the SUN BAY APARTMENTS sign and the pool, all the way to the lake with the mossy trees and smelly ducks. I stared at the water, remembering swimming in the Dnieper, which flowed outside our Kiev apartment, where I slept in the living room that doubled as a bedroom with Mama and Papa while my grandmother lived on the other side of the city and nobody ever called me Rod. I wasn't there long when Mama dragged me away by the ear.

"Dearest God I don't believe in," she said. "Tell me, what have I done to deserve this child? Did I commit murder in a past life I don't believe in? Genocide? Was I Stalin himself? Did I smother a litter of puppies?" She glared at me as we approached the apartment building, which was three stories tall and made of ugly red-orange bricks that were pretty much the same color as Baba's dyed hair. "The police are on their way, poor idiot. You must tell them everything is normal."

Baba was sitting in a plastic chair and drinking cognac on the patio, thrilled by this turn of events. Papa was in his Dino's uniform, eating pizza standing up; there was sauce on his nose. His light-brown poofy hair was matted from the Dino's hat he had to wear on the job.

Baba wagged a finger at me and said, "*I* was young and sharp once, but *you* are young and dim-witted, and one day you will be *old* and dim-witted, don't you see?"

She lifted her glass and smiled slyly. "I hope your officer has a nice juicy rump!" she added, squeezing the air with her hand for emphasis. Papa dropped his slice on the cement below him, shrugged, and picked it up and ate it anyway.

"You see?" Mama said. "Normal family."

They were knocking as soon as we walked into the apartment. The woman had short hair and the man was definitely not Officer Friendly, or even friendly. Officer Friendly was young and energetic, and this was a tired bearded man. He greeted my parents curtly and walked over to me.

"Do you realize what you've done, young lady? We could be spending our time helping people who actually need it," he said.

"Who says I don't need help?" I said.

"We are profoundly sorry," Papa said, stepping in front of me.

"Quite profoundly," Baba said, circling the man like a vulture.

"Tea?" Mama asked, but they did not look like they wanted tea.

The officer inspected the apartment—the coffee table we ate dinner on, the lawn furniture we used inside, the squat old radio with its foil antennae, which sat on a plastic crate below a poster Papa had hung up that said, IT'S NOT ALWAYS THIS MESSY HERE . . . SOMETIMES IT'S WORSE, the stained green couch that sank to the floor, and a rather severe three-headed self-portrait of Papa's dead sister, which was a part of what Baba called the "unfortunate experimental period" that characterized her final artistic years. Then he studied Mama and Papa and Baba, who, with their thick accents and garage-sale clothes, were probably even weirder to him than our apartment. I tried to make eye contact to show I was not happy being tied to this place or these people, but he didn't look at me. Though when he finished his inspection, he squatted next to me until we were eye to eye.

"Do we understand each other?" he said.

"No calling unless I need help," I said. I didn't know what else to do, so I saluted him.

"Enjoy your day," said the female officer, and they were gone. It was already getting dark out. The cicadas chirped. I had messed up big time, but I was thrilled.

"What were you thinking, you fool?" Baba said. "They could throw you in jail!"

"This feels like jail," I noted, and Mama sent me to my room without dinner.

Baba entered hours later, sneaking me a chicken cutlet sandwich, which I devoured in three bites. She was energized by the officers' visit, so she read me a letter from a suitor named Anatoly, who called her breasts "the world's ripest melons," and then she turned off the lights. When she was feeling particularly happy, she'd end the night with her favorite declaration.

"Good night, little fool," she said, reaching over to tousle my hair. "Another day closer to oblivion, here we go."

At lunch, I sat with Cassandra instead of alone for once. She had greasy blond hair and freckles and wore dresses that were so big they could have belonged to her mother. Billy Spencer grinned a wild dog's grin at me, like he was amused I had a friend, but I didn't care. Cassandra looked up from her PB&J and didn't tell me to go away, so I told her about the cops.

"What did you say?"

"I said my grandma was killing me."

She paused with her sandwich in midair, jelly dripping on her paper bag. "I didn't think you'd go through with it. You get in trouble?"

"Had to skip dinner, but food at home sucks anyway."

"Not bad, Okey Dokey."

I opened my lunch box, which had a slew of items Mama put in just to torture me: crackers with cream cheese, a hard-boiled egg, and a tomato, which were nearly redeemed by a container of herring. The cream cheese was always smeared all over the box.

Cassandra peeked inside and frowned at the herring. "Meat," she said, which wasn't technically true but I didn't correct her. "I never eat meat," she said, scrunching up her face like I was involved in something truly disgusting. I was relieved when she changed course after that. "You find out how old your grandma was?" she said.

"Fifty-five," I said, and she nodded slowly and took the last bite of her sandwich.

"My mom is forty-eight. She adopted me."

"How old is your dad?"

"No dad, no dad," she said gleefully, almost singing the words.

"You just live with your mom?"

"Basically," she said. "We barely talk, because she's always working. She sucks."

"You're lucky. My mom's always home. My grandma too."

"How annoying," she said, biting my tomato. I dipped my finger in a smear of cream cheese and licked it up. Cassandra did the same and looked like she wanted me to keep talking.

"Mama and Baba are always home but we never *do* anything. When my dad said we were moving to Florida, he was all, like, 'The beach, the beach, we'll spend so much time at the beach,' but we barely go. Anytime I ask they're, like, 'We're too tired.' And I'm, like, 'What's the point of living here if we never even go to the beach?'"

She nodded with great understanding. "Family," she said, and then she shook her head like an ancient person.

Papa brought home an unclaimed pizza from Dino's a few days later and set it on the coffee table. The table had come with the apartment; somebody had scratched FUK SUN BAY in its center. We ate on plates that said FAT IS BEAUTIFUL, which Baba had bought at a garage sale before she knew what it meant. We ate sitting on the floor with Papa's three-headed sister staring down at us.

Mama poured vodka for Papa and Baba, Sunkist for me, and tea for herself. She had been throwing up for the past few mornings and said she would switch to tea until she felt better. A jar of sauerkraut appeared out of nowhere, and so did a few boiled hot dogs and sliced tomato and cucumber. The cheese pizza looked a little roughed up. I bit into my slice and spat it out when I realized it was meat. I remembered the face Cassandra had made at my herring, as if eating meat would be as bad as biting into a cicada.

"Yuck!" I said. "There's sausage in here."

"Since when don't you like sausage? What you are given, you will eat," Mama said.

"I'm sorry, darling. I should have warned you," Papa said.

"I'll just pick it off," I said, avoiding Mama's glare. "It was a surprise, that's all."

"A surprise?" Baba said. "Ha! You know what was a surprise? Once, when my family was starving to death after the Nazis occupied Kiev, Mama baked a delicious meat pie. My brother and I said, 'Mamachka, what's in this pie? It's so savory.' And she told us it was old Syomka, the family dog. She said, 'Syomka is with us forever now,'" Baba said, laughing as she slapped the table. I spit up my cucumber.

"Oksana, behave!" Mama said. "Do not waste food."

"That's disgusting," I said.

"Disgusting?" said Baba, not without glee. "It was life, dear child. We got through the war, didn't we?" she said. "It was kind of beautiful, in fact. Mama was right. I never forgot that poor creature."

"A touching story of sacrifice," Papa said to his mother, forking a tomato.

After dinner, I waited for Papa to finish pasting a few more pictures of himself and his father and other long-dead relatives into his latest photo album so he could read *Evgeny Onegin* to me in Russian for the Mama-mandated thirty minutes and we could play *Doom* as a reward. We played and played, blasting every last hunchbacked monster and zombie in the dark caverns of an abandoned laboratory, until Baba said it was bedtime and I followed her into our room.

Her bed was too close to mine; I could reach out and

touch her if I wanted to. She picked up the photo on our nightstand, which showed her, my grandpa, Papa, and his sister holding baskets of mushrooms in the woods. Two-fourths of the people in the photo were dead, which I recently learned could be simplified to one-half. According to Baba, my grandpa had died of "being a Soviet male" when Papa was a teenager, and Papa's older sister had died of a weak heart just months before we'd left Kiev.

Alla had been a painter. She had long bushy brown hair and a loud laugh and wore thick black glasses. She'd lived with my grandmother and was always painting on her balcony, with various arty friends wandering in and out of the apartment. But at the end of her life, she'd just turned into a sick woman who smelled dusty and sour, to whom I had to bring medicine in a dark, quiet room while the adults spoke in whispers. When I heard I'd have to share a room with Baba in America, I worried that she would smell like dying, like her daughter did, but she only smelled like too many flowers.

I couldn't sleep. I hugged my doll Lacy and thought of all the dead people I had known and had not known. The police sirens wouldn't stop wailing, drowning out the insistent shrieks of the cicadas.

"The police came to my house once," Baba said after a while. "The secret police, in fact. This was just before the war. I was only half your age, darling. They came in the middle of the night and took my father away."

I waited for her to tell me what happened next. It took me a moment to understand there was no more story.

———

I went on a late drive with Papa the next weekend. Our car was a brown Mercury with a tan roof with holes Mama had taped up, and Papa was proud of it. He had never had a car or driven before we got to America. He played *The White Album* and we zipped along the highway with the windows down, hot air blowing in our faces. We picked up two hitchhikers, a couple who said they'd just gotten married. Mama hated when he did this, but Papa said he had a car, he had gas, and goddamn it if he wasn't going to help people go places.

"We won't forget this," the man said when we dropped them off near St. Augustine. We drove a little farther and parked in a deserted lot and walked across a wooden bridge toward the water. It was oily and ominous, a monster that could swallow me whole, but a dark beach was better than no beach. Papa held my hand as we passed an abandoned towel and a bunch of empty beer bottles to get closer to the shore. A bonfire blazed in the distance, the flames eating up the darkness.

"It's not all bad here, is it, Oksana?" he said.

"I like the beach. I wish we could go during the day."

"Soon, child. Soon." He looked up at the sky. "My father used to take my sister and me out to the country to look at the stars, at the constellations. I have forgotten most of their names. Though there's Orion," he said, pointing out the archer and his belt. He lit a cigarette.

"Papa?" I said after a while. "What's it like to have someone close to you die?"

He looked at the stars again as if they could give him an answer. The waves licked the shore and the tops of my feet.

"Sad," he said, and then he put out his cigarette and said it was time to go back.

He drove without saying anything. *The White Album* finished but he didn't turn the tape over. He spoke again when we were almost home.

"When you lose someone you love, they stay with you. My father and sister—they are always nearby. I can picture how they would react to almost anything, and sometimes I even talk to them. My sister loves pointing out the beauty of the landscape, and my father just says he is proud of me for plugging along in this strange land. I can conjure them up almost anytime I want. So in that way, it's not so sad, kitten, because I am never alone."

This made me spring up, like there was a serial killer in the back seat ready to slit our throats. Or, worse, a two-headed grandfather-aunt monster coming for us both. The hair on my arms stood up. I peeked behind me, but no one was coming for us yet.

Cassandra came home with Baba and me after school one day. As we walked down Prostitute Street, Baba got three honks and tossed her hair. She had started dating Mr. Trevors, but it didn't stop her from having fun. Cassandra thought it was hilarious Baba didn't know about Prostitute Street.

"I get younger by the minute, don't you see?" Baba said.

"Definitely," my friend said. Baba pinched Cassandra's cheeks and declared her a good influence.

Every morning, as sad Principal Bates said the Pledge

over the loudspeaker, Cassandra and I held hands and said the Pledge to the butterfly. Sometimes we would mix it up and say the Pledge to the pumpkin instead, since it was October. Mrs. Thomas would roll her eyes and say, "Silly hippies. Flower children," but she didn't punish us.

When Cassandra entered my room, she sneered, and I thought it was because I shared it with Baba, but it was because of my dolls.

"Dolls are stupid, Okey Dokey. They're just there to make you think all you're good for is having babies. That's what my mom says."

"I thought you don't care about your mom," I said. I saw this was the wrong answer and said, "Yuck. I hate babies."

"Do you even know how babies are made?" she said.

"Duh." I said a man and woman get naked and roll around under sheets and moan sometimes because it hurts. I didn't mention the kingdom, because I didn't know what the man put it on for.

"The man puts his thing in the woman's hole and squirts into it," she said.

I gasped and put my hands to my private parts. I would never do something so disgusting. I slowly released my hands and the world came into terrible focus. I saw all the deflated balloons on Prostitute Street in a more sinister light and understood what they were for.

"The man puts a kingdom on his thing if he doesn't want to make a baby," I said.

She snorted and patted my arm. "That's called a condom."

"A condom?" This sounded less magical. I liked "kingdom" better—a word Raluca had taught me—a mystical gateway between man and woman and family. After that, I pretty much waited for Cassandra to leave. I was tired from knowing how everything worked.

By the time Cassandra and I were saying the Pledge to the turkey, the lab where Baba worked mornings offered her a real job. This was apparently a cause for celebration, though it meant she would no longer pick me up from school; Mama would. This was slightly better but still annoying.

"A nice surprise," Baba said, putting on lipstick in the hallway mirror.

"We're very happy for you, Svetlana Dimitrievna," Mama said, not without bitterness. Her own job search had not been fruitful.

Dimitry was the name of Baba's father. It seemed unfair to me that she had to carry his name for her entire life, though he had died when she was a child. Papa's name was Ivan, but Mama only attached it to mine if I was in trouble.

"We must go out!" Papa said, clapping his hands and interrupting this train of thought. They decided on the Outback, because it was supposed to be nice and was close by. Baba put on a sparkly dress and curled her hair. As they got ready, I noticed that nobody had told me to change.

Mama said, "Do you really want to come, kitten? We may be there awhile."

"We're getting blasted!" Baba announced. "Surely you are not interested."

"Of course she should come," Papa said.

"I want to stay here," I said. If they didn't want me, then I didn't want them. Besides, I had never been alone in the apartment before. In Kiev, Mama and Papa left me home when they went to the movies sometimes. I would stage plays with my dolls and do all their voices.

"We will not be long," Papa said, squeezing my shoulder.

"We'll bring something back for you," said Baba, but she hardly cared; she was looking in the mirror.

"Goodbye, little idiot," Mama said. The door slammed shut behind her. I was glad to be rid of them and began doing all the things I could not normally do.

I danced around in my bikini. I blasted Ace of Base. I ate cold nacho cheese with my fingers, which was much better than cream cheese. I finished a *Boxcar Children* book in the bathtub. I tried to read a few pages of Baba's romance novel, but I didn't understand what was going on. I did a few cartwheels. I jumped on Mama and Papa's bed. I pulled three cicadas out of the carpet with Mama's tweezers and flushed them down the toilet. I drowned the ants by the sink. I touched all five of Papa's sister's paintings with my hands.

The darkness crept in. It was windy out and a tree branch scraped against the balcony. It sounded like a person. I played *Doom* but it only scared me, all those cretins bursting out of the darkness to destroy me. I grabbed my Amy doll from my doll pile and hugged her hard. The noises grew louder, and I was certain someone was coming for me. I decided it was one of Papa's dead. I would be smothered. I called Cassandra so she could calm me down.

"I'm home alone," I said. "I'm freaked out."

"Your family left you?"

"Not for good, just for dinner. They'll be back."

"Too bad," she said. Then she added, "That's not normal."

"It's not?"

"Not really. But it doesn't matter. Who cares if they don't love you? Fly away now," she said, and then she said she had to go. I heard laughter before she hung up; I still hadn't been to her house but figured the only laughter there came from TV.

I didn't know how to fly away. I flipped through the photo album Papa was working on, thinking it would put me to sleep. It started off boring, with pictures of Papa onstage singing in the Kiev children's choir and receiving boring math awards, but then I found a photo that filled me with revulsion and horror. Papa was my age, and my grandpa was pretty young. They stood in a field of tall grass in their underwear, holding sickles. I searched my grandfather's face for signs that he would die soon but could find none. What I did find were the outlines of his and my father's bulging things, things I now knew had brought Papa and then me into being. I slammed the album shut and screamed. I screamed again and clutched my doll but nothing happened, nobody came, not the regular police or the secret police, not the neighbors, not my grandfather, not Cassandra, not Raluca. I cried until I tired myself out and curled up on the couch, and a million years later the key was scraping in the lock.

"What's wrong, little idiot?" Mama said, putting a hand in my hair.

Papa and Baba emerged behind her. They were happy and red faced.

"I got scared," I said, sitting up. "I heard noises. I thought a robber was going to kill me."

"You are safe now, poor creature," Papa said.

"If you do not want to be treated like a child, then do not act like one," Mama said.

"Besides," Baba said, "if a robber broke in, what would you expect us to do, infinite fool, fight him off?" She didn't care about my suffering. She didn't care that I hadn't asked to get born or to be all alone one day, after everyone in my family died.

Before I could answer, she put a hand on my wrist. "You should have seen the waiter. As handsome as a young Baryshnikov! And on the way home, a man rolled down his window and told me I was beautiful." She pranced around like she was queen of the world. I couldn't be near her anymore.

"Those men think you're a prostitute," I said.

"What?" Baba said.

Papa froze and Mama dropped her purse.

"Main Street is Prostitute Street," I said. "Everybody knows."

"Well!" Baba said, clutching her necklace. She looked from me to my parents, who looked at the floor. "Of course it is, you little idiot," she said. "Of course it is. Of course I know that. You are a devil," she said, and she walked slowly toward the patio like a doll running out of batteries. Papa didn't look at me as he followed her. Did she already know, or was she just faking it so she wouldn't look stupid? I remembered how idiotic I felt when I realized I didn't know how babies were made.

Mama smacked me. "Are you happy now?"

"Delighted," I said.

Mama was so upset she didn't even lecture me. Baba returned eventually with a splotchy face. She said, "Until you apologize, I am not speaking to you, do you understand?"

"Works for me," I said, and she went to the kitchen to pour herself a drink. I watched her back as she swirled her cognac around, and I did feel a little bit sorry for her then. It wasn't the end of the world to be young and clueless, I guessed, but there was something depressing about being old and clueless. That didn't mean I felt sorry enough to apologize, though. I didn't think she'd be able to last long without talking to me.

I stayed up reading until Baba entered, carrying her heavy perfume scent. It was a cognac night for her, and she sipped from her glass for a long time while staring at her daughter's painting of the river, as if she wanted to drown in it. Then she got under her covers and turned away from me, coughing a phlegmy cough, making no mention of oblivion. Was she getting ready to die? Her back heaved and I remembered how her sick daughter had smelled and wondered if Baba had smelled like her all along, if she had just used perfume to cover it up.

When Mama and I got home after school, I told her I had outgrown my dolls. We took all the dolls from my doll pile and tossed them in a black plastic bag. She sipped a glass of wine as we worked. She had stopped throwing up recently, so I guessed she was no longer sick.

"It's nice to get rid of some things we don't need, isn't it, darling?" Mama said.

"Dolls are for idiots who want to have babies," I said.

"I don't want a baby and I don't want to be anybody's mother."

Mama laughed. "You have some time to change your mind, silly child," she said. But when we dragged the bag to the dumpster, she looked weepy. Her hand dug into my back, making me wish I still had my mullet for protection against her touch.

"Why the rush?" she said. "I don't want you to regret this later."

"I won't."

I grabbed the doll bag and dumped it in the trash. Dust and flies materialized in its wake. Mama sank her claws into my shoulders, and her face was like the ocean at night. "I have no job. I have no country. My father is long dead and my mother is across the ocean and hardly knows who I am," she said. "But I have you. You are my greatest achievement. Do you understand?"

"Ow! That hurts."

"It better, little devil, it better," she said.

As we left the dumpster, I could tell that Mama was thinking of her own mother, whom she called every week even though she had lost her mind and didn't know who anyone was. She was nothing like Baba—she was a tiny woman who called me "darling Yaroslava" when Mama made me talk to her on the phone. I never asked who Yaroslava was, though I believed that someone who stuck in her mind like that must have been from her own traumatic wartime childhood, like Baba's dog Syomka. She lived with us when I was too young to remember, but Mama put her in a place for senile people when she couldn't care for her anymore. Having a mother like that seemed worse than having a dead one, but I supposed you didn't get to choose.

When we turned the corner, a smile crossed Mama's face. I followed her gaze to the parking lot, where Mr. Trevors was escorting Baba home. Baba still hadn't said a word to me, though a week had gone by since our fight. They stopped near a palm tree and he backed Baba up against it and kissed her madly. Her hands were raised above her head like the talons of a pterodactyl. At some point, Mr. Trevors and Baba had become a real item. Her suitors' letters had disappeared from the nightstand.

"Your grandmother has a zest for life," Mama said, turning me away from this disturbing scene. "She is an inspiration to us all."

The next time Papa took me for a drive, Cassandra and I were saying the Pledge to Santa Claus. We zipped past a cracked-open armadillo drowning in a puddle of its own blood and guts. When he turned down Supertramp's *Breakfast in America*, I got nervous, thinking he would tell me something awful, that he was dying or that Baba was going to marry Mr. Trevors.

"Oksanka Banka," he said. "It seems you do not hate it here after all, am I right?"

"It's not too bad."

"You know how when you are in a maze in *Doom*, you have to walk along the same wall to ensure you are moving forward? But sometimes you may find you are in the center of the maze, going in circles instead of finding a way out."

"So what? Then you just follow a new wall," I said.

"Exactly," he said, but I didn't get it. He cleared his throat. "A Jew once said, the foxes have their dens, the birds have their nests, but the Son of Man has nowhere to lay his head."

"Which Jew?"

"We are leaving Gainesville at the end of the month."

I gripped my door handle like the car might disappear. I tasted tin. I thought of Raluca, how she must have felt when she heard the same terrible news. "Are we going back to Kiev?"

He gave me a sad smile. "We are moving to Worthington, Ohio. I found a decent job at Ohio State. The pay is not impressive, but I will not need to deliver pizza any longer."

I kicked the dashboard and wailed. "Nobody asked me!" I said. Papa pulled to the side of the road. He gave me a Dino's napkin and I wiped my face with it though it was greasy.

"This will be good for all of us. Your mother will be happier. We'll have more money. I won't have to deliver pizza. You will be happy too, in time."

"But I'm already happy here!"

"You have to think of the good of the family, dear Oksana."

I looked down at my hands. They were covered in dried-up flecks of pizza sauce.

"I would like to be an orphan," I said.

Papa pulled back on the road. "One day," he told me, "you will get your wish."

———

Back home, Mama was slapping herring on a Dino's pizza as consolation; I hadn't lasted long as a vegetarian. Baba orbited Mama, who was wiping away my tears; one of her heels crunched into a cicada. Mama said, "We already have a new home in Ohio, kitten. It's much bigger—a two-story condo!"

"Does this mean I won't have to share a room with Baba anymore?"

Baba looked like she was going to say something, but she turned away and put a hand to her face.

"You won't, dear girl. Your grandmother is staying here," Papa said.

Baba folded her arms over her chest as Papa explained that Baba loved her job at the lab and her new friend Mr. Trevors and that her independence was important to her. I looked from my parents to Baba and wondered if I factored into a single decision they made. I didn't care if I ever saw Baba again. I would live in a gigantic room without Baryshnikov or her daughter's dumb river painting and I would finally be happy.

"That's fine," I told Baba. "Because I hate you anyway!"

She didn't seem angry—she seemed amused if anything—but Mama dragged me to my room anyway. "Oh, who was I in a past life I do not believe in?" she said. "Was I Genghis Khan? Yezhov? Nero, perhaps?" She regarded me with scorn. "Were you born without a heart? What did your grandmother do to deserve such treatment?"

I knew there was no good answer, so I thought of a bad one. "Maybe she was Stalin in a past life," I said, and Mama slapped me.

"You, Oksana," she said, "cannot joke about Stalin."

"But you can?"

"I know what Stalin means. I have suffered the pain of anti-Semitism."

"Stalin died a long time ago. What pain?"

She thought for a moment and said, "Collective pain."

Instead of sleeping, I turned over in my head what Mama had told me. I figured a "condo" was different from a "condom," but I pictured Mama and Papa and me living inside a giant two-story condom in Ohio. It sealed us in until we ran out of air and suffocated. I would have preferred a kingdom, but as usual, nobody had asked me.

I searched for Cassandra in the school parking lot the next morning to tell her I was leaving. Her mom's Jeep pulled up by the side entrance. A dark-haired man was driving, her mom was in the passenger seat, and Cassandra was in the back with a big white dog. She was babbling and they were laughing, and it looked like even the dog thought she was hysterical and they were thrilled to be together, all of them. She had betrayed me.

Inside the classroom, there was more bad news. Officer Friendly was back and this time he was there to talk about drugs. He stood next to a big glass display of pills and syringes and marijuana cigarettes and other exciting things I hadn't thought about putting in my body until that moment. The display was shiny and about two feet taller than I was and seemed to contain all the secrets of the universe. He tipped his hat at me and winked. He was still tall and handsome, and his mustache was even bushier.

I could hardly look at Cassandra. She made me sick.

"I didn't know you had a dog," I snapped.

"You mean Muffins?" she said. "I love Muffins."

"Maybe if I had a dog and a nice family, I would have given up my dolls earlier," I said, but she just frowned and shrugged.

She smiled at Officer Friendly, with her dumb greasy hair and oversize dress, and I realized I didn't know her or anyone in Florida at all. I understood Raluca completely. I too would disappear without telling anybody. I wouldn't leave a trace behind.

As soon as Principal Bates got on the loudspeaker, I jumped on my chair. The students below me whispered and stared, but I didn't care. They could have belonged to my doll pile. They were garbage now. When Principal Bates began the Pledge, I shouted:

> I pledge allegiance to the butterfly
> Of the United States of butterfly
> One butterfly, indivisible, under butterfly
> With butterfly and butterfly for all!

This didn't create the dramatic effect I was hoping for, so I knocked over the drug case. It didn't even break. Officer Friendly's eyes got big as he picked it up. He seemed genuinely hurt by my behavior. Billy Spencer whooped madly. Cassandra covered her face with her hands, but the officer and his case didn't matter to me; none of it mattered. It didn't matter that Cassandra had flapped her hands and said, "Fly away, Okey Dokey," as Mrs. Thomas grabbed me by the ear and pulled me to the front office, where I had to sit and wait for my family.

"Shame on you, child," Mrs. Thomas told me. "And today of all days, what will poor Officer Friendly think? This is a good school, not without its problems, but we love our country, and so should you," she said, leaving me to await my fate. "Baby Bolshevik," she muttered.

I sat across from the principal's office, which had glass walls. Principal Bates was perched over a pile of papers, munching on a cafeteria pretzel. The only time I had been there was my first day of school, when Papa told me my name would be hard for people to say. "Now, you say 'O' as in 'Octopus,' 'K' as in 'Kite,' 'S' as in 'Sam,' 'A' as in 'Apple,' 'N' as in 'Nancy,' 'A' as in 'Apple,'" he'd said before he told me to have a good day. He took a few steps away and turned around to add, "The rest will be hard too."

Baba was gliding down the hall a while later. She wore a gold suit and her hair danced around her shoulders. She had never been inside school before and looked a little lost. She stopped and turned, talking to somebody I couldn't see. It was Officer Friendly. I worried he'd think she was weird, but he was nice—the men usually were— and she laughed and ran a hand over his badge. He gestured toward her brooch and tipped his hat and walked off. She tilted her head and admired his butt. She was ridiculous, but I didn't want to leave her, and I definitely didn't want her to die like almost everyone else in my family.

She nodded at me, grabbed my hand, and marched us into Principal Bates's office without knocking. He was a short, sad man, who watched her with his mouth open, a bit of pretzel stuck to his tongue.

"Please, have a seat—"

"That will not be necessary," Baba said, wagging her finger at him. "What a ridiculous thing to be punished for!" She led me out before Principal Bates could respond. She spoke to me for the first time in a month when we hit Prostitute Street.

"You have another week here, child," she said, kicking a lizard aside. "What would you like to do one last time?"

I got sunburned almost as soon as we hit the beach, but nobody cared. Papa blasted Dire Straits from his radio, drowning out the sounds of the gulls squawking over our heads. Mama and Baba let me build sandcastles without chasing me with sunblock. I decorated my castles with tiny pastel clamshells and we ate soggy Subway sandwiches and Papa and I kicked a soccer ball around. He'd just bought a camera and took pictures of us for a new album.

I walked to the water and looked at the horizon. The sand was warm and welcoming and I wanted to melt in it.

Baba came up behind me. "Soak it in. You won't have water like this in Ohio."

"There is nothing in Ohio."

"I believe there are lakes. But you'll have other things, child, like snow and farms and your own bedroom." She sighed. "Of course, I could go with you. But I'm not ready to give up on myself yet. I like it here. The storms, my job, the pool, my paramour . . ."

"The cicadas. I'll miss how annoying they are," I said. A plane flew over our heads with a banner for a seafood restaurant. "I'm sorry for what I said, Baba. I didn't mean to hurt you."

She laughed. "It took you long enough! But I forgive you, dear. I know all this has not been easy for you either."

"You do?"

"Of course. Poor girl, anyone could see that moving out here was quite a shock to your system. But you have no idea how you have lifted my spirits. All of you," she said, sweeping her hand past me to my parents, who sat on the hood of the Mercury, drinking beers.

She had lost everything: her country, her youth, her father, her daughter, her husband, and soon she would lose us, and yet she hummed and toed the water and wiped her face and said she was going for one last swim. I watched her plunge in with her head rocking above the waves and knew she was happier than I had ever felt.

Mama lifted her beer bottle at us when we returned to the car. She was drunk and happy and didn't look at all like she was going to be sick. "Dearest God I don't believe in, what have I done in a past life to deserve such bliss? Was I Florence Nightingale? Perhaps Akhmatova . . ." She gave Papa a kiss that made me squirm.

We picked up a hitchhiker on the way back, and Mama didn't complain. He was young and limp-haired and he bobbed his head like he was listening to a secret song. I sat between him and Baba in the back, and she kept reaching over to squeeze his biceps. He told us to drop him off near Flagler Beach, and when we got there Papa made us all get out on the side of the road and asked him if he would take a picture of us; it was our last trip together. My face burned from the sun as we posed. Then I asked the man if Flagler Beach was where he lived and he laughed and said it wasn't, but maybe it could be, and he thanked us and walked through the brush to the ocean.

Back in the car, Papa put on "Ticket to the Moon," and as Mama and Papa and Baba sang wildly with the water brimming around us, I knew I would never have a family of my own. I would never be able to carry the weight of other people's pain or get to the bottom of it. One day they would all be dead and I would make sure I felt nothing. When the song ended, I closed my eyes and imagined I was drifting up into the sky, and by the time I opened them we were almost home.

PRIVATE PROPERTY

"I need your help, Konnikova."

Until that morning at the bus stop, I didn't think Sammy Watts knew my last name, let alone how to pronounce it. We had developed a kind of mutual respect on the bus since he and his sister had moved to Worthington last year, but he had never asked for my help before. We were unlikely allies. I was in Gifted and he was a jock whose second home was Principal Peterson's office. It was rumored he'd gotten held back twice in his old school in Cincinnati, which was why he looked much older than the rest of the sixth-graders. He approached me holding his kid sister's hand, looking like he meant business.

I hoped he didn't have some kind of tutoring in mind, because frankly, my final year of elementary school was shaping up to be quite packed. For one thing, I was running my best friend Nicole's presidential campaign, and for another, there was a baby ready to burst out of my mother's vagina at any moment, and I would be expected to help out when he did.

"What can I do for you?" I said, studying my nails.

"I need you to look after my sister."

He told me he needed someone to keep an eye on her on the afternoon bus rides because he'd be at football. Kelly Watts was a scrawny girl with a teddy-bear backpack and a persecuted look. She orbited around her brother while holding his hand and wouldn't look at me.

"What's in it for me?" I said.

He laughed. "I guess I'll have to think of something."

Sammy's arms were bulkier than I remembered and his mushroom cut had grown out and his hair fell into his eyes like a derelict Taylor Hanson's. We didn't have anything else to say to each other, so we kicked rocks toward the creek. The creek had a bridge over it; to the right of the bridge were the crappy apartments where I lived, and to the left were the still-crappy-but-less-so houses where Sammy lived.

Fat Jack approached from the less-crappy side. He gave me the finger. Seeing him was a comfort, in a way. When I'd moved to Ohio in the middle of third grade, he'd called me "Commie" and "Russian Spy," but he'd lost all power over me long ago, when Nicole had taken me under her wing. Now our spats were more of a formality. I almost enjoyed them.

"Hey, Big Red."

"That's what you need to chew, because your breath smells like dog shit," I said.

"Fuck off," Sammy told him, and Fat Jack gave him the finger too but did what he was told. "You see? Threats everywhere. Do we have a deal?" Sammy said.

"I'll think about it."

"It's gonna be a long year, Konnikova," he said, letting go of his sister's hand.

"The years are long, but life is short," I said.

It was something Papa said and I wasn't sure what it meant, but it made Sammy laugh. The bus finally pulled up with old Mr. Romano, a hardened ex-con, behind the wheel. Sammy took out a Polaroid and snapped a photo of his sister standing in front of the bus as the students filed on. She looked desperate and paper thin, her skin nearly translucent in the morning light. Sammy waved the picture to make it develop faster and I didn't see why he was in such a rush to see the sad image of his little sister, but I supposed this was something I wouldn't understand until I had a sibling of my own.

I went to Nicole's a few days into school to work on her campaign, with the Shoemaker twins. She lived in a mansion on the other side of town. It had a statue of a glass swan in the living room, vases filled with pastel rocks, a white carpet, and at least five bedrooms. I understood how things worked by then. If your dad was a real estate agent, you got a mansion. But my dad was just a physicist and my mom was only a part-time accountant. We lived in a condo in a building that looked like a roadside motel, with a tiny bathroom monopolized by Mama's nervous vomiting, and neighbors who fought so hard their furniture blasted through our cheap walls. Nicole's walls were so thick that her mom would call her on a personal landline when dinner was ready.

"I have neat handwriting. I have the best hair. I'm nice to ugly people," Nicole said, ticking off her positive qualities on her manicured nails. "If I can just get this speech down, I'll have it all." I was in charge of writing the speech and coming up with the poster slogans, and the twins with drawing the posters. Nicole did not do much herself; she was more of a figurehead.

"You already have it in the bag," Melinda said.

"Definitely," said Bridget.

Melinda was prettier but Bridget was more artistic, and their hair was as black and shiny as the trash bags where Mama kept my old clothes.

"It's like you've already won," I told Nicole, clarifying what Melinda said, because Nicole was not always familiar with turns of phrase.

"You can never get too comfortable, Oksana," Nicole said, chewing a strand of blond hair.

Her bedroom had recently undergone an alarming transformation. She had ditched her pink wallpaper and dolls in favor of posters of Nirvana and Oasis and Gwen Stefani and replaced her princess bed with a wooden bed with plaid sheets. She'd kept the mountain of stuffed animals on her bed, which was a relief. My favorite part of her room was the bay window with a ledge covered in pink pillows. If I'd been Nicole, I would have spent all day sitting there, reading and looking out into the thick, dreamy woods across the street, woods that had a PRIVATE PROPERTY sign in front of them because they belonged to Nicole's family. But I never saw her sit there.

It was a good thing she had this gorgeous house and a gorgeous family to go in it, because she had other problems. She was not a bright girl; her mother regularly visited Principal Peterson to keep her out of Basic Ed, but after sixth grade, we'd be in middle school and she wouldn't be able to stay in the regular classes forever. I was desperate for her to win the election, to trounce Isabelle Lee, though the girl was smart and regrettably even nice. But Isabelle Lee had a life of success ahead of her, while this might be Nicole's last chance to win at anything.

"Plus, if the speech doesn't clinch it," I said, "then my routine will do the trick."

We spent recesses tumbling in the grass, and though I had no formal gymnastics training, I had quite an impressive repertoire. Over the summer, I had coordinated a routine I would perform as Nicole finished her speech, which ended with me clapping my feet in a handstand as the audience burst into applause. My clapping feet would communicate what words could not: that Nicole was generous and loyal, that she had silenced Fat Jack the moment she saw him teasing me, that she'd helped me find matching clothes and saved my life, basically. But the twins exchanged an ominous glance when I mentioned the routine.

"About that . . ." Nicole said. "I've done some thinking, Ox. And, well, I think we should scratch the routine. I want to project a mature image as a leader, and I think your antics may send the wrong message."

"What antics? It's a highly sophisticated routine," I said.

"Don't get all mopey," Nicole said.

"I'm not mopey," I said, looking away. "I'm just working on your speech."

The twins were no help, as usual, just smugly coloring in their signs. I kept my mouth shut after that. I thought of Sammy Watts knowing my last name and wondered if my friends even knew how to pronounce it, not that I would ask them. I finished the speech and wrote down more poster ideas, which included *Got Nicole?* along with *Nicole Summers All Year Long* and *Summers Is Never Over.*

Nicole's brother, Lionel, waddled into the room as we were wrapping up. We called him "the Lion" for his mane of blond curls. He was cute, for a kid, much cuter than the devil who lurked in my mother's womb, I was sure. The Lion was followed by Mrs. Summers, who produced a plate of cookies from the ether. She was radiant, a mom who could sell Minute Maid on TV. I only watched it at Nicole's—Papa had banned TV from our house because he felt it was for fools who lacked imagination, though he would still play *Doom II* with me if he had a particularly bad day at work.

Mrs. Summers scooped up her son and turned to me. "I bet you can't wait to have a little brother," she said. "Your mother, when is she due?"

"In a month."

"So exciting!"

"I can't wait," I said, flashing my best smile. She chased the Lion to his room, and for the first time I wondered where the baby would live in our tiny condo.

"I only told you about nine times. I was helping Nicole work on her campaign," I said to my parents at dinner. "Remember?" We were eating Mama's specialty, something she called Turkish rice, which was really just rice smeared in ketchup.

"Lovely," Mama said, flipping through *What to Expect*

the First Year, which was perched on her enormous belly. She was reading in English so she was speaking English, which made me cringe. "But that girl, she is as dumb as a doornail."

"Dumb as a post," I said. "Dead as a doornail."

"Indeed," Mama said.

"A corpse would make a better president than most. Andropov certainly," Papa noted, taking a generous sip of wine from his Buckeyes mug. "When anybody chooses to be in a position of power, I am inherently suspicious." Papa lifted a finger. "In the Soviet Union, this is something you are born knowing, like how to bribe a bureaucrat."

"It's different here," I said.

"You can certainly trust Clinton more than Andropov," Mama noted. "What a charming man. . . ." She retreated to her child-rearing book, ignoring me as Papa rambled on about how he'd been lucky he didn't have to bribe too many people because he was the Math Olympics champion in high school, which opened a lot of doors for him. Mama didn't pay attention to this either, because she was Jewish and Papa was not, and she said that everything had been easier for him in Kiev than it had been for her. I poured water on my rice and stirred it around just for kicks. We sat under the only one of Papa's sister's paintings my grandmother hadn't kept, which featured Papa's head rising from a fruit bowl. His bulbous nose was a pear and his ears were orange slices.

Mama looked up from her book, shook it at me, and said, "An American-born child, can you believe it? So much advice on how to raise an obedient creature! We'll get it right this time, won't we, Oksana?"

"You are hard on the girl," Papa said with a chuckle, though I didn't see what was so funny. He stroked my hair, but it was too late.

"What room is the baby going to stay in?" I said.

"Pardon?" Papa said.

"The Lion has his own room and he's only three."

"If you are so fond of this zoo animal, then why don't you move in with him?" said Mama, resting a hand on her belly. "The baby will sleep with us, and when he's old enough—oh, who knows where we'll be. . . ."

"Who knows what the world has in store for us?" Papa said. "My work at the university is temporary. A dead end, perhaps . . ." Papa had been interviewing for finance jobs in New York, though nothing had panned out yet.

Mama ignored Papa's ominous declaration about his current career. "At your age," she told me, "I shared a toilet with my parents and four families in a nice *communalka*. Each family had a cupboard with their own toilet lid in it, so we did not rub butts with strangers—it was really quite civilized. Did I ever complain, foolish girl?"

Mama had a point. In Kiev, I never minded sharing one big room with Mama and Papa, but here it was embarrassing to not even have my own bathroom. But I would not give in to her.

"If Kiev was so great, then why did you leave?" I said.

"Oksana," Mama said, putting her head in her hands. "Dearest God I don't believe in," she began, but she gave up on this train of thought. She settled on, "Do not suck my blood."

"My girls," Papa said, putting an arm around each of us and splashing wine from his mug onto the carpet.

"Why don't we enjoy the present? We cannot look into the future."

"Indeed, dearest Vanya," Mama said, looking at my father. "It is a blessing not to know what will happen next."

"It's too bad," I said. "Because I really don't want to share my room."

I could only see about five minutes into the future. The neighbors were raising their voices, which meant they'd be shoving furniture into our wall in no time. Mama stopped clearing the table when the bottom of a chair leg came through the kitchen wall. White dust exploded onto the floor.

"I really wish I could drink," Mama said.

"That is why I am drinking for two," Papa said as he dumped the remaining wine from the bottle into his mug. He gave us a goofy smile and nodded at the cries behind the wall. "You see? That's love."

A few days later, Fat Jack taunted Kelly Watts on the bus ride home. He was yanking her pigtails like the shithead that he was. Papa always told me to feel empathy for others, and I tried to think of how much it would suck to be Fat Jack, but I couldn't see past his looks. He was so fat it was hard to think anything else about him.

"If you want me to stop, just say so," he told Kelly.

"Stop," the girl said, very quietly.

"I can't hear you. . . ."

"Why don't you pick on someone your own size?" I said. "Oh, wait. There are no sumo wrestlers on the bus."

"Why don't you lick Stalin's nut sack?" he said, but

Mr. Romano turned to us with a steely gaze, and the boy ceased his taunting. It was rumored that Romano had spent thirty years in prison for killing his wife, so he was not someone to mess with.

Kelly gave me a grateful smile. But as soon as we got dropped off at our stop, Fat Jack yanked the girl's hair again while the other kids and parents scurried away.

"Leave her alone," I said.

"Or what?"

"Or I'll curse you with my commie voodoo," I offered, and he snorted and snatched her backpack. He spun it in wild arcs over the water, which was suddenly a raging river instead of a charming creek where Nicole and I hunted for crayfish.

"If you want it, come and get it," he said.

"Stop," she whispered.

"Give it back, dipshit," I said.

"Fat chance, commie!"

"You're the fat one," I said, as Kelly began to cry. I could see I would make a terrible older sister. I picked up a big stick from the side of the road and held it up. "Give it back," I said.

"Or what?" he answered, having already exhausted his bully vocabulary.

His arm was the size of my body and he didn't take me seriously. Nobody did. Nicole thought I was a baby for wanting to do my routine. My parents only cared about my future brother and were ready to shove him in my room and maybe even toss me out to boot. I was nobody's first choice, the Ross Perot of real life. And yet this girl was depending on me. I launched the stick toward Fat Jack, hoping to scare him away.

It didn't happen in slow motion—it happened fast, actually. One minute the stick was in my hand and the next it had sliced through his cheek and he was on the ground with his face in his hands. I hadn't even wanted to hit him with it, let alone have the thing rip through him. He'd seemed so far away from me when I threw it.

"What did you do?" he wailed. "What did you do?" I crept up to him, grabbed the bag, and tossed it to Kelly.

"Thank you!" she said, as loudly as I'd ever heard her speak, and she ran away. Fat Jack lifted a hand from his cheek and was puzzled at the flesh that fell off it. His cheek was white in the way of skin that was about to bleed, hard, and I wasn't going to hang around to see it happen.

"I didn't mean to hurt you!" I said as I took off. I ran and ran until I reached my apartment and sat on the curb to catch my breath.

Mama greeted me from the couch when I walked in; her belly looked ready to swallow up her tiny arms and legs. A cup of half-drunk tea was on the coffee table in front of her, along with some work papers and a phone she'd probably used to call her friends in New Jersey or her sick mother in Kiev earlier. The corners of the neighbors' bookshelf and TV poked through the wall behind her, and the carpet beneath her was the same brown as the tea—you could have bled out an entire person right there and no one would have noticed. But she smiled like she was genuinely happy to see me. Mama could be nice sometimes.

"My dear little fool," Mama said, patting the space beside her. "I'm so glad you're home. I was starting to worry."

"It won't go on her record," Principal Peterson assured my parents the next morning. "Like a stone dropping to the bottom of an ocean. It's the best I can do," he said, smiling though he was saying sad things. Papa winked at me as the principal uttered his strange turn of phrase, while Mama acted like he was being normal. He went on to say that the best he could do was kick me off the bus and give me two weeks of in-school suspension, which I'd spend in the side room by his office, completing my schoolwork and drowning in self-loathing.

"We understand," Mama said. She put a hand on her belly, as if to guard her unborn child from his sister's mistakes.

Principal Peterson was a tall man who appeared to always be on the brink of apologizing. I knew he didn't like doling out my punishment; he seemed particularly ill-suited to be a school principal, or even to socialize at all. Based on the strange way he talked, I wondered if he had wanted to be a poet. A few students claimed to have seen him at an Ohio State game alone, which sounded like the saddest thing in the world.

"I only wanted to scare him, not hurt him. He was going to throw Kelly's bag into the creek," I said.

"Behave, Oksana," Mama said. "This is a sentencing, not a negotiation."

"My daughter is foolhardy but not monstrous," Papa declared. He had been watching two squirrels chase each other around a tree outside the window, confused about his role in this drama. Papa was my comrade-in-arms, my teammate; he did not know what to do during my punishment. The night before, he'd winced painfully when he said we couldn't play *Doom II* together anymore because it was too violent.

"I understand your daughter's intentions," Principal Peterson said. "Still, there's a boy with a broken face, and something has to be done. Seventeen stitches down his cheek," he said, and I sucked in my breath. I couldn't believe I had done this to somebody. "I would say an apology is in order, but the boy doesn't wish to see your daughter," he continued.

Though I was relieved I didn't have to face Fat Jack, I now felt even worse. I wished Nicole or the twins would appear so they could tell me I was not some dirty criminal.

Mama and Papa left and Principal Peterson and I were stuck staring at each other. Through the window behind him, I saw my parents walking toward Papa's new used red Honda, his pride and joy, holding hands. Mama stopped to touch her belly and Papa kneeled, put an ear to her stomach, and kissed whatever living thing was under there. A thing too amorphous to be monstrous, one that they hoped would turn out better than me, a creature desperate to break out into the world, and who knew what for.

My teacher, Mrs. Ferguson, delivered my classwork after my parents left—rather smugly, in my opinion; she already hated me because I'd complained that the books she made us read were too easy. She was the Gifted teacher, and her room was connected to Mrs. Davis's non-Gifted class by a private bathroom the students were not allowed to use. Naturally, we believed this was the site of spectacular, wild lesbian orgies between the two teachers, which took place when the students were at recess.

I finished my work and spent the afternoon snipping my arm hairs with my plastic scissors and reading the latest *Fear Street* book. The only person I saw all day was Mrs. Summers, who visited Principal Peterson for a long time to rally for her daughter. I left twice to use the bathroom and crept around like a burglar to avoid Fat Jack, even though I knew he was in Basic Ed at the other side of the school. I was already losing my grip on reality in my isolation and felt a kinship with Mr. Romano, our bus driver.

When the final bell rang, I saw that Sammy Watts had been in another side room all along. He gave me a knowing, almost businesslike nod; he was there for cheating. He was wearing a Michigan T-shirt to be controversial.

"You're a hero, Konnikova," he said. "Don't let anybody tell you otherwise."

"I only wanted to scare him," I said.

"I saw him this morning," he said, shaking his head slowly. "You did a number on him. If he didn't look so bad, I'd hit him again."

"I didn't want to hurt him."

"Not even a little?"

"Maybe a little."

"Can you come by later? I want to show you something. I promised to pay you back, didn't I?" I had spent the day veering between intense guilt and self-pity, and it was a relief to have someone be nice to me.

"Fine," I said.

I was pretty sure a silence fell over the halls as I walked toward the exit, though maybe I was just out of it after my confinement. I was looking for my friends, hoping they would tell me I was only being paranoid, that nobody was actually talking about me. I saw Nicole and the twins leaving Mrs. Davis's classroom and caught up to them. They confirmed my worst suspicions when they looked at me like I was personally responsible for the death of Kurt Cobain.

"What a shitty day," I said anyway.

"We're on a tight schedule here," Melinda said.

"Yeah," said Bridget.

"I love you, but I can't afford to be associated with you right now," Nicole said. "I have an election to win." They walked by my SUMMERS ALL YEAR LONG poster without acknowledging it. Nicole looked back just to show how much it hurt her to hurt me.

Sammy's tiny house stood about two inches from the houses on either side of it, but a house was still a house, and there was no way a neighbor's shelf could make it through its walls. His kid sister and her friends were doing weak cartwheels under a plastic basketball hoop, and his mom smoked on the porch. Sammy wore his practice jersey and there was mud on his forearms. I looked around for Fat Jack, though I was pretty sure he didn't live all that close by.

"All right, Konnikova, it's time to show us what you've got," Sammy said, rubbing his hands together as I approached.

"Excuse me?"

"I've seen you doing flips with your girlfriends at recess. So come on, give us an education."

"We don't do that anymore."

His sister gazed at me so hopefully that it seemed easier to do stunts than to protest. I did a roundoff to warm up, then an aerial, followed by a roundoff–back handspring, which didn't feel right, something I hadn't done for too long, something I would one day forget how to do completely. I then went for something a little easier, walking on my hands. I could see my upside-down shadow in the waning sunlight.

Kelly laughed aloud, and some of the boys even whooped a little. I felt pretty good, so I did what I wouldn't have the chance to do for Nicole: I walked in circles and clapped my feet. It was fun to ham it up for a change. Sammy cheered for me. I came down, not because I couldn't hold my balance but because my forearms were starting to ache.

"Not bad," he said. He shooed the other kids away. It was time to get down to business. "I said I would pay you back. Are you up for a potentially dangerous mission?"

He gave me a soulful glance through his bangs. I could feel the sweat pooling at the back of my neck.

"What do I have to lose?" I said.

He grinned. "I knew you were all right, Konnikova."

I hopped on my bike and sped after him—he rode fast. We zoomed down his street and past the middle school, where we'd be forced to go the next year. It looked like a square submarine and didn't even have a playground. The houses got bigger and farther apart, until we got to Nicole's. We crouched in the woods across from her house, facing her bay window.

"Peterson should be here any minute," Sammy said, producing his Polaroid.

"Why would he be here?" I said, and he snorted.

"You really are clueless, aren't you? He's fucking Nicole's mom."

"Principal Peterson?" I said, and he nodded gravely. "How do you know?"

He shrugged. "I know a lot of things."

A car pulled up a house away from Nicole's. At first, I didn't think the man who emerged from it was the same one who'd doled out my punishment. This version looked excited, confident. But Principal Peterson tilted his head enough for me to recognize his apologetic presence. Nicole's mom opened the door and Sammy snapped a picture before the house swallowed them up. I imagined what they would say to each other in bed. "My penis in your vagina is like a stone dropping to the bottom of an ocean," he'd tell Mrs. Summers. "So exciting!" she would reply.

Sammy inspected his photograph and handed it over.

"What should I do with it?" I said.

"You're supposed to be smart, aren't you? You'll figure something out."

"Gifted," I said, "is not the same as smart."

As we pulled our bikes out of the woods, I wanted him to kiss me, or at least to hold my hand or promise to call later, but he seemed above all that, maybe because he was so much older. At the end of the block, he gazed back at Nicole's mansion.

"Private property," he said, shaking his head. "How can you own woods?"

Nicole looked unsteady as she approached the podium in tiny heels, drowning under the bright lights of the auditorium. I sat in the back, flanked by Sammy and Principal Peterson. Principal Peterson looked like he was holding in a big shit. It must have hurt him to look at Nicole, since she looked so much like her beautiful mother. Her beautiful mother, in fact, was sitting near the stage with her handsome husband, who had his arm around her. If I didn't know better, I would think they were happy together.

"If I am elected president," Nicole began, her voice shaking, "I promise to bring change to our school. I promise. . . ." I could barely listen as she stumbled over her words, having cut all of my witty phrases. I pictured how it would play out if I had walked on my hands behind her and saw how stupid that was, how it would make her look even worse.

She seemed so scared that I forgave her everything. My heart heaved when she said, "Remember, a vote for Nicole is a vote for . . ." and struggled before adding, ". . . a better place for everybody! A stronger community!" She looked up like she was lost and waiting for someone to give her directions. Her parents clapped heartily up front.

Sammy laughed. "You didn't help her with that nonsense, did you?"

"Tried to."

"Should have tried harder."

"That's enough," Principal Peterson snapped. He was talking to us, but he was looking at Nicole's parents.

Isabelle Lee trotted onstage and was as competent and on point as a stapler. Then the vice president and secretary candidates spoke, but nobody cared about them. The only thing I paid attention to was that Sammy and I were sitting with our arms insanely close together but not touching, reminding me of the neighboring houses on his street. The hairs on my arms sizzled.

The moment was wrecked when I spotted Fat Jack as the front rows filed out. His cheek was puffy and looked like it had a hideous black caterpillar crawling along it. I was scared by how scared *he* was when we locked eyes, as if I were someone to be reckoned with. He walked past me, almost running, really, before I could figure out what to say. He looked back, horrified, and nearly tripped before he disappeared into the crowd.

"Your mother is resting," Papa said when he picked me up from school on the final day of my punishment. I was glad to have time alone with him, though he didn't say much as the car pulled away. *Dark Side of the Moon* was playing in his Honda. The car was his sanctuary. After work, he'd go on long drives by himself, or park by the creek, where he would smoke and read my grandmother's letters from Florida, which he kept in the glove box. I only noticed that he had been crying when he turned down the music.

"Your mother will need time to recover," he said. "She has lost another baby."

"What do you mean, another?"

Papa sighed. "Her fourth. And her last. We were so hopeful about this one—none of the others had made it this far . . ." he said as his voice broke. "But it is too dan-

gerous now. We aren't going to try anymore, do you understand?"

I nodded and tried not to cry. Why did he have to tell
me the truth? It all made sense—all those years when I
thought Mama was puking just because she was just sick,
my parents whispering late at night, secrets I assumed
had to do with how broke we were. I had always thought
I was enough for them. I felt the tears stinging my eyes,
not because I was mourning my last chance to have a
brother but because my parents had tried, again and
again, to have another child, to replace me. But now the
child was erased, like he hadn't been resting in Mama's
belly at all. "Like a stone dropping to the bottom of an
ocean," I thought but knew better than to say.

"I understand perfectly," I said.

"The important thing," he said, "is that you be kind
to your mother."

He looked away and rolled down the window. He lit a
cigarette without asking if I minded, for once. He looked
so helpless that I did not want to stop talking to him. I
opened my mouth, but when I tried to form words I
began to cry, which was exactly what I'd wanted to avoid.

He squeezed my hand and said, "We are only children, you and your mother and father. Lone soldiers in
the universe. No brothers or sisters to call our own.
Rogue warriors."

This rogue warrior cast a vote for Nicole Summers at the
beginning of class the next morning. Mrs. Ferguson
picked up my ballot and told me she was glad to have me

back, though her face said the opposite. I tilted my head toward her sexual bathroom to show she didn't have one up on me, but she didn't notice. I thought of Nicole on the other side of the wall, getting nervous, sucking on a strand of hair. I marched to Principal Peterson's office when the recess bell rang.

"I have something that might interest you," I said.

"Is that right?" he said. He looked tired, even for a principal.

I slid the photo of him and Mrs. Summers in his direction. His face drained of color, just like Fat Jack's cheek after the stick had ripped through it.

"What do you want?"

"I want Nicole to be president. You don't want this picture in the wrong hands."

He stood and adjusted his tie. "Get out of my office, Ms. Konnikova."

"But—"

"You must be accountable for your actions. You can't un-ring a bell. What lesson would I be teaching you if I took the bribe? I am a role model," he said, his voice quaking. "Don't you understand that?"

"Some role model," I said, and he flinched at this, like he was bracing against a cold wind, but I did not let myself feel sorry for him. "Besides," I tried again, "don't you want to make Mrs. Summers happy?" But he just looked angrier, so I returned to my original approach. "If she doesn't win, I'll tell everyone your secret," I said.

"My my," he said, regarding me with near admiration. "I didn't think you had it in you." When he turned away from me, toward the window, his shoulders heaved.

There were creases all over his suit, around the elbows and down his back. There were creases in the skin at the back of his neck too. He was creased everywhere.

Principal Peterson announced the results of the election over the loudspeaker at the end of the day. Isabelle Lee had wrested victory from Nicole's hands in what he assured us was a very close election. "As close as . . ." he began, but he could not think of an adequate metaphor and told us to have a good afternoon as the class snickered. After the final bell rang, I heard a stuck-pig sound emanating from Mrs. Davis's room, followed by a shuffling and slamming, which told me that Nicole had run into the sex bathroom, and I ran in too, from the Gifted side.

She sat on the toilet and the twins crouched on either side of her, rubbing her shoulders. She looked like an overwatered flower. I felt terrible for her. This was the worst thing she had ever had to deal with, and it would only get worse from here.

"I can't believe this," she sputtered.

"I really thought you would win," I said.

"Same," said Bridget.

"Leave her alone," Melinda told me, but Nicole pushed her away.

"I'm sorry I didn't let you onstage," she said.

"It's all right. I'm over it," I said. I couldn't believe it had ever mattered to me.

"What am I supposed to do now?" she said. "What am I supposed to do?" She hiccupped madly. This had been her last chance to be on top and she saw it as clearly as a comet shooting across the night sky. Maybe she wasn't as dumb as I thought.

She cried louder as I looked around the room where the teachers supposedly did their illicit deeds. There was a periodic table, a map of Paris, a few rolls of toilet paper, and the teacher pay schedule for the 1996–97 calendar year. It was hard to imagine anything remotely wild or spectacular going on in here.

"Chin up," Melinda said.

"Try to smile," I translated, but Nicole wasn't listening. "You go home. I'll tear everything down," I told her.

She nodded gratefully, and the four of us emerged from the non-Gifted side to face an unhappy Mrs. Davis. I could see her deciding whether or not to punish us.

"Just get out of here," she said. "I have a lot of work to do."

The twins led Nicole to the lobby. She had an arm around each of their shoulders and hobbled forward like she had sprained an ankle. I was left to tackle a wall of lime-green signs that read NICOLE 4 PREZ—lazy mind-farts of the twins, no doubt. For the first time, I walked down the halls without being afraid of seeing Fat Jack. I tore down rows of uninspiring signs until I reached Principal Peterson's office. I couldn't believe he hadn't caved. I hadn't even asked for that much.

Just before I turned the corner, I saw Sammy leaving Principal Peterson's office with his mother. When he saw me, he told her to wait outside for him and she walked out the front door. I peeled Nicole's last poster off the wall, ripping it in half for dramatic effect. It said, NICOLE IS YOUR GOAL! That had been my handiwork.

"Tough loss today," he said with a smile. "My condolences."

"She's devastated."

"She'll get over it," he said. "Anyway, I'm glad I caught you. I'm leaving town tomorrow."

"For how long?"

"For the foreseeable. My mom's shipping me off to my grandma's in Cleveland. She hopes she'll whip me into shape," he said with a dark laugh.

"What did you do this time?"

He shrugged and held up a bloody knuckle. "Thanks for everything, Konnikova. You're not so bad."

I knew it was the last time we'd see each other, that Cleveland might as well have been in Alaska when you were eleven. I tried to find a decent way to say goodbye.

"Are you really thirteen?" I said.

He threw back his head and laughed. "Twelve, actually. And only because I have an early birthday. I wasn't held back, if that's what you're asking." He put his non-bloody hand on my shoulder. "You can't believe everything they tell you."

"Who is 'they'?"

In the space where he was deciding whether or not my question was rhetorical, I kissed him. I felt the tip of his salty tongue before I pulled back, because I got scared, and because I didn't want him to pull back first. The small bit of his tongue had lodged into my mouth and stayed there like the corner of the neighbors' bookshelf that lingered in our wall. I wanted more of him, though. I wanted to lick his bloody knuckle. I wanted him to say, "You're sucking my blood," and for me to say, "Yes, yes, I am."

He gave me a sleepy, lazy, sweet smile. He pulled out his camera and snapped my picture before I could figure out how to pose for it.

"Did you use what I gave you yet?" he said. It took me a second to realize he was talking about the photograph.

"Soon," I said. "Still waiting for the right time."

Nicole called late that night with devastating news. Principal Peterson had stormed her mansion and told her father everything; he said he was tired of keeping secrets. "I can't help who I love," he said. "No more than a snake can help shedding its skin." I was happy to hear Nicole laugh a tiny bit when she reported this, glad she had a moment of relief before her world came crashing down. Apparently Principal Peterson had spewed romantic nonsense until Mr. Summers punched him in the face, at which point he left; Mrs. Summers stood in the driveway as he drove away—filled with dreadful longing, I imagined.

My parents had fallen asleep hours ago. They were holed up in the cavern of their bedroom with the radio on, men cheering for faraway goals in my native language, so getting to Nicole's was not a problem. As I climbed on my bike, I saw our next-door neighbors walking into their home, looking even older and more tired than my parents, hardly capable of passion.

The mansion was a wreck. Nicole's mother was raving in the kitchen and her father sobbed with his head in his hands. I had never seen Mrs. Summers with even a bra strap showing, but now her face was puffed up and she was holding an empty wine bottle like she planned to break it in a million pieces and stab herself with the shards, and it was all because of me.

"I don't know how it happened!" Mrs. Summers was shouting. "I'm so sorry. . . ." She gave me a weak nod as I passed her. It was a shame they were so far away from their neighbors that no one could hear them. I hated being so close to ours, but right then the idea of someone else being there was kind of nice, some nice rich neighbor coming over with a casserole or just words of comfort to distract them from their pain.

The white carpet leading to Nicole's room was suddenly the dumbest thing I had ever seen, a bright space to showcase your messes. Nicole was in bed, holding her brother in her lap. The Lion looked too big in her arms and he was trying to wriggle out. She released him when she saw me. She sat in the center of a stuffed-animal mountain, oblivious dogs and cats and Beanie Babies flanking her like soldiers awaiting instruction. For once, her mother didn't need to call her personal landline for Nicole to know what was going on downstairs.

"Oh, Oksie. Can you believe this?"

"I can't," I said, joining her under her plaid covers.

"I knew I could depend on you. The twins—they didn't even come. They said they had a curfew! Can you believe that?" she said, and she burst into tears at the word "curfew," a vestige from her ordered life. I tried not to bristle when I understood she had called the twins first.

"Your parents will work it out," I said.

"You really think so?"

"Definitely," I said. I looked away, because I had never lied about something that mattered before. I knew she wanted more from me. "We are rogue warriors," I told her. "Lone soldiers in the universe."

Nicole nodded and closed her eyes, slipping deeper under her covers, and I knew she understood me this time. The Lion climbed on her bay-window nook and stared in the direction of the dark woods with his hands pressed against the glass. I moved toward him and saw that his face was filled with wonder, bathed in light— a light whose source was not the moon or a celestial being but the headlights of my parents' fucking car. I would never be able to escape them.

Eventually, they cut the lights. Papa had his arm around Mama and they stared at the house like that alone would summon me. They wanted the world to be safe for me, and I hated them for it. I pounded on the glass to signal to them, not to say I was coming but to tell them to go away. But they didn't see me. They just kept sitting there, knowing I would have to leave my friend eventually. Who were these people, and what were they thinking? Were they disappointed with their only child, with how their lives were turning out? What did they think I needed? Why didn't they just leave me alone?

AUTOGRAPH

Papa had been the U.S.S.R. Math Olympics champion when he was sixteen, but all he'd managed to achieve was working for Goldman Sachs. He had competed all over the Soviet Union, from Tallinn to Vladivostok, and had even gotten to shake Brezhnev's hand in a big ceremony when he won. But nobody cared about the Math Olympics in America. Mama loved to remind me of all of Papa's sacrifices for our family and told me to go easy on him, especially when he did things that were "good for his soul," like blasting classical music in his car as loud as humanly possible without caring about his passengers—namely, me. That morning, I massaged my temples, hoping Papa would get the picture, amazed that even classical music could be offensive at a high volume.

I ran out of patience once we hit the Parkway. I said, "Can you turn it down a notch?"

"Turn it down, rabbit? But this is the only way I like to hear it," he said with an exaggerated frown that made him look as dumb as the boys in eighth grade. Lately he had replaced all the songs with English in them with classical music whenever he drove, and I hoped the phase would pass. But I felt guilty when he grunted and turned the music off completely.

"I'm just not awake yet," I said.

"Here," he said, thrusting his coffee mug at me. "This will do it."

I was almost fourteen and had never had coffee before. I took a sip and struggled not to spit it out.

"Disgusting," I said.

"You get used to it, like everything else," he said. "You'll see."

I was skipping school for Take Your Daughter to Work Day. It had taken some wrangling to convince Mama to let me go, but Papa was excited to show me the Wall Street office where he had been working for the past few months—the reason my family had left Ohio for New Jersey. I cared more about ditching class than seeing the place that kept Papa from making it home in time for dinner or playing computer games with me. Only after I accepted did I realize I'd have to leave home at six instead of seven in the morning. I took another sip of the disgusting slush as we pulled into the garage, which was just past the twin towers. It tasted like mud. Papa put his hand on my back as we walked to his office.

We passed Battery Park, which was where Papa had taken me and Mama on our first trip to New York, when I was eight. Papa saw me slowing down and said, "We can walk around here at the end of the day. Perhaps even get some ice cream," and I said that sounded like a good idea, though I was pretty sure you were too old for ice cream with your dad once you got full boobs. A garbage truck stopped in front of us, blocking our path. My friend Lily had told me garbage men made a ton of money, way more than Papa, but I wasn't sure I believed her.

The Goldman Sachs building loomed in the distance like a brown cheese grater. Papa lit a cigarette as the truck roared away and finished it by the time we reached the building. He nodded hello to two of the security guards and we stepped inside. The ceilings were infinitely tall, the lobby made of shiny marble. I got a name tag at the front desk and we waited for an elevator to take us all the way up to Papa's floor. We were let out into a room at least five times the size of my school gym. There was a table with bagels, orange juice, pastries, and coffee on it, and a few daughters picked at the food. All of the suited-up dads stood in clumps, looking considerably older and more tired than my father. The daughters giggled in a circle, and I wondered how they spoke so freely together. Papa and I looked at the people and back at each other.

"Would you like to see my desk?" he said.

I grabbed a bagel with no cream cheese and followed him. The floor had no offices at all, just row after row of desks crowded with more computer screens than I had ever seen in my life. Enormous TVs hung from the walls, and clocks showed the time in London and Tokyo. As Papa led me toward one of these rows, it occurred to me that this meant he didn't have his own office.

"Here," he said, gesturing toward a desk with only two computer screens on it. "I sit here all day long. Except when I smoke." It looked so pathetic—hardly twice the size of my desk at school. I noticed a photo of me holding my brother just after he was born a year ago, and it made me cringe. I almost never thought of Papa when

I was at school, going about my life, while he looked at this picture of my little brother, Misha, and me every single day. We idled back to the chattering daughters and dads, and I picked at my bagel until a gray-haired lady mercifully rang a bell and announced the order of events. The only thing I gathered was that some famous basketball-player lady was giving a speech after lunch. Other than that, we'd spend most of the day in "workshops." This definitely sounded worse than school.

Only when a different gray-haired lady came over to separate me from Papa did I realize he would not be joining me—he would have to work. This didn't seem fair. The other dads were already rushing to their desks, answering their phones. Papa lifted a hand as he backed away from me and said, "See you at lunch."

"I was, like, *obsessed* with Mallory Hazzard when I was little," a big Italian-looking girl from a place called "Shahlin" was saying to anyone who would listen; it took me a moment to realize she was talking about the basketball player. The girl had curly black hair, Tiffany's jewelry, and a perfect French manicure she'd probably gotten just for the dumb occasion. The other girls wore dresses, billowy flowery things. I wore a Spice Girls T-shirt and cargo pants that were too short, showing too much of my Skechers, which looked ridiculous in the plush conference room. I hadn't dressed up, specifically because Mama kept telling me I should, which I figured was only because she was a real accountant now and had to dress up for work so she thought I should be fancy too. The girl rambled on about this basketball legend I had never heard of—I didn't even know women's basketball was a thing.

Our "Grrrrrl Leaders!" workshop was completely useless; each girl had to share some kind of "entrepreneur" idea. I didn't know what "entrepreneur" meant and said I just liked to read, not lead, thank you, and the instructor quickly moved on. After it wrapped up, I was stuck listening to the girls comparing *NSYNC to the Backstreet Boys. It was pretty obvious they were nothing like me; they were from places like Basking Ridge and Short Hills, places where all the friends my parents knew back in Kiev lived now, while we lived in average Edison, where Mama claimed we would "get on our feet" before we could move somewhere more stuck-up. Once we were dismissed, I followed the girls into an elevator for the next workshop. Three men hovered over us, smiling smugly.

One looked at "Shah-lin" girl's name tag and said, "You're not Kenny Rizzo's girl, are you?"

"Guilty as charged," she said, and the men got excited, introducing themselves and shaking her hand, like they had never met somebody's daughter before. Then, because they sensed they were ignoring the rest of us, they figured out who all the other dads were, declaring, "Great guy," "Love that guy," "Sharpest man I know"—how many floors did this building have?—until the first man put a hand on my shoulder and said, "And who's your father, honey?"

I swallowed. "Ivan Konnikov," I said, standing taller.

The man frowned and said, "No, I don't know that

one," and the others chimed in to agree. The jovial atmosphere disappeared completely, as if I had said my father was Joseph Stalin.

I said, "He only started working here a few months ago," and then they nodded a bit more enthusiastically, grateful for this excuse. I could have told them more. I could have said he would still be a hotshot scientist if we had stayed in Ukraine, but Mama was Jewish and decided we were all Jewish refugees and made Papa schlep our family to America, where he'd hardly made a dime as a physicist, and then my brother was born and he realized he had to make yet another sacrifice for his family, so here we were. And *here,* I was finding out pretty fast, kind of sucked.

Mallory Hazzard was not what I expected. For one thing, she was white. For another, she was gorgeous and insanely tall, a specimen from an entirely different breed of woman. Her blond hair fell to her waist—I assumed she'd have it pulled back because she was an athlete. She had a big nose that was somehow perfect and an adorable gap between her front teeth. She began by saying, "I never had it easy, growing up. I lived in a dirt-poor town in West Virginia with nine brothers and sisters. My dad died in the mines when I was a kid, but he gave me my first basketball for Christmas. Shooting hoops was the only way I could get out of the sticks and help out my poor mom. . . ."

The fathers were seated away from their daughters, on the other side of the room. It reminded me of the dances at school, girls on one side and boys on the other. Papa, who could rarely hide his emotions, had a constipated look on his face, though he stuck his tongue out when he caught me staring. If I hadn't known there was a women's basketball team that people cared about, then Papa probably didn't know what basketball was. I was pretty sure the only thing he'd ever done for sport back in Kiev was shooting beer bottles in the woods—though even that pastime had been cut short after he shot his cousin in the foot. As Mallory Hazzard talked about how proud she was that her American team took the bronze in the 1992 Olympics, Papa was probably thinking this woman's life hadn't turned out so bad, that at least all her hard work had gotten her something she wanted.

"I'm so glad to give back to the community today and so honored to have the opportunity to speak to so many young, talented women. Maybe a few of you will be a part of the WNBA someday," she said, and this even got a laugh. I laughed too, but not because I thought she was being cute. Though I didn't know everything about America, I was pretty sure there weren't too many basketball players with dads who worked at Goldman Sachs. We applauded, and then a swarm of girls got in line to get their picture taken with the celebrity and to get an autograph on the big posters of her face they had stacked up. I saw the "Shah-lin" girl up there, posing for a photo with the star, which was the first time I saw her smile, revealing big blue braces that made me almost feel sorry for her.

When the girl returned to my group, she said, "Oh my God. She was, like, so freaking nice. I can't believe it . . . I'm never going to wash my hand again." She clutched her rolled-up signed poster like it was a magic wand, but it didn't impress me. I had stopped being scared of her once I realized "Shah-lin" was only Staten Island. While her minions cooed around her, the girl zeroed in on me, like she was wondering why I wasn't tripping over myself to suck up to her too. But I turned away from her, toward the dads, and wondered how they didn't suffocate after staring at screens all day in their thick, itchy suits. Garbage men were far better off, I decided; they wore comfy, loose-fitting clothes and were constantly on the move.

"Garbage men," I said to the girl. "I hear they make a lot of money. How much do you think they make?"

Her eyes got huge. "Garbage men?" she said. "I mean, they probably make, like, minimum wage."

"Sounds pretty good to me," I said, backing away.

She narrowed her eyes, trying to figure out whether or not I was insulting her; I guess I wasn't sure either. The other girls glared at me, like they had some personal biases against garbage men.

Just to cover her bases, the girl managed to say, "You know you, like, totally clash, right? Did you get dressed in the dark or what?"

"Brace face," I managed, before fleeing the scene.

I wandered up and down the building for a while until I found the best view from the top floor. I looked down on the city, which was kind of gross but kind of beautiful too, with a few boats drifting into the harbor, not a cloud in the sky. Spring was all around us; the trees below had sprouted pink and white flowers. I peeked into the windows of the surrounding buildings, but all I saw were offices and more offices, and who knows what people did in any of them. One woman whose desk faced the window sat with her head in her hands. I promised myself I would never work in an office, especially not in a big room with endless desks and no barriers between them.

I didn't want to have any more awkward conversations in the elevator, so I took the stairs. After I went down about a dozen floors, I heard a strange noise below, and I followed it down to the next landing. It sounded like . . . crying? Choking? At first I didn't think it was her—for a number of reasons, like her red eyes, but mostly because her gorgeous blond hair was up. She sat hugging her legs like a child, and her big leather purse was wide open, revealing scattered makeup, some crumpled paper, and a half-empty water bottle. It was Mallory Hazzard.

What do you say to somebody famous? I scratched the back of my knee and heard myself say, "I like your hair up."

"Thanks," she said, giving me a small smile. She didn't seem all that surprised to see me. I guessed that when you were famous, people were always sneaking up on you.

"Do you usually wear it like that?"

"I do. Except when I have to do this . . . promotional bullshit. Sorry," she said, patting the ground. I sat down without hesitating. It was the first interesting thing that had happened all day.

"Why do you have to do that stuff?" I said.

"Do you always ask so many questions?"

"You sound like my dad."

"What's your name, kid?"

"Oksana."

She smiled. "Like Oksana Baiul. Nice. I'm Mal," she

said, reaching out to shake my hand. It was quiet in the stairwell but not in a bad way. Did no one take the stairs anymore? "Any particular reason you're not doing the whole father-daughter thing?"

"It turns out it's not really a father-daughter thing. They separate you from your dad all day. And all the girls are snobs. I don't have anything to say to them."

"Don't let them get to you, kid," she said, taking a sip of her water. I tied and untied my sneaker, waiting for her to say more. She sighed and said, "I do this nonsense for the money. To tell you the truth, I don't have much going on. I make ends meet by dealing with assholes at places like—Goldman Sachs. No offense to your old man. I'm sure he's a nice guy."

"He is," I said. I searched for a way to show her my dad was special, nothing like the fools in the elevator. "Back in Ukraine, he was kind of a big deal," I began, and her eyes widened. Telling her he was the Math Olympics champion would mean nothing; I had to think outside the box. "He was in the Olympics," I said.

"The Olympics?" she said. "For what?"

This gave me pause. I pictured Papa, who was broad-shouldered and somewhat tall but not exactly athletic-looking, and considered the options available to the members of my track team.

"He threw the javelin," I told her. "He was a gold medalist in javelin."

"Seriously?" she said. "Man, what I would have given for the gold. That's beyond amazing. You should be incredibly proud of him."

"Oh," I said, "I am."

She took a sip from her water bottle and I asked if I could have some too. She said, "That's not water, honey."

I grabbed the bottle and took a swig anyway. It was sharp and bitter and left my stomach feeling queasy and warm. It must have been vodka. What my parents drank. "Gross," I said. "That's even worse than coffee."

"You don't need that stuff yet," she said.

Before I could answer, I heard a voice say, "Oksanachka? Is that you?"

"Oh shit," Mallory Hazzard said. She snuck out of the stairwell, leaving me all alone. Papa was about ten floors down and he was coming up fast. I got up and pointlessly adjusted my shirt.

"Where did you go? I was worried you ran out to Battery Park. What's the matter with you?"

"I got lost, Papa. I was just looking for the bathroom."

"Does your father look like a complete fool to you?"

I shook my head and scuffed the stairs with my shoe. We stood there looking at each other. I was deciding whether to tell him about the weird men who didn't know who he was.

"It's my fault."

We jumped at the sound of Mallory Hazzard's voice. She'd returned to the stairwell, looking radiant, like she hadn't been crying or drinking at all. Her hair was down and her lips shone with freshly applied gloss. Papa was starstruck, stumbling backward, awed by her beauty—and her celebrity. It surrounded her like a force field. I didn't know what she wanted to say, but I knew my heart would break if she incriminated herself to Papa.

I stepped in front of her and said, "It's not her fault. I

left because . . . the girls were being mean to me, and Mal made me feel better."

But Papa barely heard me. He put a hand on the railing. "I am sorry that my daughter troubled you," he said. "She likes to follow her own path. . . ."

"It's no trouble," she said, sounding completely not drunk. "She's a good kid."

Then Papa smiled shyly. He pulled out the notepad he kept in his back pocket. "For my daughter—would you mind?"

"Of course not," she said, smiling as she signed her name. Then she grabbed a scrap of paper from her bag and handed it to my father. "Would *you* mind? I hear you were in the Olympics."

Papa laughed. "Well, yes, but—"

"Your daughter told me all about it."

He looked at me like I had just won the National Spelling Bee.

"Oh, nonsense," he said, blushing, but he signed the paper anyway. "What a day! I thank you for giving me the greatest pleasure. My daughter will not forget this," he said, shaking her hand.

"The pleasure is all mine," she said, tucking the page into her bag.

I stepped back, into the corner. Those two had lost something that was very precious to them a long time ago, and I couldn't help them get it back. There was an understanding between them, and I had no business being there. Why was this day taking so long to end? The three of us regarded the stairs winding above us. The building must have had fifty floors, at least. For a moment, as Papa cleared his throat, I had the terrifying fear that he would burst into song, though he hardly ever sang, he only listened. But they just stared at each other. Papa was not unhandsome—at least he was better-looking than the dead-eyed men he worked with. His sandy hair was thick and his blue eyes burned bright.

I couldn't stand there any longer, so I mumbled something about needing the bathroom and left them alone. I found an empty hallway and I walked on my hands from one side to the other until I got dizzy and had to stop, watching the spots flickering and flickering before my eyes until the world returned to normal.

I found Papa at his desk a little while later, admiring his family photo; thankfully, it was time to go. When we left the office, I saw the elevator jerks standing outside with the other "Grrrrrl Leaders!" and their dads, who were not just older than my father but fatter and uglier too. Staten Island girl was beside her dad, a big dark-haired guy holding a paper cup of coffee, and just the sight of the bitter drink made me almost gag. Papa lit up with the security guards, and while they were making small talk, I wandered away, toward the elevator-jerk group. I marched toward the head creep as the girls raised their brows at me.

I said, "My dad is Ivan Konnikov, remember? You may not know who he is, but he was the Soviet Math Olympics champion once." I stopped and took a breath and prepared to exaggerate a bit. "He had dinner with Brezhnev to celebrate his victory. People all over the Soviet Union knew my father's name—he was famous!" I took a step back, catching my breath, embarrassed I had said so much.

The man said, "That's wonderful, honey. We'll look out for him."

They gave me these amused smiles, like I was just some dumb kid they were humoring.

"Dinner with Brezhnev, huh?" one said, nodding. "Is that him?" We turned toward my father, standing with the guards. He smiled and lifted a hand, cigarette smoke rising above him.

"Who the heck is Brezhnev anyway?" Staten Island girl said.

"That's him, all right," I said, ignoring her. "Ivan Konnikov. Don't you forget it."

I made sure I was out of Papa's line of sight, and then I lurched slightly toward the Staten Island coffee dad and made him cry out as he spilled some of the brown slush on his sleeve, though he had done nothing to me.

Papa put a hand on my shoulder when I returned to him. "My daughter," he said to the guards, and they smiled at us as we walked away.

In the parking garage, we waited for someone to pull our new Passat around. Most of the other cars in there were not like ours—shiny BMWs, Lexuses, and Mercedeses—because Papa hadn't had time to make real money yet. But that day, Papa could have been going home on a parade float. When we drove off, he had this dopey grin on his face and didn't say anything for a while. He was so happy he didn't even complain that we spent a good ten minutes behind a fire truck, unable to see a thing. Squares of yellow light flicked on all over the city as the sun went down.

Papa said, "Today was nice, wasn't it, Oksanka Banka? It's not every day that you meet a star! This job has some advantages!"

"She was such a great role model," I said, knowing this would add some pointless comfort to his day. I was getting pretty good at lying by then and wondered if it should alarm me. But why should I care if he couldn't see who she really was—or if she really knew about his past?

"I found the woman to be quite inspiring," Papa said.

He smiled again, as if all his pounding away at the computer and the hours he spent on the road that made him come home like a zombie Mama had to bring back to life were worth it after all. He turned on the classical music at a reasonable volume and drummed the wheel, staring off into a newly bright world. But after we pulled into the Holland Tunnel, I realized that we hadn't gone back to Battery Park. I hadn't wanted to go back there when he'd suggested it, but I suddenly felt I had missed out. I remembered the long-ago day when Papa and Mama and I had gone there for ice cream and asked a stranger to take pictures of us with the Statue of Liberty in the background. That was what we thought we did, anyway. After the photos were developed, we cracked up when we saw that we were blocking the statue in every shot. You could just barely make out her torch shining over our heads, hovering below the dirty clouds.

LIGHT YEAR

The word was "transient."

"Temporary," I said. "Fleeting."

Mrs. Donovan sighed. We were at her kitchen table, going over my SAT flash cards for the millionth time. I tried to pay attention as I watched her neighbor tearing down his Christmas decorations through the window.

"You really don't need me. I'm just stealing your money, kid," she said.

" 'Transient,' " a voice said. "Also a word for 'bum.' "

"They won't use it like that on the test," Mrs. Donovan said, turning toward a scruffy green-eyed man who wore a HARVARD CLASS OF 1993 sweatshirt. She introduced me and said he was her son, Benny, who was staying with her for a little while. He picked up my binder and studied my full name, which I had written on the top.

"Nice to meet you, Oksana . . . Konnikova," he said as he shook my hand.

"Nice work," I said. "No one ever says it right on the first try."

"Most people don't try hard enough."

We stared at each other until Mrs. Donovan said, "Benny just signed on to coach the track team, so you'll be seeing more of each other."

"How do I hate winter track," I said. "Let me count the ways." This made him laugh. I said, "Did you like Harvard?"

"Of course," he said, but his voice fell flat. "I studied English like a good son." He lifted the book he was holding, which was *The Stranger*.

"I love reading," I said idiotically. "*The Stranger*'s one of my favorite books," I added, though I hadn't exactly read it. He smiled like he knew I was lying. I wanted to ask what he was doing coaching track in Edison, New Jersey, if he'd graduated from Harvard, but I didn't want to act like I cared too much in front of his mom. He peered in the fridge as she picked up the next flash card.

" 'Avuncular.' "

It was such an easy one that I waved it away. So was the next one. And the one after that.

"The milk's expired," Benny said.

"Don't just stare at it. Throw it out," Mrs. Donovan said, but he was already walking away. She stood and poured the milk down the drain as her neighbor dragged a deflated reindeer into his garage.

"Now," she said, returning to the table. "Where were we?"

I felt her son's hand still burning into mine as she held up the next card. Though Mrs. Donovan had been my teacher all of sophomore year, she had only mentioned her son once. That had been a year ago, when I returned to her class after my father died. "It's not a fair thing,"

she'd said, hugging me after the other students filed out.
"It was so awful when my son lost his father. . . ." Now I
wondered: How had her son reacted, and when had it
happened? I was so distracted I said I didn't know what
the word on the next card meant. She gave me a puzzled
look and told me the definition. I laughed because it was
so easy. It was "dilemma."

The next day working at the school library was slow. Mrs.
Grundy was giving a tutorial to an AP bio class in the
back, and people weren't exactly falling all over the poetry display I'd spent hours perfecting. A few Korean ju-
niors were memorizing the answers to an old calc test.
They got their tests from the Korean seniors for free; I
got mine from them in exchange for Mama's sleeping
pills. Mr. Ferraro stopped making new tests after his son
died in 9/11 that fall.

I was working in the library when I found out about
it, after Mrs. Grundy wheeled out a television with the
grainy image of the burning towers on it and we heard
the students with parents who worked in the city get
called to the front office one by one. I tried to feel something, some kind of fear or horror for our fucked-up
world, but I didn't have any pity left for anyone outside
my family. I found Mrs. Donovan after her class let out
that day, and she gave me a big hug. "The world's full of
nasty surprises, kid," she had said, and then she shrugged
and added, "That's all I've got." I didn't realize how
much I missed her until that moment. I asked her to be
my SAT tutor later that month, though I didn't really
need help.

It didn't take long to find Mrs. Donovan's son in an old yearbook, though most of the students were white back then, instead of Indian or Asian with a handful of Russians like me. Benny was in practically every picture, a smooth-faced baby. I stroked his face, wondering at the arbitrariness of time, how he happened to be born fourteen years earlier than I was. There was his pale, muscular body as he crossed the finish line in a race, his jaw clenched and his head back like he was defying gravity. The goofy look on his face as he gave a speech as student council president. The smirk in his photo for Most Likely to Succeed.

But even then there was an emptiness I recognized in his eyes, because I saw it in Mama. I wanted to own it, that sadness, to embrace it until it warmed me up and hugged me back. But I didn't get it. What did he have to be so sad about?

The bell rang and I jumped. My boyfriend, Koz, approached the front desk. He grabbed my copy of *The Stranger* and my calc book, though I could have carried them myself.

"You look cute in that sweater," he said. I was wearing one of my mom's concoctions.

"Maybe I don't want to be cute."

"Too bad, Calf. You can't help it. Like Lito can't help hitting the bottle between classes."

"Shut up," I said, but I laughed anyway.

In spite of his remedial math classes and frosted tips, Koz won me over by making me laugh on the track bus just after my dad died. I was feeling extra emo right then, reading *The Bell Jar* and itching to write my own moody poems, "High and Dry" on repeat on my Discman. He put on my headphones and said, "Now, that's some music I could really slit my wrists to." I cracked up, and by the end of the ride he had his arm around me. The only time we had spoken before was when he started calling me Calfnikova, after he saw my huge calves when the season started. As we got off the bus that day, he said, "I can tell the guys to stop calling you Calfnikova." I said, "Don't. I'm used to it."

Now he said, "Did you know we're getting a new coach? He's Mrs. Donovan's son."

"Oh yeah?" I said, not sure why I was lying. He made fun of Lito some more, but I didn't feel up for it. My brother had woken me up with his nightmares twice the past night, and I was exhausted.

We stopped outside my calc class, where Mr. Ferraro was wiping off the board, getting chalk all over his belly. This was the part where Koz and I made out, but I could tell we both wanted to skip it. I squeezed his hand and said, "See you at practice."

Every season, the new runners lined up by the bleachers, shivering as they waited to get their warm-ups from Mazzo. With his gold chain and forever tan, he looked like a Seaside bouncer as he judged the new crop. He sent the black kids to sprinting, the white and Asian kids to distance, and he scrunched up his face at the Indians, like it took every brain cell he had to say, "Try mid-distance." Someone always complained about Mazzo's antics, but I found it hard to hate someone that simple. It was like how people got worked up about Bush. Why bother?

Koz ran by and squeezed my shoulder. "Ready for a new season, Calfzilla?"

"Born ready."

Benny—Coach Benny—stood in the center of the track, timing 400 splits. Coach Lito, booze addled and wobbling like a bowling pin that refused to go down, was showing him the ropes. Benny nodded smugly, like being a coach was a role he was trying out. They didn't have a uniform for him yet, so he wore the hoodie Lily had designed for our team fundraiser. It read, BURN, BABY, BURN! THE HOOVER HAWKS ARE ON FIRE! Below that, she had drawn a sneaker with red and orange flames exploding out of it, licking their way up to the top like tiny fiery tongues, consuming everything in their wake. Benny lifted a hand in my direction and I ran up to him.

"Look who it is," he said. "My mom's favorite student."

"I don't think you're supposed to say that. Besides, she's not my teacher anymore."

"I don't care about what I'm supposed to say."

"Good for you," I said. We stared at the other side of the track, where Koz and Lecky were pretending to stab each other with the javelins. "Why is it so easy for some people?" I said.

"That's a question I've been asking myself for a long time, Oksana Konnikova."

"At Harvard?" I said, trying to recover from the sound of my full name in his mouth, like he was tasting every syllable. "Was that something you asked yourself there?"

"Only every day," he said, fiddling with his stopwatch.

"I'd love to go to Harvard."

"Why?"

"It's the best," I said, knowing how dumb this was. It had to do with Papa's idea of America. If he was going to abandon his physics career to suffer on Wall Street—just a short walk from the Towers—then it would be for the family, so my brother and I could make something of ourselves. If I went to Harvard, it would prove he had done something right. He'd worked so much that he'd spent more time driving to and from work than with his family, so if it wasn't for us, then what was it all for? I said, "My dad . . ."

"So you're one of those," Benny said, which really pissed me off.

"I'm not one of anything," I said.

The night after our first meet, which we won by a hair, Koz came over after Mama and my brother fell asleep. We made out in bed for a while and then he folded his arms behind his head and stared at the glow-in-the-dark stars on my ceiling, childish idiot stars Papa had put up long after I was too old for them.

"I should really take those down," I said.

"Maybe you should," he said, and for some reason I was annoyed.

"I kind of like them."

He laughed. "Suit yourself, Calf. I was just trying to be agreeable."

"Here's something you can agree with," I said.

I reached into his pants and stroked his dick. Though his friends didn't know it, Koz—a Catholic—didn't believe in sex before marriage. He didn't even believe in blow jobs, though Lily had given me an extensive tutorial, using a Popsicle, just in case. After I finished, we were quiet, until I felt a jolting pain in my leg.

"Fuck," I said, and I flexed my foot and stretched forward until the pain stopped.

"Let me help," Koz said, but I gently shoved him away. I guess I wasn't so gentle, because he looked hurt. He said, "You all right?"

"Of course."

I got cramps in my calves a lot, usually at night. Though Papa had barely been home during the day, I could always count on him in the middle of the night, when I'd wake up crying out, and he'd rush to my room and flex my leg until the pain went away. "There you go, my dear girl," he'd say. "All better."

Koz got up and zipped his jeans. "It's pretty musty in here," he said. "I would open up the window if I were you."

"When it gets warmer," I said, but he was already walking away.

Later that night, my brother cried out and I ran to his room. The blanket Mama made was soaked and Grisha the hamster was agitated, banging into his wheel. My brother read more books than any almost-five-year-old and was full of knowledge about presidents and dog breeds, but he didn't know how to stop wetting himself. I cleaned him up and took him to my bed. He only let me take care of him after his nightmares now, which had started after Papa died. Me, I never remembered my dreams. I would have traded with my brother in a heartbeat.

"Papa got stuck on the train tracks and I couldn't pull

him off. You should have seen his face. He looked so sad," he said.

"His face was like that because you're sad, Mishka. But he's not sad. He's somewhere up there, laughing at us."

"Up with your glowing stars?" he asked, nuzzling into me, his voice thick with sleep.

"Higher than that, silly," I told him, tossing a semen-stained tissue in the trash. "He's up there with the real stars."

I was late for gym. Lily had me trapped by her locker, rambling about her latest fight with her boyfriend, Vinay. She was saying, "The fuck is his problem? If he wanted to date somebody who gave him head all the time, then he should get with a white girl . . . no offense." I wasn't offended. I was mostly counting down the minutes until practice. I did find it funny that a Korean girl was telling me white girls were slutty when she was the one who wasn't a virgin.

I only realized I said what I was thinking when she said, "What's the matter with you, OxyContin? You think you know everything now?"

"All I know is I'm late for gym."

"Whatever," she said, nudging me as she slinked off to the art wing. Lily never stayed mad for long. I speed-walked down the hall until I heard a voice behind me.

"Oksana Konnikova."

I moved into the dark, narrow corridor that led to the auditorium stage, until there was just an arm's distance between me and Benny. He grabbed the ends of my scarf, pulling me closer. Static jolted from it and I could feel my hair flying up. I tried to smooth it down but it only crackled more.

"Cool scarf."

"My mom made it." I felt dizzy and short of breath. "She made me, like, five this month alone. The only thing she does anymore is make scarves and mittens and sweaters for me and my brother. You'd think we live in Siberia or something. . . ." He smiled like he knew I was rambling.

"It's all right," he said, dropping the ends of my scarf. "I like hearing you talk."

"I finished *The Stranger*. I mean, I read it again. It's pretty dark."

"Is it?" He scratched the back of his head and gave me a grown-up smile. "You ready?"

"For what?"

"To kick South Brunswick's ass tomorrow."

I considered jumping into coach-athlete banter, but I knew it wouldn't impress him.

"Not really. But it doesn't matter what happens. I can win or lose, and it won't make a difference. I just run so I don't sit at home and go nuts."

He smiled. "That sounds about right to me."

The final bell rang but I didn't move. I was embarrassed about talking so much. I said, "Can you write me a pass?"

"I'm not a teacher."

I walked away holding the ends of my scarf, feeling the heat on the back of my neck. I studied myself in a display of football trophies in the lobby and barely recognized the girl with the rumpled hair who felt wild in front of her teacher's son.

The 9/11 memorial was next to the trophies, showing a picture of Ferraro's son along with ones of two dads of kids I didn't know. Every few weeks, Mr. Ferraro would cover the memorial with NEVER FORGET posters, which the administrators usually tore down. His son stood on a porch wearing a plaid shirt and a dopey smile that seemed inappropriate for such a solemn display. In the picture his father chose to represent him, taken who knows how long before he jumped out of his building to avoid getting burned alive, the man looked almost lovesick.

I spent lunch helping Mrs. Donovan grade sophomore quizzes on *The Odyssey*. The final question was: *How many years went by before Odysseus returned?* Someone wrote, *two thousand light-years,* and she chuckled as she drew a red line through his answer.

"Benny seems to be doing well," she said, studying my face.

"He's great," I said. "The team loves him." This wasn't strictly true, but it was better than "Everyone thinks he's stuck-up but I might be obsessed with him."

"I'm so glad," she said, smiling big. She hummed to herself, not even caring when her kids had clearly not done the reading.

When she taught *The Odyssey* last year, she once stepped away from her desk to stare out a window during a discussion. "Penelope's one lucky broad," she had said. "She got her man back." Then she stared at us, bewildered, as if we could relate. I didn't know when her husband had died, but I loved her even more after that.

"I'm so glad," she said again. "I was so worried. I just want—I want to make the world safe for him, but there's only so much I can do, and it terrifies me."

"There's no need to worry." She didn't look convinced, so I changed the subject. I said, "What is a light-year, anyway?" I didn't hear her answer, because I saw Benny walking down the hall, looking at his stopwatch like it could tell him something important.

Plainfield was a joke. I placed first in the mile by five seconds. Misty O'Farrell, Plainfield's blond elf of a miler and one of the only white girls on the team, normally put up more of a fight. Plainfield was the only school around in shittier shape than ours. Cracks ran through the track like varicose veins.

Koz was doing his comedy act on the ride home. As we passed a water tower, he said, "Why do they put the water up so high? So nobody steals it?" The guys cracked up, but Benny interrupted him before he had a chance to riff.

"The elevation makes it flow into the pipes."

"Right," Koz said, offended. "Thanks for the pro tip, man."

We passed Bollywood Cinema, formerly Hollywood Cinema. They still had movies for white people, but they served samosas along with popcorn. I liked samosas better than popcorn anyway, but Koz didn't like going there anymore. I expected him to complain about it, but he just shook his head and let go of my hand. I pulled out my

SAT book and refreshed myself on geometry, or, as Lily called it, "white-people math."

The bus passed the front of our school, a two-story slab of cement that looked like a mausoleum. I was glad Papa wasn't buried, that he was in an urn in our living room, though I didn't like how it was above the TV Mama got after he died, because he hated TV and found it far inferior to the stereo. The inside of the urn looked like the jar where he threw his cigarette ashes.

"What does the school look like to you?" I asked Koz.

"I don't know what the right answer is, Calf. It looks like a fucking school."

"There's no right answer."

"Is that right," he said. "Then why do I feel like I keep getting everything wrong?"

He tried to get me to go to the Rutgers food trucks, but I passed, though he was my ride. I waited outside for Benny to leave his office and asked him to take me home.

"Your boyfriend can't take you?"

I shrugged. My hair flew up in the wind. My sweat had cooled, making me shiver.

"All right, kid. Get in."

I climbed into his musty car. "I looked you up in the yearbook," I said. "You had everything back then. What happened to you?"

He laughed. "You don't waste any time, do you?"

"What happened to you?"

"Why do you care? What, you're worried you're going to lose it too?"

"Maybe I already have."

He drove out of the lot as I told him where I lived. And then, in a monotone he could have used to tell me the distance workout for that day, he told me what I wanted to know. At Harvard, he'd spent all his time reading, didn't see the point in going to class. In high school, there had been too much noise for him to see that. He said, "The edges blurred. It wasn't anything romantic. I broke down during my senior year and went away for a while. I spent most of the time reading, really. I read all of Proust. The pills helped a little. I finally graduated and moved to the city and tutored rich kids. But last summer, I got tired again, so I moved back in with my mom. She thought it would help to get me back here, to remind me of my glory days. . . ."

I waited for him to mention his dad, knowing he must have played a hand in all this. I wanted to ask when he'd died, but instead I said, "Is it helping?"

"I'm not you, all right? You're just a kid. I know you love the fucking *Bell Jar*, but you're gonna be fine. Trust me." I turned toward the window, and he squeezed my arm. "Most Likely to Succeed," he said. "More like Most Likely to Smoke Weed."

"How about you get to know me before you tell me who I am?" I said. I hadn't meant for it to come out so mean. Until then it hadn't occurred to me that he didn't know about my dad, that this fact that dominated my existence wasn't written on my face, that his mother hadn't mentioned it.

He parked in front of my house. "You're right," he said, resting his hand on my thigh. "I do want to know you. I'm just—trying to keep my distance."

My brother stood at the kitchen window, watching us. His blond curls were getting really wild. I would have to give him another haircut soon.

"That's my brother," I said. "And my mom's probably on the couch, watching *Law & Order* and knitting more shit I don't need."

"Where's your father?"

"Papa died a year ago," I said as my brother pounded on the glass. "Or maybe it was yesterday."

Mama was on the couch as I predicted, under a blanket she had made, watching *Law & Order*. Papa's sister's painting of his head rising out of a fruit bowl hung behind Mama; before, I'd just thought it was kind of weird, but it seemed to mock us now. There were spools of yarn at Mama's feet. She was knitting, always knitting—something she never did when Papa was alive, when they spent evenings drinking wine and listening to Soviet music. I would give them their privacy, but sometimes I'd walk by and see Papa saying, "Shhh," and lifting a finger when he heard the raspy croon of Vysotsky or the tortured howls of Viktor Tsoi, as if he were in the presence of something holy, and Mama would dutifully listen to whatever melody delivered him to this sacred state. Now she just came home from her accounting firm, freed the sitter, flicked on the television, and picked up her yarn; she was like Penelope, except the shroud was for herself, there was no chance her husband was coming back, and there were no suitors. Her best friend, Valentina, kept trying to set her up with random Russian bachelors, but she said it was too soon.

My brother came in from the kitchen. As I kicked off my shoes, he said, "That was a Nissan Sentra." This made Mama perk up.

"Who took you home in a Nissan?" She knew Koz drove a Ford. I told her it was a friend from the team and she went back to knitting.

Mama used to be a real person, with friends, a job she actually cared about, and a sense of humor. She would worry about me and my brother getting cold, as Jewish mothers do, as if that was the only thing left, her covering us in layers of wool, as if the warmth would fix everything. The last time I saw Mama's mother before we left Kiev, when she was already deep in her dementia, her remaining concern had also been keeping me warm; her parting words to me had been, "Bundle up, darling Yaroslava." Mama returned to Kiev to bury her soon after Misha was born, and though I knew it was too early for her brain to follow suit, it worried me. It made me wonder what would be left of me if I fell apart. Would I spend my days holed up with a book? Running laps? Studying until I went blind?

My brother opened his book on the presidents. He could already name all the states and capitals. And fifty breeds of dogs, every car that passed our house, the trees and plants in the woods; in the summers, he sat by the creek out back, naming all of the fish and even the rocks. Where had he come from? When I was his age, I was always running, running, running. Next year, he'd go to kindergarten, leaving Mama alone.

I pulled him up and said, "Let's get some air. We have an hour before dark."

"Be careful out there, little fools," Mama said, but she didn't mean it. The worst thing had already happened, so she didn't really need to worry anymore. We kissed her on the forehead before stepping out into the cold.

A few boys played basketball at the park; one kid shot and missed wildly and the others cracked up. When we got close, my brother dropped my hand.

"Did you know that William Howard Taft was the fattest president?" he said.

"That's quite an honor."

"He once got stuck inside the White House bathtub even."

"How did they get him out?" I asked as we reached the frozen creek. Scraggly trees swayed behind it and my brother's face clouded over. He didn't like not having all the answers. "What a thing to be remembered for," I said.

As we turned back, I saw that even the laziest people had stripped their homes of holiday decorations. Which was too bad, because the strung-up lights made the town look almost pretty.

Neel Shah was playing piano in the house across from ours. Papa had loved hearing the boy play. On one rare evening when Papa was home early, our family stood outside Neel's house, listening to song after song. We went back inside after I said I was tired, which was something that kept me up at night a few weeks later, after Papa's brand-new BMW was crushed by a Dodge Neon during his morning commute. Would it have killed me to stay out a bit longer, hear a few more notes, give Papa another moment of peace? I couldn't forget the look on his face as he put an arm around me and my brother and said, "That, my dears, is the sound of perfection." I nodded, though I'd never understand why it made him so happy. It just sounded like a lot of noise to me.

I sat in the car Mama let me borrow, in the junior lot after the next meet, not ready to go home. It had been an indoor meet and my lungs burned from running through the thick dead air. I don't know how long I was sitting there when Koz tapped my windshield.

I rolled down the window. "You scared me," I said.

"My bad." He still wore his jersey, and the white-blond hairs on his arms pricked up from the cold.

"Where's your coat?" He shrugged and I said, "Get in. I don't want you to freeze to death."

"That's the most you've cared about me in a while. Ever since your coach showed up," he said, though he did get in, pushing aside my mostly unread copy of *Swann's Way*.

"Stop it," I said. "He's practically twice my age."

"That's what makes it so fucking gross."

Koz's minions walked by, humping the air when they saw us. I honked and they jumped away. I pulled out of the lot, and the remaining cars receded in my rearview. We cruised down Tingley Lane, passing the strip of tired restaurants by the fire station.

"Did you see that?" Koz said. "They're tearing down Carmine's for another Indian restaurant. Fucking A."

"Carmine's was kind of gross anyway."

His lips got tight. Carmine's was where we'd gone on our first date. After we'd split a giant bowl of tortellini he'd said, "Big calves, big eyes, big appetite. I like it," and I heard myself telling him how Mama joked that I had big calves because I always stood on my toes around Papa to try to be as tall as he was when I was little. I don't know what I had against Carmine's all of a sudden.

"There's something you should know," he said. "Lecky's cousin went to Harvard with Coach Benny, and apparently he, like, went psycho there. You know what he did?" I put a hand on his shoulder but couldn't stop him. "He jumped on a table in the dining hall and started shouting at the top of his lungs. Took out a knife and started carving up his neck. Blood was spraying all over the place. They had to drag him away—"

"That's bullshit," I said, braking hard at a stop sign. "He doesn't have any scars." I tried to focus on the road. There were piles of snow on either side of it, already black and slushy.

Koz's voice shook. "You and me have something special, Ox. I don't want you to get caught up with— someone dangerous."

"That's sweet of you, but I can hold my own. I'm a big girl."

"I don't want you to think you're invincible. I love you."

"Stop," I said, but the look in his eyes was so helpless that I squeezed his hand. On his street, the snowbanks were cleaner than on the main road. The snowman on his neighbor's lawn was melting, flashing a demented smile. I saw his tiny mother in the kitchen, making dinner for her husband and only son. The American flag Koz's dad had put up after 9/11 flailed in the wind.

"Here we are now," I said. "America."

Koz dropped my hand and said, "I want you to know who I am."

"What?"

"That's what he kept shouting," he said as he opened the door. "Over and over and over."

"Would you like a hug, sweetie? A Xanax?" said Mrs. Donovan, peering into me.

I was at her kitchen table, suffering through a passage about "The Hollow Men." I knew Benny was there because I smelled pot.

"I'm just nervous," I said, after too long. "Just a month to go before the test."

"You have nothing to worry about, kid."

The phone rang and Mrs. Donovan said it would be a minute, so I followed the skunky smell up the stairs. Photos of my teacher and her husband crowded the wall; in one, they stood in the Grand Canyon, looking tan and impossibly young. I remembered Mrs. Donovan crying for him in class. With his big nose and bulky camera, Mr. Donovan didn't look like a man who could inspire much passion, but I guessed that was how most people seemed when you weren't the one who loved them.

I walked down a dark hall until I saw a room with a fish tank and lava lamp, which bubbled around like an angry fetus. Benny stood by the window, smoking a joint. He faced the neighbor's house; the chimney sent puffs of smoke into the night air.

"Hey," I said, and he turned to me as he fumbled with his joint.

"Jesus. I didn't see you there."

"Sorry. Your mom's on the phone."

"Right."

"I don't mean to be in your way."

"No," he said, grabbing my wrist. "Stay a minute."

I came closer. I couldn't see his scars, because he wore a turtleneck. Now that I thought about it, he always wore a turtleneck or a sweatshirt—it was cold now, but he couldn't hide forever.

I said, "Can I be honest?" He nodded. "I couldn't get past the first page of *Swann's Way*."

He laughed. "Me neither."

"But I thought you said—"

"It made for a better story. I was too sedated to read much at the hospital. You know what I read? Comic books."

"Oh," I said.

He put out his joint and said, "This is a bad habit I'm trying to break."

"We all have them."

He brushed a strand of hair away from my face and said, "Not you, my dear."

He put his other hand around my waist and pulled me toward him. He kissed me and kissed me. His tongue was warm and ashy. My bones were turning to liquid. It was nothing like being kissed by Koz, who was sloppy and eager to please. I cupped his face and that was when I felt them, the small cuts under his ears. They didn't make me want to leave. I pulled down his turtleneck and ran my hands down his neck, feeling the rough, jagged skin underneath.

"What the fuck are you doing?" he said, pushing me away.

"I just wanted to see, that's all. It's not a big deal."

"So somebody told you," he said, his eyes narrowing.

"It all makes sense now. What was this, some kind of bet?"

"It's not like that. I just wanted to know if it was true." He looked so hurt that I didn't know what to do next. I tried conjuring the literary characters who'd instructed me over the years, but what popped into my head was Lily ranting in the hall. "If he wanted to date somebody who gave him head all the time, then he should get with a white girl."

I pulled down his sweatpants, got on my knees, and put his dick in my mouth. It was tender and almost hard. He put his hands on my shoulders to push me away, but they just stayed there as I tried to bring him to life. He moaned softly, and I was surprised by how much he sounded like Koz when I touched him, all the world's men reduced to the same boyish sound. But then he became completely limp and let out this strange, gurgling cry, and I pulled away. "I'm sorry," he said. "It's just been so long."

"A light-year," I thought, though I still didn't know what it meant. As I stepped into the hall, I remembered the pictures of his father.

"When did your dad die?" I said.

"Ten years ago," he said. "Or maybe . . ." I walked away before I could hear the rest.

On the bus to states, Benny blandly wished me luck, like I could have been anybody. Anytime I tried to talk to him, his eyes just glazed over and he gave me an empty smile that shattered me. With my head against the window, my hoodie up, I read through some poems I had written the night before, and I decided they were crap. I was thinking of the crying sound Benny made in his room. What had I done? What was I hoping he could give me?

That year the championships were in East Orange. A patchy field of grass separated the track from the Parkway, where cars zoomed behind a wire fence. Koz took second in the boys' mile, and the girls were called before I finished warming up. I got to the starting line and moved into the second row, behind Misty O'Farrell and her ponytail. Lito gave me a look like, "Are you nuts?" I shrugged. Why should I always be the one setting the pace? Let someone else do the work for once. I didn't care about Lito. What worried me was that Benny wasn't watching.

I took the first lap nice and easy. After the first 400, there were five girls in front of me. Benny wasn't near the starting line. He was walking toward the Parkway. By the second lap, it was just me and Misty, that Irish waif. I was tired of watching her blond ponytail bobbing up and down like a halfhearted whip striking at nothing— I passed the dumb bitch. Then I did the stupid thing I always do: I searched for Papa in the stands. He was always asking if he could watch me run, but I'd always told him, "No, no, you'd just make me nervous."

I was still ahead as the bell clanged at the final lap. I could still see Benny in the distance. He had almost reached the fence before the Parkway. I didn't think he would try to climb it, but Koz's story made it seem like nothing was off the table. Whatever he was doing was my fault. I ran off the track two straights from the finish. I ran past the coaches, past Koz, past the crowd, past the patches of icy grass, and past a few ducks, stopping just behind Benny. I tried to catch my breath. It came out white and dusty, like car exhaust. He wouldn't look at me.

"I didn't finish the race," I said.

"Another mistake. But you're young. You'll make plenty more." We watched the cars flying past us. He picked up a rock and lobbed it over the fence, just missing a truck.

"What's the matter with you?"

"A lot. But you know that already. You had your fun, didn't you?"

"I wasn't just having fun. I liked you. You let me be who I am."

"Just who you are right now. Don't worry. It'll pass."

"I'm sorry."

"I bet you are."

More cars zipped by: two taxis, a small truck with a horse swinging its tail in the back, and a beat-up minivan with thick black tape over its back windows.

I saw Koz running up with a medal around his neck, looking pale and cold.

"Leave her the fuck alone, man," he said, coming at Benny fast. I'd never seen the two of them standing together until then and didn't realize how much bigger Koz was.

Benny held up his hands and said, "I'm trying."

"Stop it," I said, making an attempt to move between them. "It's my fault. Please."

"Too late," Koz said. He cocked his arm, hesitated for a second when he saw the blank look on Benny's face, and punched him anyway. Benny fell and moaned, cover-

ing his face. Koz stared at his hand, Benny's blood dripping down his fingers.

"Are you coming with me or not, Calf?" He reached
his mangled hand out to me.

Benny looked up, his face wrecked. "Why don't you
ever call her by her fucking name?" I looked at Benny and
back at Koz.

"Shit," I said, falling over my leg. "Fucking cramp."

It was a cowardly move, I knew. Koz wasn't buying it.

Benny said, "Here. Let me help you," and he slammed
his head against the fence one, two, three times, before
we pulled him away, his forehead and cheeks streaked
with blood and rust. I looked for an authority figure. I
pictured Detective Olivia Benson from *Law & Order*
coming to save the day. But it was just Coach Lito running up with his fists clenched at his sides, reeking of Jack.

"What the fuck?" he said, and a few coaches followed
him and escorted Benny to the bus.

Koz wouldn't talk to me. I followed him to the bleachers, where the rest of the team was sitting. I watched him
rubbing his hand and saw how badly I had messed everything up.

"At least put on a sweatshirt," I said.

The Hawks ended up placing third—it would have
been second if I had finished my race, and first if Koz
hadn't gotten DQ'd for punching Benny, though the
coaches argued it wasn't fair because all that happened
after his race. Mrs. Donovan arrived in the Nissan Sentra
as the team dragged our equipment onto the bus. Benny
climbed out in a daze. He and his mother looked hunched
over and old as they bucked the wind. I wanted to go up

to them but I knew I would only make things worse, so I got on the bus and watched their car recede into the traffic.

Benny was in the hospital after that, first for his face, then for his mind. I knew I had ruined him enough and didn't consider visiting, though I did spend the weekend standing outside Koz's house, under his American flag. He wouldn't answer the phone or the door.

By Monday, the entire school knew what had happened. Everyone went quiet anytime I turned down the hall. I walked by Mrs. Donovan's room four times before I went in. I was afraid to ask about Benny, so I asked if we were still on for our last SAT session the next evening. Her face was pinched and stony, and I knew I shouldn't have come.

"We're done, kid. You'll be fine without me. And I'll be more than fine without you."

"I'm so sorry." I didn't know how much she knew and didn't want to find out.

"Yeah, yeah," she said, returning to her quizzes.

Koz sat on the other side of the cafeteria, avoiding my gaze. I ate the chocolate chip cookies Lily stole, which were gooey and underbaked, just perfect. Lily and Vinay were memorizing the answers to Ferraro's latest test, their lips moving silently. She kept glancing at me, but I just stared at Koz. She put an arm around me and said, "Damn girl, you must be hungry."

"I'm fine," I said, knowing I'd break down if she kept being nice.

"Suit yourself."

Lunch was almost over, and now was my chance. I needed to get Koz's attention. The teachers were already congregating by the exits. I climbed up on the table, nearly losing my balance. "What the—" Lily said, and I waited a beat until hundreds of eyes were on me. I even got the attention of "The IQ of 2 Crew," Lily's name for the cheerleaders and football players. The problem was, I had to say something. I hadn't thought far ahead. Koz was looking in my direction at last.

"I want you to know," I said, holding his gaze. He put down his sandwich. I tried to channel Benny, to think of what was going through his head when he jumped on the table in his dining hall and began cutting himself. But I didn't have it in me. I saw it was a popular day for Lily's hoodie, that dozens of kids wore the black sweatshirts with fire climbing up their chests. "I want you to know how proud I am of track and field. We got third in states!" I said. "Burn, baby, burn! The Hoover Hawks are on fire."

I jumped down to tepid applause and I walked away fast. Just before the front lobby, I heard footsteps behind me. Koz was rubbing his bandaged hand.

"Nice job up there."

"I'm sorry, Koz."

"It's too late for that. You made your choice on the field."

"I guess I did," I said, scuffing the floor with my sneaker. "I didn't mean what I said about Carmine's. You know I loved that place. The tortellini was amazing."

"Tortellini? Do me a favor. When you get home, open the fucking windows. Tortellini," he said again, shaking his head, and then he disappeared around the corner.

I passed Mr. Ferraro in the lobby. He was putting up another batch of NEVER FORGET posters around the 9/11 memorial. "Why not forget?" I wanted to say. "What good is it to remember?" I helped him put up the rest anyway. It didn't take very long.

He stepped back to admire his handiwork. "What do you think?"

From the angle where I stood, it looked like his dead son was perched on his shoulder. I moved away from him. "I think you need to make up some new test questions," I said.

My brother woke me up at dawn the day before the SAT. I kissed his forehead and wiped the sweat off his face. He hadn't wet himself this time.

"Everything's fine, rabbit. You were just having a bad dream." I climbed into bed with him and stroked his hair.

"Sana? When will the dreams stop?"

"Soon, soon. You'll see. Just go back to bed."

"Will you stay with me?"

"Of course," I said. "Of course I'll stay." Then something occurred to me. "How long is a light-year?"

"A light-year is a measure of distance, not time," he recited.

"What does that mean?"

He shook his head and closed his eyes. He didn't know everything.

Grisha ran in jagged circles in his cage, thinking he'd get fed because we were awake. I watched my brother close his eyes, wondering how much he remembered Papa, knowing that one day, Papa would be out of his dreams, that he wouldn't remember a thing about him. I was devastated for him, but I also thought he'd be lucky to have his head forever cleared of someone he loved. But maybe I was wrong. Maybe he wouldn't forget.

There was only an hour left before I had to get ready for school, and the sky was turning purple, the moon growing faint. The only house that was lit up belonged to Neel the piano maestro. Every morning, when I got up for school, I saw him finishing his routine, stretching his fingers. I opened the window as he began to play, though I was too far away to hear a thing, not that it would have made a difference. As the sun crawled up, his father pulled out of the garage, probably leaving for the city. He waved goodbye to his son, but the boy didn't look up, not even once, because he was so determined to finish his song.

ONWARD TO THE
BRIGHT FUTURE

I.

"Congratulations," Beeman said with a bow. "You are both free."

Beeman was Delta Chi president, so he had the honor of unlocking the plastic handcuff that connected Kornberg and me after we each tipped our bottles of bubbly upside down, proving we had consumed our allotted share. I was Kornberg's date to Champagne and Shackles only because an anorexic frosh named Stefanie with an F had bailed last minute, but I took what I could get. Our hands had been touching for so long that I was just about ready to combust. I thought I might explode right there, leaving Oksana particles all over the walls and ceiling and dirty couch.

"Not a moment too soon," Kornberg said, shaking off the cuff.

"Man is born free," I said. "Yet everywhere he is in plastic handcuffs."

"I wouldn't take it that far," he said, but I had made him laugh.

A few of us were crammed on the leather couch at the Delta Chi house on Teaberry Lane, my home away from dorm for the last three years. Beeman was with Ellie, who lived two floors below Rachel and me in a Gothic clocktower, a place we fondly called the Cocktower. Ellie was a wild girl who had supposedly taken a dump in a fish tank one night freshman year. Frankie was with Becky, a freckled girl I didn't trust because she didn't drink and people called her "chill."

I was decidedly not chill, particularly not that night, since I had snorted too much of the Adderall Frankie traded me for the sleeping pills I had swiped from Mama over spring break. My heart was already pounding, and Kornberg watching me with his hound's eyes and sandy Pushkin hair made it worse, so I started telling a story about a guy I'd brought back to the Cock the night before.

"We already had our clothes off," I said. "Coldplay was on. We were moments away from the act. He leans in and whispers in my ear—you know what he says? 'You're so sexy, Olivia.'"

Beeman leaned in too close. "What did you do next?"

I shrugged. "What was I supposed to do? It was either tell him my real name and kick him out or finish what we started."

"That's awful," Becky said. "I wouldn't know what to do either."

"Really?" Ellie said. "I would have kicked the fucker out. If you want to fuck me, you should at least know my name. It's not like he needed to know your sign."

"Did that really happen?" Kornberg said.

"Unfortunately," I said. But he was shaking his head like he didn't believe me; my story had failed to work its magic on him. I got up to regroup, kicking aside a bunch of plastic handcuffs on the way to the bathroom. I broke the seal and considered that I had been holding in my pee for so long and it had begun to hurt so much that it felt good to finally let it out, which was not unlike holding in my love for my date. I stared into the toilet for a long time but decided against puking.

The party had accelerated at an alarming rate in my absence. Three boxes of cheesy bread had materialized and a gaggle of freshman skanks were devouring it with abandon, hot melted cheese dripping into the cleavage of their lacy tops. Beeman was shooing a still-shackled happy couple off the rotting wood near the TV. Frankie was taking a hit from a tie-dye bong. Three seniors threw darts into a board with George Bush's face on it. Macy the dog lapped up salsa near the back door. *American Psycho* was on, and we were at the part where a bloody Patrick Bateman chases a prostitute with a chainsaw.

Kornberg was talking to Ellie like he had never seen a blonde with a tiny nose ring and a spray tan before. The girl was frankly too hot to be there, but she had exhausted her options, so she had to pick off the low-hanging fruit at the frat house. She belonged not with girls like me but with the clan of put-together Duke girls who had pin-straight fake blond hair, wore real pearls and Lacoste polos, majored in public policy, and overstayed their welcome on the ellipticals. Korn caught me staring and even winked, that bastard, and then he took Ellie's hand and led her up the stairs to his room.

Beeman was in the kitchen, looking defeated after losing his date, though encouraged by the fact that I had
also been ditched by mine.

"I should have held it in," I said.

"You couldn't hold it in all night."

He pulled two Coronas out of the fridge and even
handed me a lime wedge, a sign he was working me hard.
He was wearing a striped polo with black sweatpants
and green Crocs, trying to look like he was so rich
that he didn't need to bother with real pants or shoes. He
had been hoping for seconds ever since we'd hooked
up on Halloween, when I was dressed as a slutty Anna
Akhmatova and he was a Tootsie Roll.

"Why do girls love Kornberg so much?" he asked me.

Where could I begin? Zach Kornberg had held my
fragile post-Soviet heart in his hands since the moment
he read the first poem I had ever shown anybody, freshman year, and called it shit. He could see into the darkest
crevasses of my soul without judgment, and whenever he
laughed at something I said, he laughed with his whole
body—his throat, his shoulders, the light hairs on his
head—and it made me feel immortal. But this wasn't exactly the kind of thing I could say to Beeman.

I shrugged, trying to be "chill." I said, "He's kind of
tall."

"What about when he's sitting down?" he said, but he
didn't want an answer this time. He set down his beer
and moved closer to me. "Wanna check out my new video
iPod?"

My options were rather limited at that hour. It was too
late to call one of the prospects in my phone. My friends

were probably done giggling on Sarah's floor and recounting their wild nights, which meant Rachel was asleep so we couldn't spoon. I supposed I could always leave my baby brother a voicemail about how much I missed him. Or I could climb under the last blanket Mama had ever knitted for me and listen to Modest Mouse and miss my dad.

"Why not?" I told Beeman, and his eyes lit up like the flecks in Goldschläger.

Korn and I parked behind our old freshman dorm to eat Cook Out. I felt like I'd just gotten to college, but somehow we were two months away from officially being seniors. I dipped my greasy fries in ketchup and stared at the squat brick building and pictured the kids in there gearing up to face the night. Korn and I had met in the common room when I was mulling over the first poem I'd written about my father.

The poem was called "Onward to the Bright Future," and it was about how when I was a kid in Kiev, Papa would get me to stand on a chair at parties, lift my arm toward the sky in an imitation of Lenin, and shout his favorite Marxist catchphrase: "Onward to the bright future!" The party trick cracked up the guests every time. I wrote about how I couldn't get this image out of my mind whenever I was drunk at parties, thinking of how disappointed my poor dead immigrant father would be if he knew how frivolous I had become in this free land.

Kornberg had scanned the poem and frowned. "Do you really feel this way when you drink, or is this just

how you think you should feel? Most people drink pre-
cisely to forget shit like this," he had said, slapping me
awake. I ended up never turning the poem in.

I watched him to see if he too was feeling nostalgic.

"Ellie was fucking wild last night," he said, and I tried
not to look put off.

"Did she shit in your fish tank?"

"Do you have to be so vulgar?"

"I'm sorry," I said. "Did she defecate in your fish
tank?"

He sighed. "No, man, she was just wild," he said, but
he didn't elaborate. "How was the Cock? Get any action?"

"Pen-to-paper action," I said. I didn't feel like telling
him about my repeat performance with Beeman.

"When will I see it?"

"It's not ready."

Earlier that day, I had written the first thing I would
never show him. Post-Beemitus, I read Chekhov in the
gardens and was depressed I wasn't Chekhov, so I began
a joke poem based on his story "The Darling." Instead of
describing a woman who falls in love with a series of men,
mine depicted a girl who wastes her life watching her love
take a new girl up a staircase every night; he dies when
she's an old woman, and she has to carry his body down
the same fucking stairs and bury him on her own. I called
it "The Dumbass."

"When will it be ready?"

"A writer's work is never done."

"Suit yourself, Kon Artist."

"I don't wear suits."

I scooted up, but I still couldn't see much of the dorm.

Our view of the first floor was blocked by a cement wall that separated the freshman campus from the town. Some thought it was elitist and even racist given the racial makeup of Durham, but I just found it useless; there were a few points of entry and it wasn't even that high, so it wasn't really keeping anyone out. I didn't give it all that much thought, though. Kornberg put an arm around me and I felt his finger grease getting in my hair. I could have drowned in it.

Teaberry Lane was tense and musicless when we pulled up. The house was tan and ravaged like an irresistible older man slightly past his prime. All the guys plus Stefanie with an F—who was already making eyes at Kornberg—and Becky were crowded around the TV, watching the news. I knew something terrible had happened when I saw nobody was drinking.

"A stripper said she got raped by the lacrosse players last night," Frankie told us.

"Exotic dancer," Becky said.

"This is terrible, terrible," Beeman said, pacing around. This, coupled with the thirty people crowding his rotted floor, seemed too much for him to bear in one night.

Kornberg got the last floor spot and pulled me onto his lap. The reporter stood in front of the unremarkable white lacrosse house and delivered the news: The previous night, the lacrosse team had called two strippers-slash-exotic-dancers to the house, and one of them had accused three of them of raping her later that night. Neighbors had heard them shouting racial slurs at the women as they ran off. The police didn't reveal her iden-

tity or the identity of the accused guys. They were comb-
ing through the house for evidence now.

"She probably wants to be paid off."

"First we get robbed in the Sweet Sixteen and now
this."

"Innocent until proven guilty."

"Yelling racist shit isn't great, though."

"Different category of not great than raping somebody."

"That still doesn't excuse their behavior. Guilty or
not, we shouldn't root for them. They're the reason people hate Duke," Becky said.

"That's bullshit," Kornberg said.

It was possible those guys did it, even likely. Duke ath-
letes were a different species, which I didn't think about
much except during basketball season, when I pretended
to care. The lacrosse players, especially, were part of the
world Papa had entered when he went to Wall Street for
the sake of his family, and they weren't exactly on my
radar.

As people continued to debate whether or not the
guys did it, I slowly became aware of the fact that I was
sitting on Kornberg's lap for the first time in my life. I felt
his hot breath on my neck and could hardly breathe myself.

The arguing had dissipated into the latest screening of
American Psycho. Kornberg kept looking at me from the
corner of his eye like he was waiting for me to say something, maybe to point out that I had room to move from
his lap now that half the people had gotten up for beers.
But he just kept staring at me, or at least I was pretty sure

he was, and for a microsecond I wondered if he was waiting for me to tell him to take me up those same fucking stairs, but this couldn't have been true, this was not the right moment, and I was so overwhelmed and scared and freaked out that all I could think about was that I wanted him to stop staring at me.

I looked back at the screen, where Patrick Bateman was axing poor Paul Allen, a fountain of blood spurting over his chic banker's apartment, and thought of my father again, of how he had never watched a minute of TV in his life. The one time Mama had dragged him to a movie, he came home rubbing his eyes like a newborn, saying, "So many bright images—what do you do with them all? The horror! I will never sleep again!" This made me smile.

"Television is the opium of the pupil," I said, quoting my father.

Kornberg laughed, but then he patted me on the side, indicating that I could move off him. Then he said, "Don't you have anything better to do?"

I nodded toward Stefanie with an F and said, "Don't you?"

He laughed again and we watched the movie for a while, and when I got up to get a beer I came back and he was talking to the damn girl, who had red hair and sadly looked like a nice person but who was definitely not Ellie hot, not hotter than me. Just as I was getting ready to peace out, Beeman settled at my side.

"A few of us are going to check out the house. Wanna come?"

"I'll pass," I said. "Too tired."

He said it was only a few blocks away, but I didn't budge. What was there to see? I grabbed a slice of to-go pizza and left.

I had to cross the quaint colonial freshman campus to get to West, and by the time I entered the more menacing and Gothic upperclassman world, I was stuffed and sad. I walked up the six-floor shaft of the Cock, already feeling nauseous, so I was pretty pissed when I opened the bathroom door and saw that I had company.

Ellie was on the floor, hugging her knees, blocking my path. Her long, rumpled blond hair touched the ground. She looked up like she wasn't sure what I was doing there.

"Sorry," she said.

"It's okay," I said. I faced her for a moment, wondering if I should ask what was wrong, if I should sit next to her and stroke her hair and hear about whatever heartbreak had led her down this dark path. But I was tired and needed to puke and, anyway, she wasn't my friend.

"It's fine," I said pointlessly, as she put her head back down. "I'll just . . ."

I stepped around her to grab my toothbrush, and I could smell my shampoo on her. Earlier that year I had discovered she had been using my shampoo, but it seemed too late to move it out of the shower. The shampoo predicament signified some terrible flaw within me, not her, and I hated her for exposing it, even then. I got out of there fast and made it to the downstairs bathroom just in time to puke up the pizza.

I dodged reporters and news trucks to get to poetry workshop to see what people thought of "The Dumbass."

Allen English was a sacred space, separated from the Cock by the chapel and library, which was blocked by a man standing on a podium, yelling at a small crowd about how the Durham community would not stand for the disgusting behavior of the lacrosse players. "We need accountability! We need some answers, and we need them now!" The people cheered and held signs that read, STOP THE VIOLENCE! RESPECT THE COMMUNITY! NO MORE LIES!

"Excuse me. Sorry," I said, weaving through the people. I was sweating by the time I reached my creative writing class on the third floor.

Dr. Monroe wore a flowery dress and sat cross-legged with her wild hair falling over her shoulders, her tan, freckled skin vibrating with the auras of previous lovers. She had risen to relative fame by writing a memoir about spending her youth in a sex cult in California, where she had slept with men and women of all ages and proclivities in a variety of shocking combinations. She wore no makeup and was somewhere in her forties and was absolutely breathtaking. I hoped to be as weathered by love as she was, one day. I waited for her to acknowledge the sounds of the protesters, but she just jumped right into "The Dumbass."

"This is really relevant to hookup culture," said a pink-haired girl named Brooke.

"There are some strong immigrant themes in here. They could be played up, though," said a boy named Cooper, who thought he was Jack Kerouac.

The roar of the protesters kept me from focusing.

"Yes, yes," Dr. Monroe said slowly, after my classmates lost steam. She even closed her eyes, which was something she only did when she was making a particularly important point. "There is some humor here. It's all very funny, really, isn't it? We need humor, especially in difficult times, but we need to feel the hum of humanity below the surface. We can't just laugh into the void, can we, now? We have to ask ourselves, what is worth noting about this wild life?"

I didn't want to ask myself anything. I wanted someone to give me the answers.

The news released the names of the accused players a few weeks later: Collin Finnerty, Reade Seligmann, and David Evans. Someone also leaked an email written by a player named Ryan McFadyen after the strippers left. It said, *I plan on killing the bitches as soon as they walk in and proceeding to cut their skin off while cumming in my Duke issue spandex.* He was riffing on the way Patrick Bateman talked in *American Psycho,* though nobody cared about the context. President Brodhead suspended the team after that; the coach resigned before he could get fired. A bunch of community members, students, and faculty were going to protest at the house.

I thought about going, but I wanted to write a serious poem first. I couldn't focus. I went for a run through the gardens to clear my head, but it didn't help. When I came back, I just sketched Kornberg's face about ten times before I realized it looked more like Pushkin than Kornberg. Then I snorted some Adderall and tried to avoid writing about Kornberg and wrote about my recent return to Kiev, after my grandmother retired there last year, when she and her brother, Boris, got me so drunk on the banks of the Dnieper that I puked. I wrote about how much my grandmother loved returning to the Motherland, how I wished there was a place, or maybe a person, that could make me feel at peace like that. The poem was sentimental and stupid, so I shoved it in a drawer. By the time I looked up, the darkness was creeping in from outside.

Everyone was in a festive mood by the time I showed up at Teaberry. Beeman had just gotten hired at Lehman Brothers and was as high as a kite, deliriously happy he could move to Manhattan and wear a suit and eat twenty-two-dollar sandwiches and probably die of a heart attack by fifty. I congratulated him and Kornberg gave me a look, as if he thought I was going to tell him what I really felt. To be honest, I was glad there was something to celebrate.

Kornberg and I took a break from flip cup and went to his room to get high. He rolled a joint on a copy of *Das Kapital* and we climbed on his roof and he told me about his encounter with Stefanie with an F, who wanted to cuddle after they fucked. I told him about my recent night with a senior named Conrad Champion, from my British Romanticism class. He was doing Teach For America next year and his bed had been littered with handouts and textbooks. As he'd cleared the educational materials so our romance could take off, he had said, "Can you believe I'm going to be somebody's teacher?"

"What a tool," Kornberg said.

"It was actually kind of sweet."

The boy's name stopped being funny eventually, and afterward he'd talked about growing up on a ranch in Montana. He would go off into the world and become somebody's husband, and I would be his anecdote. I saw his eager face floating before me and knew I was having a benevolent high.

I pictured each boy I had been with as a thick-stemmed flower I was delicately placing into a giant vase. There was room for many more. It was startling and beautiful and wild and sad.

It couldn't be more different from the life my parents had; they'd married at nineteen so they could get their own apartment and, as Mama insisted on telling me, "a place to make love at last!" Now Mama was moving in with her boyfriend, Sergei, a serious, bearded, and rich banker who actually seemed to enjoy his criminal job. She seemed happy enough, but I couldn't imagine that finding a place to make love was a big priority for her now. I guessed it was better for her than being alone, but I would rather be like Dr. Monroe, alone and free instead of settling.

Kornberg leaned back on his roof with his hands behind his head, and I did the same. Our elbows were touching and I felt electric. The roof felt like sandpaper and the stars were gratuitously bright. A big, friendly tree rose above the roof, and its leaves rustled with the wind.

I said, "I can't imagine marrying the first person you've ever been with."

Kornberg laughed. "It's too late for either of us to do that, isn't it?"

"Just a bit."

"You, Kon Artist," he said, "are the kind of girl I could marry by the time I'm, like, twenty-five."

I turned toward him to make sure I wasn't hallucinating. I said, "What, you'll be done fucking around by then?"

"That's not what I mean."

"Twenty-five is so old," I said. "Twenty-five is in forever."

I tilted my head closer to his to try to see what he did mean, but he just looked at the stars again. I was feeling too good to push it right then.

Nobody hooked up that night. We listened to Guster and played about fifty rounds of pong. I was on fire, I was burning up, my fingers were flames, and the plastic white ball sailed into those red Solo cups with a vengeance. Kornberg didn't try to get with anyone, Frankie was too high to try, and Beeman fussed around installing black lights in the living room. When they finally flickered on, everyone screamed, because the leather couch was covered in a million stains. Everyone acted like it was the most disgusting thing they had ever seen, but that was where I crashed that night, the lights still on, thinking it was kind of wonderful.

II.

When I got out of the Cock shower the next morning, Ellie was standing right where I had found her curled up just days ago. But she wasn't crying this time. Her hair was falling all over the place, still unstraightened, but she had full makeup on and the orange glow of her spray tan was brighter than ever.

"I know Kornberg is your friend, but you should be

careful around him. He raped me a few weeks ago, back at the house. I thought you should know."

"Kornberg is my friend," I repeated. I took a step back and put one hand on the wall.

"Your friend raped me," she said. She stared at me like she expected me to launch into a long defense. When I didn't, she said, "The lacrosse case made me realize I can't stay quiet about this. I wasn't going to do anything about it, at first."

"We don't even know if they did it."

Ellie narrowed her eyes. "You're so in love with him it's pathetic."

"Why are you telling me this?"

"I'm looking out for you."

"I already have a mother who does that."

She stretched her arms out toward me, palms up. The bones stuck out below her wrists. "You can't see them now, but I had crazy bruises on my wrists," she said. "From when he held me down."

I tried to stay calm, knowing that if I balked it would make her think I believed her. There was nothing on her wrists. Were they bruised the last time I'd seen her in the bathroom? I had been too drunk to notice.

"You should have taken a picture," I said. I felt terrible after that and searched the high-ceilinged, nearly private bathroom for a way to make up for it. "I've been letting you use my shampoo all year long," I said.

She laughed bitterly. "It's easy to share when you have a lot of something," she said.

———

Dr. Monroe was standing up when I got to class a few minutes late thanks to Ellie. Her hair was combed and she was wearing lipstick and a solid-colored dress. She closed her eyes before she spoke.

"I have tried to keep this a sacred space for art, but that seems impossible now, doesn't it? It is impossible that you have not noticed the cameras, the reporters, the papers—the world out there," she said, waving at the window. "Words. There are so many perverted uses for them. Words will sell you things. They will make you feel like less of a person. They will lull you when you should be alert. They will make you believe the wrong things. Words have a different purpose in literature—an exalted purpose. Literature reminds us that there is more that binds us than tears us apart," she said. We nodded tentatively, awaiting further instruction.

I stared at my notebook, in which I had most recently written a stanza about my grandmother as a child, watching Kiev burn for five straight days when the Nazis first took it over, and then a page-long ode to Kornberg's forearms, and thought I was beyond fucked. Somewhere along the line, I had decided that writing was what I believed in, the only thing. The email Ryan McFadyen had dashed off in probably two minutes would define him for the rest of his life, while nobody would care that much about anything I ever wrote, even if I kept at it until my dying day.

"Go home," Dr. Monroe said, opening her eyes but making no move to sit down. "Write something true. Write something that makes the reader feel as if a hand is emerging from the page and clutching his heart. Give it your full consideration," she said.

We had many questions for her.

"Should the poem follow a particular form?"

"Do we need a rhyme scheme?"

"When you say true, do you mean factual?"

"Writing is a privilege," she said. "What will you do with that privilege?" Then she waved us away.

She turned to the window, where a protester's voice blared through a megaphone. Dr. Monroe was one of eighty-eight professors who had signed a petition against the players, which appeared in *The Chronicle* that week. I wondered how she could be so sure those guys did it, how I could be pretty sure they did it, and yet how I could be certain Kornberg would never rape anybody, and how this certainty was like a rock I could feel in my shoe.

"What's up, Konnikova?"

Kornberg was waiting for me on his roof. I could see by the smirk in his eyes that he hadn't heard, that I would be the one to tell him the news. His smile crushed me. I couldn't put up with a moment of banter with him. I picked up a stray plastic handcuff and opened and closed it.

"She's saying you raped her," I said.

"What?"

"Ellie. She's saying you raped her."

I told him everything I knew and watched him lower his head into his hands. The sun was setting and a few boys gathered by a fire pit in the yard. The boys cheered inside the house. His eyes were brimming when he looked up.

"My dad always told me that respecting women was the most important thing in the world," he said. "He kept saying it before I left for school. And I promised him I would never, ever, treat a woman badly. Not ever." He moved closer to me. "I didn't do anything she didn't want to do. You have to believe me, Oksana."

"Of course I believe you."

"Then why didn't you ask? Don't you want to know if I did it?" he said.

"I already know you didn't."

He was biting down on his lip so hard I thought he'd draw blood. I needed to fill the silence, so I added, "She was saying that the lacrosse case inspired her to speak up."

"That's fucking crazy," he said, slamming his hand on the roof. "Fuck," he said, punching it this time, bloodying his knuckles. "What do those guys have to do with me?"

"Absolutely nothing," I said. They were fifty times as rich; they were not Jewish; they wore Lacoste polos; they hung out with super-tan six-foot-tall scary model girls; they did not know how to do laundry. He was just a normal kid from Philly.

His eyes were watering. Snot leaked down his left nostril. I wiped his nose with my sleeve and then I pulled him up by his bloody hand and led him to his room. It was messier than last time. Three trays of takeout were stacked over a Domino's box and a few Bud Lights, and Cook Out shakes were stationed on his desk like soldiers, guarding books he might never finish. Phillies and Blue Devils tickets were taped to the wall. A photo stood on his nightstand of him and his parents and brother squinting into the sun outside the Roman Colosseum. A few stray bright earrings were scattered at the foot of his bed, none of them pairs, none of them mine.

We climbed into his bed and he closed his eyes and wrapped his arms around me. We stayed like that all night long and I was awake the entire time, feeling his chest rising and falling against my back. I didn't move an inch, because I didn't want to ruin the moment, such as it was.

Kornberg received official notice from the school board that his case would be going to trial. It would be kept out of the papers, unlike the lacrosse case, which was all over the national news; that week, Jesse Jackson had come to protest in Durham, and a reporter for *The News & Observer* wrote an accusatory op-ed that started with the words *Members of the men's Duke lacrosse team: You know. We know you know.*

Kornberg's name, however, or Ellie's, would not be revealed. He would make his case before the end of the semester—there were two weeks left before summer vacation. Ellie would speak behind a screen, and they would never see each other. That was all he told me. As far as I could see, nobody else knew; it seemed cruel that I had to. After I'd told him, he said he would never have another sip of alcohol.

"I feel so much better now," Kornberg said when we drove to the airport for no reason a few days later. "I finally feel like I'm doing what I'm meant to do. . . ."

"And what would that be?" I said.

He shrugged. "I've been running more. Becky's teaching me to cook."

"That's cute," I said. Boring Becky was cooking for him? What, did he not think I knew how to cook? Well, I didn't, but that was beside the point. I could always learn.

"I've almost finished *Das Kapital*," he added, all excited about his sober life that didn't include me.

"What was your favorite part of the book?" I finally said, trying to sound as uninterested as possible, but he was undeterred.

"This one part has been haunting me," he said. "Marx wrote that when a worker finishes a product, part of him becomes congealed in that thing. I just got this image of myself walking around with all these bits of people congealed inside me, you know?"

"That only happens to me when the condom breaks."

"Jesus, Konnikova. What is the matter with you?"

"What?" He seemed more pissed than the occasion called for. "I was just joking."

"I thought you'd have more insight," he said. I didn't know if he was referring to my dumb poem about me as a kid imitating Lenin or my family's sad history or if he just meant I was being an idiot.

"What insight?" I said. We pulled off 85 toward campus and he slowed down. "Marx had a decent idea, Lenin fucked it up, millions of Jews died, my family left the Soviet Union, and now I get to write poems and fuck people named Conrad Champion."

He sped up again and sighed. "You have it all figured out, don't you?"

He didn't say anything else after that, not even after we pulled up at Teaberry. He found Becky in the kitchen and began playing with her necklace and whispering in her ear, and I wasn't sure why he hadn't taken me back to the Cock.

I should have left, but I sulked on the couch next to Beeman instead. The news was on, and the pearled girlfriend of Reade Seligmann talked about what a great guy he was, how there was no evidence against him. She was so slick, with her straightened hair and Lacoste shirt. I was pretty sure I could find more common ground with an eggplant than with her. Beeman seemed alarmed by how intensely I was glaring at the screen.

"You all right?" he said.

"Do you think she bleeds if you cut her, or do pearls come out?"

"Probably blood?" he guessed. He was so stupidly sincere. I ran my hand up and down his arm, as if to ignite a spark between us.

I returned to my dorm the next morning to an email from Dr. Monroe. *I've been thinking about you,* she wrote. *Have you considered applying to MFA programs?* I hadn't given it much thought, but I was flattered by her suggestion and determined to write the best and truest poem I could for her class. But I was out of Adderall. I paced around campus, hoping to get inspired while walking, just as Mandlestam had, but all I did was dodge a reporter putting a mic in my face and a guy I'd hooked up with at a foam party sophomore year.

In the end, I returned to the "Onward to the Bright Future" poem I had put in a drawer freshman year and tweaked it until I was convinced there was nothing false, and certainly nothing funny, about it.

I got to class early and volunteered to go first. Dr. Monroe was in her usual position, cross-legged and wild-haired. As I began to read, I could picture her face without looking up. She would glow with stern approval and say, "Your work is really maturing, Ms. Konnikova." But when I finished, she appeared slightly bored, even angry.

"Lies," she said, waving the poem away.

She kept looking out the window as the students read their poems; none seemed to satisfy her. She waved us all away and told us to try again next week.

Kornberg and Becky went public at the house, holding hands and whispering like conspirators. They weren't all over each other like two horny people on the verge of fucking either, which was the only way I had ever seen him be with any other girl. He even let her wear his dumb Phillies cap. No, this was definitely something new. Those two had the confident maneuvers of people in love. Of people who didn't drink either.

"You have an eyelash," Becky said, brushing a hand over his cheek while he smiled like a farting baby. "Got it," she said, blowing it off her hand. "I made a wish."

"Don't tell me what it was or it might come true," he said.

"It already has," she said.

She kissed him where the lash had been. Or phantom lash, for all I knew. This was some kind of love porn—it felt indecent to watch.

It was enough to make you puke, which was exactly what I went to the bathroom to do, though to be fair it had more to do with the Jell-O shots than with my broken heart.

Afterward, I wiped my face and stared at myself in the mirror. I pictured Kornberg standing behind me with his hands on my shoulders. "You have vomit on your cheek," he said to me, stroking my blotchy face. "Let me get that for you."

I saw the real Kornberg standing in the kitchen by himself, holding a Coke, looking like the king of his manor. He was waiting for Becky to finish her intense conversation with some girl with short bangs on the couch. I thought of Tsvetaeva's "An Attempt at Jealousy":

> Are you bored with her new body?
> How's it going, with an earthly woman,
> with no sixth sense?
> Are you happy?

I took a step toward him, wanting to blurt out such poetry to echo my pain and show him what a fool he was.

"Are you happy?" I said, as harshly as I could.

He smiled and shook his head. "Happy doesn't begin to describe it. Man, what did I do to get so lucky?"

"Nothing," I said. "That's what makes it luck."

He didn't seem to hear me. He was just looking at the room, waiting for his girl to emerge. I could have been talking about eating a koala's asshole, or getting fingered by Dick Cheney. I wanted to get his attention. I lowered my voice. "Does she know about this thing with Ellie?" His verdict was coming in by the end of the week.

"What the fuck does that have to do with anything?" he said. He took a long sip of his Coke and said, "Yeah, she knows." That was it, the only trump card I had over the girl gone. I was just a Cook Out wrapper, a skunky Bud Light, a king's cup nobody could be coerced into drinking. He was pretty pissed until Becky returned, evaporating the creases in his face. Had he really told her everything? I couldn't be sure. He put a hand on my shoulder.

"Don't let anybody call you Olivia," he told me.

If he hadn't walked away, I would have told him he'd been right earlier—I had exaggerated the story for comedic effect. What really happened was that the poor boy did forget my name and had a bewildered look on his face, as if he were trying to conjure me, a look that changed to gratitude once I told him what I was called.

I crawled out of Beeman's room with a top-ten hangover on the morning of the biggest drinking day of the year. I scrubbed my face and saw that I was wearing his oversize T-shirt that said LEHMAN BROTHERS: WHERE VISION GETS BUILT. My dress and shoes were MIA, so I put on Beeman's green Crocs. I grabbed a slice of pizza and kept my head down during my stride of pride back to the Cock as I devoured it. This was the state I was in when I found Ellie at the bottom of the stairs, holding a tower of boxes.

"Fuck!" she said, both at me and at the shit she was about to fall under.

"I got it," I said, grabbing a few of them, and she didn't stop me.

"Whatever," she said.

I hadn't seen her in our hall or bathroom since our last chat and assumed she had been using a different one. But her hair looked so greasy and her collarbone protruded so much that I wondered if she had left her room at all since then. She was transferring to Oberlin for her senior year. I followed her to the lot behind our dorm, where her car was parked, its trunk open to reveal a box of biology books and a pink blanket. I was surprised that she drove a beat-up Volvo instead of an Audi or something, and even more surprised to see her Michigan plates; I had assumed she was from California or Connecticut.

"My friend Lily loves Oberlin," I said. "Well, she dropped out last year, but, like, she said it was this incredibly welcoming school."

She would have none of my pleasantries. "This place is diseased," she said, practically spitting the words.

"I'm getting an MFA after this," I told her. "I'm not going to end up like these people."

She snorted. "Good luck with that."

It was the last day of classes and I had already wrong-night partied. The students had started drinking on the quad, and "Gold Digger" was blasting from a room above us. Girls were out with their pearls and pastel dresses and gladiator sandals. Soon everybody would get liquored up and head to class anyway, a time-honored tradition I would uphold after I showered.

We put the boxes and a lamp into her trunk and she shuffled her things around in the back seat, trying to push them down. I pictured myself getting in the passenger seat, joining her at Oberlin next year, where I would drop acid and roll around naked in a cornfield, reciting Elizabeth Bishop, and have women tenderly going down on me—a place where I wouldn't wear fake pearls, where I could stop shaving my legs.

I tugged down my shirt to make sure it covered my ass.

"I'm sorry," I said. "You shouldn't have to leave."

"This is my choice."

This was the first time I had seen Ellie without makeup and she looked prettier without it, her face as fresh and lost as a high school girl's. She had stopped with the spray tan too, and her skin was pale and wonderful and I wanted to touch it.

I tried searching her face for signs she had been raped; would she really go through all this trouble if it wasn't true? Why couldn't I learn the truth from looking at her, or at Kornberg? What the fuck else did I not know? Asking her would be pointless, invasive. But I wanted her to confirm it, to tell me what a terrible person the love of my life had been all along. I wanted her to release me.

"Did you really shit in a fish tank?" I said.

She narrowed her eyes and said, "I guess I'm the only person who ever made a mistake around here." She opened her car door and gave me the finger, or gave the whole place the finger, or maybe it was all the same to her.

III.

By the time the Delta Chi spring formal rolled around a year later, I thought I would never graduate. I was browned out and solo when we got to the bar; Frankie, my sort-of boyfriend, got too high to leave the house after the pregame. Kornberg and Becky were guzzling water at the bar, and he stared at her like the world had been ravaged and she had risen out of the ashes with her brown hair and modest green dress and cute little nose and he couldn't believe she was his. They had signed a lease on a place in the West Village, which basically made them married. I'd spent the previous summer interning at a literary agency in Manhattan and didn't care for the city. It was just a place to escape Mama and her now-fiancé, Sergei, hook up with randos, and work on my MFA applications. Most of the places I applied to were in remote, artsy towns that wouldn't have many Duke types in them.

But it didn't work out. I got rejected by all the MFA programs I applied to except Iowa, which I still hadn't heard back from; I was trying not to get my hopes up. If I didn't get in, I decided, I would go to California to start my life, just as Dr. Monroe had done. I wasn't adventurous enough for a cult or a commune and didn't know what I would do there. I wanted to just go.

The charges against the lacrosse players were dropped that week; they never even went to trial. The prosecutor was disbarred for dishonesty and fraud, and the string of allegations against him and his team was long and convincing. The stripper, an NCCU student whose name and identity were revealed, faced no charges for her false accusations. Of course it wasn't fair that she chose those three guys at random from a messed-up photo ID process, but it was hard for me to get pumped about this victory for Duke and the players. They transferred to play lacrosse at other colleges and were heading to Wall Street just fine, not to mention the millions they got in the settlement. The only one who had a rough go of it was the emailer; he was suspended for a few months and then allowed to return to school, but no one could forget what he wrote. I had been thinking about Ellie a lot during that time. Had she been following the case? What would she do next? I pictured her entering the Peace Corps or going to law school to become the good kind of lawyer.

I approached Becky and Kornberg as the night wore down. He and I were cordial, but there were no more drives to Cook Out and he hadn't read a word I had written since he'd gotten a real girlfriend. He'd spent all year cooking with Becky and reading *The Decline and Fall of the Roman Empire* and applying to law school. I'd spent most of the year writing in my apartment or getting high in Frankie's car. Kornberg and I were friendly enough when we saw each other, but we weren't friends.

He said, "Can you believe it's all almost over, Kon Artist?"

The nickname stung me. He hadn't used it in a long time, and he didn't have the right to, all of a sudden. "It's been over for a while," I said, and he narrowed his eyes. I turned to Becky. "Why don't you drink?"

She gave me a small smile. "My dad's an alcoholic."

I sucked down my drink, resenting her for her acceptable reason for not boozing; I was hoping for a sordid tale of an addiction, a dark and skanky past.

"My dad's dead," I offered cheerfully.

"I know. I'm sorry." The cunt, she even put a hand on my shoulder. "I just read your poem about your dad in *The Archive*. The one about you standing on the chair, reciting Lenin? It was so beautiful and sad."

"Thanks," I said.

"I read it," Kornberg said. "It still didn't sound like you."

"What do you want me to sound like?" I said. I was pissed but he was right, that bastard. I had spent the better part of the previous summer trying to resuscitate my poem from freshman year, but after all the work I'd put into it, I didn't think it sounded like me either. But it was the poem I had sent to all the MFA programs. I had nothing better. I stared him down and eventually he left for the bathroom. I watched him walking away in his suit and tie, looking handsome, almost adult, like the lawyer he would be one day—and not the good kind, I was sure. I knew I might just melt into the earth if I saw him casually drape his arm around Becky one more time. I drained my drink and wished for oblivion. Why wouldn't this feeling die?

"Bergy's a little harsh," Becky told me. "I loved the poem."

What the fuck was a "Bergy"? I couldn't let her get away with calling him that.

"I can't say I'm all that thrilled the lacrosse players are free," I said. "I mean, I know they didn't do it, but they were still rich and racist pricks, you know? I'm not as relieved as I was when Kornberg got off," I said, and only when Becky's eyes got big did I see what I had done. I had only suspected she didn't really know before, but now I was certain. "You know, because he didn't do anything wrong. Everyone knew Ellie was crazy," I said.

"What?" she said, putting her hand on the bar.

Kornberg returned and we continued to stare at each other. Becky looked a little wobbly, but she managed a smile for her boyfriend.

"I have to go," I said. "So long, Bergy."

I carried my heels and began the trek home to my

apartment. It was a warm night. The moss hung lazily off the trees and there was a sharpness to the stars, as I walked along the wall of the freshman campus, that reminded me there were a few things about this place I would actually miss. I needed to see the lacrosse house before I graduated. It didn't take long to find it. I hadn't realized how close it had been to Teaberry the whole time.

It looked so clean and ordinary on its dried-up patch of lawn under the dim streetlight. Nobody had lived there since the investigation, so there was probably nothing to see. I stepped across the front lawn and cupped my hands to the window and looked in anyway, but it was too dark to see anything. I tried the front door, but it didn't give. There was a door around the back, though. It opened easily, as if the house had been waiting for me all along.

There wasn't much inside. The walls were bare, the counters were clean, there were no signs of the cops or of an investigation. One chair stood in the center of the kitchen. I sat down on the carpeted floor and pressed my back against the wall. It was scary quiet in there. It didn't occur to me to turn on a light, because there was enough to see by with the moonlight streaming in, and anyway it didn't take long for my eyes to adjust to the darkness.

My Iowa rejection came in the mail a week later. There was a typo in it. I got drunk after that. Luckily it was the last day of classes, so my behavior was socially sanctioned; Rachel and I made Popov punch at Sarah's first thing in the morning. My last poetry workshop was that day, so I was tipsy as I faced Dr. Monroe for the last time. I scanned the room and noted that none of the other seniors had even applied to MFA programs. Brooke was going to Wharton—no more pink hair for her—and the other writers were working at *GQ* or *Rolling Stone* or going into finance. It was like they all got a memo I missed.

"Well, this is our last class, but your journey is just beginning," Dr. Monroe said. She spoke about nourishing our talent once we were out in the world and told us we had a responsibility to do good work. "You will be your own advocates," she said. "You'll have to motivate yourselves, because no one else will care if you stop writing. Not your friends, not your lovers, and certainly not your family. In fact, they will all probably be a bit relieved if you stop. The question is, what path do you want to take? I cannot answer that for you."

Her eyes were open the entire time, which made her words hit harder for some reason. Her speech, combined with the potent effect of a few cups of punch, slightly lifted my spirits. As the other students filed out, I noted that no one else was drunk. How had that happened? I faced my teacher, hoping she didn't smell the booze on me, and tried to find a way to thank her for everything.

"I didn't get into Iowa," I said.

She nodded. "Don't let it discourage you."

"I don't need an MFA," I said. "I'm just going to work hard, like you said. I know I'll get there eventually. I might even go to California, you know, to get away from all this."

I had never stood so close to her before. I was surprised by how old she looked up close, barely younger than my mother.

"You'll need an MFA to get anywhere as a writer these

days. Honestly, you should keep trying Iowa if you want anyone to notice you."

"But you just went to California—"

"Yes, dear, but after the cult business, I was a Stegner Fellow."

I watched the students carousing on the quad through the arched windows, and though I had been desperate to leave all day, all year really, now I wanted my teacher to embrace me. I didn't want to return to the world.

I said, "Remember that day you told us to write something true?" She nodded weakly. "Did you have a specific answer in mind?"

"It was a hard time for everyone on campus. I was not very generous with you all then," she said. She clutched my wrist and her face broke into a smile. "What was that lovely poem you wrote about the girl watching that boy take those girls up the stairs? It was written in a Russian tradition? 'The Idiot'?"

" 'The Dumbass,' " I said glumly.

"Of course," she said, clasping her hands together. "That's the one that stays with me. It was funny and moving at once. Harness that energy. When I remember you and the work you have done here, I will always think of 'The Dumbass.' "

Kornberg had called nine times while I was in class. I called back and understood he had broken his sobriety pledge. He told me what I hoped and feared was true: Becky had dumped him. She'd found out about Ellie and felt betrayed because he hadn't told her. It didn't seem like she'd told him how she knew.

"I'm on the roof," he said.

"Don't move, don't drink."

I ran through West and the freshman campus, dodging clumps of pastel-clad people milling about their dorms' decorated benches, their beers sloshing onto the manicured lawn. I could barely pick out Northgate before I cut through the back and sprinted to Teaberry, passing a cop pulling somebody over.

I caught my breath outside the house, knowing I needed to act carefully given that my wildest dreams had come true. The guys were playing pong on the front lawn, future bankers and doctors and lawyers and world-conquerors. They were oblivious to the fact that I was standing there, a currently unemployed writer, trying to calm down. A few guys tossed a Frisbee to Macy the dog, and she happily caught it in the air. I could hear "Santeria" blasting inside, drowning out the sound of somebody actually playing a guitar.

Inside, a couple was making out on the couch, and the carnage of the day's festivities was on full display: a few stray balloons and scattered confetti, a collapsed beeramid, a tower of pizza boxes, a small pile of cardigans, a baseball bat, an explosion of glowsticks. There was finally a hole in Beeman's rotted floor, just the size of a footprint, and I missed him for the tiniest second. I poured myself a cup of Stoli and went to Kornberg's room, which was even more of a wreck than the rest of the house.

His bookshelf was knocked over, vomiting Hemingway and Pliny the Elder and Herodotus, which mingled with Cook Out wrappers and a milkshake that had exploded over his family photo. Thick shards of glass were scattered across the room, reflecting the harsh light. By the window, which had been punched, there was a trail of blood along with brown liquid from a shattered bottle of Jack, and there were three more holes in the wall.

"Oksana?"

I brushed some glass off the sill and climbed onto the roof. He wore a COLUMBIA LAW shirt and cargo shorts, and his face and arms were covered in blood. I took off my cardigan and wiped him down. He looked ruined, and I was the one who had done it to him. When I looked up, I saw that there was a balloon caught in the big tree that rose above the roof.

"I hope you weren't counting on getting your security deposit back," I said.

He gave me a sad smile that said my comment didn't deserve a response, and I couldn't have agreed more. Jack Johnson came on after Sublime, which made it ridiculous to feel feelings. I moved toward him. I didn't see the point in lying.

"I'm the one who told her," I said. "It was the only way to get her away from you."

"I know." He staggered up, teetering dangerously. "But why?"

"You shouldn't have said that thing about marrying me when we were twenty-five," I said. "I lost my patience."

"You have to be fucking kidding me," he said. "You didn't get what I meant at all. I meant I hoped you would take yourself more fucking seriously by then. I gave you so many chances. What did you do anytime we were alone? Start your comedy act. Recount your latest sexual misadventure. You were impossible."

Down below, the boys whooped wildly. "Why didn't you just tell me?" I said.

"I told you over and over and over. You refused to listen." He sighed and shook his head. "You kept laughing at everything like your life is a big joke. Like nothing at all matters to you."

"That's just how it looks," I said.

How could I tell him that everything mattered to me? That it all mattered so much that I couldn't help but laugh or I would explode?

His jaw was firm. I waited for him to tell me to fuck off, to set me free, to give me permission to get away, to leave these soon-to-be-spackled walls for California and never look back. But he didn't look mad, only exhausted and dirty. How could I have missed everything? I had missed so much, there wasn't anything left over for me to get.

"I'm sorry I didn't see it," I said.

He nodded, a nod that said he agreed and goodbye all at once. His floppy hair was on fire from the day's last specks of sunlight, and his eyes were red and lovely.

As I backed away, I saw the faces of the men I had loved or been with up to that point not as flowers but as balloons that smiled down on me. Well, I had only loved one, but I knew there would be more of them, many more, even if it didn't feel that way right then. One day there would be so many that when I held them all by their strings, they would lift me off the ground and carry me up into the sky.

KEY TO THE CITY

Lee and I buy a stack of books at the Strand kiosk outside Central Park and take them to a sunny rock above a lake crammed with rowers and lily pads next to kids running around like they are never going to die. I should be excited to see Lee for the first time in half a year, but I'm still pissed from my fight with Mama that morning back in Jersey, where I was supposed to stay to help out with my stepdad's birthday tomorrow. I thought returning to the city and seeing my old friend-lover and soaking in the only scrap of green in Manhattan would soothe me, but it doesn't. I can't stop staring at the Freedom Tower looming in the distance, with cranes pecking at the few unfinished floors at the top, which thrust pointlessly toward the sky.

"Eyesore," I say. I glare at Lee and dare him to challenge me, but he just laughs. I say, "Nothing says freedom less than a building called the fucking Freedom Tower."

"I believe they changed the name."

"Nobody uses the new name," I say. "It's too late."

"You're the expert," he says.

"Hardly an expert."

"You're so salty today, O," he says, and he reaches into his tattered red backpack to pull out *Breakfast of Champions* to counteract my foul mood. He reads and reads in an exaggerated version of his Dallas drawl, and I'm cracking up in spite of myself.

Since we met at a summer writing workshop right after I graduated from college, I've seen him when he leaves Dallas to visit his boarding school friends, and we occasionally talk on the phone in between the visits, but not that often, because we don't need to. Though sometimes when I fail to lure some poor horny boy home, or fail to get lured, I drunk-dial him and he reads to me until I fall asleep. He was kicked out of two boarding schools and one college, and once or twice a year he goes into a stint of what he calls "gentle rehab." He's four years older than I am and works for his doctor dad as a glorified receptionist, which means he reads all day—he has read more than any person I have ever met, and that doesn't count for nothing.

When he gets bored of his performance, I pick up the copy of *Fathers and Sons* in Russian that my grandmother gave me, to read something good for my soul instead of the dreck I have to wade through every day at the literary agency where I work. I grabbed it on impulse after feuding with Mama, because I wanted to read the part where Arkady's poor father wanders around his farm, feeling lost and disconnected from his son; I remembered it being so beautiful in English, the poor old man filled with longing and despair in a way only a Russian man could be, but I can't find the fucking passage in my native language, so I snatch Vonnegut out of Lee's hands.

He pulls out *Catch-22* and reads with his nose about an inch from the page. He looks like a lost little mole. His mushroom cut is a bit longer than usual, strands of hair falling into his eyes. I put my book down and drift off, soaking in the day's lovely light, and when I wake up he is sitting with his hands folded over his knees, watching the kids on the other side of the pond, and I don't like it one bit, him looking wistful at the sight of other people's kids as if he wants some of his own.

"Let's go," I say, grabbing his hand. We leave the park on the west side and cross the street toward the Dakota, which is always under renovation.

I blink and I am sixteen again and my brother is almost four and we're in the city with Papa, who has taken a day off work to show us around. Most people see the Dakota and think John Lennon, but Papa's talking about Tchaikovsky, who came to America to visit a friend who lived in the building. He puts his arms around us and says, "Poor Tchaikovsky did not understand America. When he returned to Russia, he declared, 'The man lives in a palace bigger than the czar's. In front of its own private park!' Imagine, he thought the man owned all of Central Park!"

I laugh and say, "Why would anybody think that?"

"Who's Tchaikovsky?" my brother says.

"An important man," Papa says, and he seems sad for some bottomless reason. As if he knows he will die in a few weeks.

But I'm not with Papa; I'm with Lee, who is liking the hand-holding a bit too much.

I nod in the direction of the Freedom Tower. I say, "Monstrosity. Abomination."

"You can't blame people for trying to move on, O," he says.

I walk faster and consider pointing out that the two beams of light they had kept up in place of the towers were stunning. Instead, I say, "There's no moving on from that."

This time, he's staying at the place of a friend who's away at a bachelor party. He fucks me on the hardwood floor, which I chose over the leather couch by a gargantuan TV or the cushy bed. He pulls my hair and I claw at his neck and he holds me down, thrusting so deep inside me I swear I can feel the tip of his dick pushing up to the bottom of my throat, and I get a rise from seeing myself in the wall-length mirror with my head thrown back, Lee's hand over my mouth. I come hard, once, then twice, and he pulls out and comes on my stomach just in time.

"Careful," I say. I am pretty sure my uterus will stage a walkout if I take one more Plan B. I imagine it crawling out from between my legs, holding a poster that says, WILL NOT WORK!

"If you really wanted to be careful, you'd tell me to use a condom," Lee says.

"Fuck off," I say, smacking him, and he laughs big and wipes me off and puts his head on my chest. When he lifts it, I give his pretty white throat a gentle lick and tell him to shower first. I aimlessly make myself come again in this banker's apartment, because why not, a neat little hat trick for the day. But the sweet afterbuzz is ruined when I look in the mirror again and see my indignant mother popping in, lifting a finger as she says, "A classic case of too much freedom." I shake her off. That's when I notice I'm still wearing the necklace my brother gave me that morning. I've kept it on this whole time.

Lee gets out of the shower in a towel and gives me a sad little smile. He is as pale as a baby's ass, and his shoulders are broad and dotted with freckles. He is the definition of Ugly Hot, with a face like a car accident you can't stop staring at because you can't put your finger on why it attracts you, which I prefer to the eager, open-faced douches of Murray Hill. He puts on his glasses and they make him look like an old man with owl eyes, so fucking helpless that I want to either cradle him or put him out of his misery.

He has a small tattoo of a wave on his upper back, a tribute to his sister, who drowned when they were kids. We only talked about it once, but he wrote a beautiful, thinly veiled story about it back at the writing workshop, which was when I fell a little bit in love with him. Now he's staring at me and for a moment I expect him to talk about his sister.

He says, "Can I ask you something, O? Do you fuck everybody like that?"

"Like what?" I say, flashing a smile.

But he is suddenly serious, and maybe it's because he's really done with the pills and coke this time, I don't know—I'm just glad he doesn't press me on it. He opens a bottle of red wine from his friend's stash and lets it breathe while I shower in a bathroom with gleaming bamboo plants on the windowsills, and then we're sitting on the balcony overlooking the park. My phone rings and it's just Mama, so I silence it. It's the third time she's called, no doubt to beg me to come back.

Lee raises a brow. "Some man is really itching to talk to you tonight."

"Can you blame him?" I say. I consider telling him what happened that morning—Mama saying ignorant shit in front of my brother—but it seems easier to play along.

"You're too good for him, whoever he is," he says, squeezing my knee. His eyes settle into determination and I worry he's going to say more.

"If you could own all of Central Park, would you?" I say.

He laughs, though I'm not really joking. "I don't think so, O," he tells me. "I don't need all that much to be happy."

"Right," I say, though I don't believe him. If he had everything he needed, he wouldn't keep returning to drugs, but I see no use in pointing this out.

I gaze at the lush park. An old lady walks two poodles, tired-looking couples push strollers, and teenage girls in empire-waist dresses lick ice cream cones. Though I swore I'd never move to the city like all of my college class-mates, I've been living here and working at the literary agency for three years now, and orbiting it for much lon-ger than that, but I have never felt at home here. But now that I'm finally on the brink of leaving, I wonder if it will be impossible to go through with it.

Lee preps me on the party in Gramercy Park on our way there, and the half bottle of his friend's wine and another glass at dinner have made me feel up for the adventure. It's a bunch of his buddies from Exeter he wants to see, and the host, a guy called Shifty, is apparently a tool who played water polo for UCLA, but he has a sick apartment, one that allows him to have a key to Gramercy Park, the only private park in Manhattan.

His friend lives on the third floor of a building with a shiny marble interior, exactly the kind of Ivy League grad apartment I've avoided by living in Greenpoint and hanging with vaguely literary people, people who wouldn't be caught dead sitting around watching *American Psycho,* like these guys probably still do. When Lee opens the door, the party's already in full swing, though it's not even close to midnight.

"My man," says a tall blond guy, rubbing Lee's head and putting him in a headlock.

Lee says, "Look at this handsome ball sack," and introduces me to the guy, who I have already gathered is Shifty.

"Welcome to my humble abode," he says, shaking my hand. He seems sweeter and less full of himself than I expected, wearing his hotness like a borrowed sweater.

"Not so humble," I tell him, and he has a nice, easy laugh. His place has glass shelves, a black-and-white poster of fog blanketing the Golden Gate Bridge, a mammoth liquor cabinet, and a signed baseball on a gold stand.

Lee is dicking around with the guys he really wanted to see, some of whom I've met during his previous visits: Parker, Highbridge, Nickers, Zuckerman, and two of their wives, two different tall bony beautiful women named Taylor, their wedding rings winking at me like stars. Man-boys like this make me relieved my barely teenaged brother is gay, that he will have an infinitely more interesting life that won't involve blood diamonds, though it will be harder. They give me a once-over and I know I don't fit in, with my BP tank top I'm five years too old to be wearing, high-waisted floral skirt, sparkly black Toms, and chunky turquoise brother necklace.

Lee and I pour some whiskeys in the kitchen and take them to the balcony. Gramercy Park is bigger than I expected, with a black metal fence surrounding a leafy oasis. It seems almost staged under the streetlights. Even looking down into it feels like a slight violation, something I should have to pay for. I tell Lee I wouldn't mind having a key to it.

"Me neither," he says. "Though when I move to New York I won't be anywhere near this place. Somewhere in Bushwick if I'm lucky," he says, and that's how he tells me that Nickers helped him get some marketing job, so he's in the city to scope out apartments. Then I tell him I applied to PhD programs in Slavic studies, mostly on the West Coast, and he takes a long sip of his drink.

"You never told me you were leaving," he says.

"You never told me you were coming."

He sighs and puts his head in his hands. "I don't see you as a stuffy academic, O."

"I don't either," I say. I tell him I've basically stopped writing or reading for pleasure because of work and that in a PhD program I'd get to read my favorite books instead of submissions. But he doesn't buy it. I say, "What do you see for me, then?"

He drains his glass. "I see you here with me."

"I don't know if I'll get in anywhere," I say. Yet another lie. I have been accepted to a program in Davis, California, but I have two more weeks to decide. My family has no idea I'm doing this. He's the first person I've told.

"You can't leave," he says. "You belong here."

I can't argue, because he gives me a boyfriendly kiss that scares the hell out of me. The Taylors' wedding rings materialize before me, shining menacingly. I want them to gouge my eyes out. I don't want to see anymore.

He tries again. "Sometimes I think it would have been easier if I didn't have a sister. It's hard to say goodbye to someone you love. But I'm grateful for all the time I had with her."

"That's family. You don't have a choice with family."

"I don't have a choice with you."

"Of course you do," I say. "I do too." I don't know if I believe what I'm saying. I want to tuck a strand of loose hair behind his ears, but I stop myself. Will they have guys like him in California? I can't be too sure.

We sit without talking. Two drunk girls on the balcony are complaining that they don't get enough vacation days. Then Mama calls again.

"I need to answer this," I say, getting up, though I have no intention of taking the call. Lee shakes his head and puts a hand on my wrist.

"I haven't done a line in over a year, Oksana," he says, like he is giving me flowers.

I've been talking to Shifty for eternity by the fridge, which is plastered with save-the-date magnets, couples posing maniacally, smiles strained as they desperately try to prove they haven't made an epic mistake. They pose on the beach, in Hoboken with the skyline behind them, in a field of wildflowers, on an artfully arranged pile of logs beside a creek, and they look exhausted, all of them, like they have been trapped inside the magnets, forcing those smiles for months. As for me, I prefer to hook up with men who are already married, to avoid the possibility of appearing on a magnet and everything that comes with it. All those men remind me of Mama's husband, and I'd rather be alone than with a man like that.

"These people look diseased," I say, and Shifty laughs.

He puts a hand on his chest in mock concern. "Should I call a doctor?" he says, and he gives me a big easy smile. He cranes his neck toward the balcony, where Lee is charming one of the girls who were there earlier, his hair flopping up and down as he gestures. Shifty says, "And, uh, you and Lee . . ."

"Oh," I say, still feeling Lee's hand on my wrist. "It's nothing serious."

Then someone dims the lights and starts blasting shit from an iPod. A dance party begins, which I'm pretty sure means everyone but Lee has snorted their fair share of blow, and though Lee and I are normally united in never dancing, because we suck at it, I am drunk enough to go for it, to sway to all the manic nothing songs blasting through the apartment: "Tik Tok," "Sexy Bitch," "Bad Romance," "Rude Boy," and "Empire State of Mind." Though I know I should be moved by the raspy lyrics of the rebel Russian bard Vysotsky or the Soviet rock my parents listened to during their final years together, nothing makes me feel more pain than a perfect pop song after a few drinks, when I am open to the world's ecstasy and horror, dancing like I have ten arms and ten legs and ten different hearts for breaking. The crowd thins and it's just me and Shifty and the Taylors now, and suddenly I am making out with one of them and she tastes like cigarettes and lipstick and she even cups my ass, but someone yanks her away and the room is spinning and I'm back with Shifty. I can feel the firmness of his chest through his collared shirt. The music stops and I hear myself say, "What was California like?"

"I loved it," he says. "Especially the weather."

That's it? I let go of his arm. "Was it different?"

"Not really. Same people as here, just more palm trees. Better Mexican food. And good hiking," he says. "Pretty hot girls too," he adds with a demented grin, and then talks about how much he loved working at a start-up that made an app that let dogs tell their owners when they needed to use the bathroom. I realize how much my head is pounding and how badly I want to leave, and though the music is back on, Ke$ha singing about her own bad habits, it doesn't thrill me anymore. It's time to give Lee a civil goodbye and peace out.

"Excuse me a sec," I say.

But Lee's not on the balcony anymore, though the balcony girls are still bitching. I go down the hall and open the door to a room where one of the Taylors is getting fucked from behind, her husband's jiggly white ass shaking up and down as he mounts her against a dresser.

I hear Lee's laugh in the next room and find him with his bros. He springs up after doing a line, and when he sees me, his face goes from excited to upset to kind of pissed. Nickers and Parker stand on either side of him, looking equally moon-eyed and jumpy, or maybe it's

Parker and then Nickers. His boys are quiet and I don't know what to say. I cross my arms and he follows me to the bathroom since there's nowhere else to go.

"What the fuck is wrong with you?" he says.

"You said you haven't done a line in over a year," I say.

"That was very true two hours ago." He paces madly. "What do you care? I fucking pour my heart out to you and you go eye-fuck that low-voltage douche."

"Is that why you came here? To pour your heart out to me?"

"Every time I come here, I come here for you, O. Isn't that obvious?" he says, his chest rising. "What do I have to do to make this stick?" A poor choice of words. I think of him coming on my stomach, a spitball slicking down a chalkboard, the time a girl stuck gum in my hair in second grade and Mama had to chop a chunk off, laughing the whole time. His hair is wild now, a bit sweaty, his eyes bulge a little, and he won't stop moving.

"You're fucked up right now," I say. "We'll talk later."

"I'm perfectly fine, darling," he says. But he is not done with me yet. "There are other ways to fuck people, you know. You might even enjoy feeling another person close to you."

"Is that right?" I say, backing away from him. And I'm already looking at Shifty and he's looking back at me.

I sit on the floor of Shifty's shiny minimalist man bathroom and send Mama a text to say I'll call tomorrow, the most I will give her. She instantly writes back. *You do not have to help with party. Just be there please. Love, Mama.* I'm getting the spins and the tiled floor is crawling up and down the walls, so I hold on to the toilet but I can't gather the courage to puke. I lean against the sink and stare at myself in the mirror. Mama pops up again, wagging that same damn finger and declaring, "A classic case of too much freedom." Then it's not just Mama I see but all of us, my brother and stepdad and me at the fucking breakfast table this morning.

Mama and Sergei are going over the guest list for his birthday party and Mama says, "Of course Yuri and Matthew are coming; they wouldn't miss a chance to dance." Yuri is Mama's childhood friend who immigrated at fifteen, a decade before we moved here, and Matthew is Matthew Mussolini, third cousin of evil Mussolini, owner of a dance studio, and Yuri's partner.

"Poor Yuri," Mama clucks. "He came to America at a vulnerable age and was confused and lonely, and naturally he was desperate for love. If he had stayed in Kiev longer, he would have developed a stronger sense of self and met a nice woman eventually. But in America, he was lost; he thought anything was possible. A classic case of too much freedom."

"You know that's not how it works, right?" I say, eyeing my brother, who barely looks up. Since he came out to me a few months ago, I can't let these things slide.

"Of course, Oksana, you know everything," Mama says, and then I throw my plate into the sink so hard it cracks in two and I tell them I changed my mind, I won't be staying for the party, I have to go to the city to see a friend after all.

"A lesbian friend," I add when Mama tells me to behave. "A big, hot butch lesbian. If I'm around her long enough, I'll turn gay and then I won't get to have a great fucking family like this one." This, at least, gets a chuckle from my brother.

Sergei leans toward me. "Have you no pity for your mother?"

How I hated him! This man whose idea of a fun evening was putting his arm around Mama and grumbling at the TV news while she sat with an amused look on her face, like she couldn't believe he could get so worked up about the state of the world. Sure, he loved my mother, but could she really be enjoying herself? Sergei had never even been married before Mama's friend Valentina set them up, and he didn't drink. How could you trust a man like that?

I lean toward Sergei, unafraid. "Actually," I say, "I pity Mama quite a bit."

"Foolish girl," Mama says, understanding me perfectly. "What, in the name of Karl Marx, have I done to deserve her? Why does she insist on sucking my blood?"

Then my brother stands up and I'm terrified of what he's going to say.

"I just don't believe he's related to Mussolini," he says.

I follow him up to his room, which is a mess, with words in French and Japanese scrawled on his crooked whiteboard, math textbooks opened on the floor, piles of bright dirty clothes scattered near his bed, and some kitsch items from our recent trip to visit our grandmother in Kiev on his windowsill: a regular nesting doll and one of Putin as a dog, a Ukrainian flag and broom, and a generic painting of the Maidan, the plaza in the center of Kiev. My brother isn't starting high school until next fall, but he's already trying to make himself more interesting, and I applaud him. He's losing his baby fat and it's appar-

ent that he's going to be very handsome soon, which
Mama thinks is the reason all of his friends are girls.

He reaches under his pillow and gives me the turquoise beaded necklace.

"I got this at the mall. I thought it was pretty," he
says, and I try to keep it together when he puts it on me
and it really does look pretty, brightening my dull eyes.
Then he says, "Don't worry about me. I know they're
clueless about that stuff."

I bite my lip and wonder if he is lying. He must need
me. I run a hand over the necklace.

"It's beautiful," I say. "One day," I tell him, "you'll be
able to leave too. You'll get to go anywhere you want."

Shifty leads me to the gate of Gramercy Park a few
shots of Grey Goose later. He pulls out an intricate silver
key that fits neatly in his palm, curlicues blooming from
its sturdy base, and eases it into the lock. The gate creaks
open for us. The park is silent on this warm night, with
its green benches and birdhouse and a statue of a man in
a robe with his hand to his chest, looking down slightly,
like he can't believe what we're thinking of doing there.
It's like a park in a movie set. Shifty takes my hand and I
try not to trip.

He puts the key in his pocket and I say, "How much
does it cost to replace it?"

He looks slightly embarrassed. "A thousand," he says.

"Have you ever lost it?"

"Never," he says. "And I've lived here for almost a decade now."

"That must be nice," I say. His blond hair is slick with
gel; his green eyes are shining. The statue, I am sure by
now, is glaring at me, and I redirect my gaze.

"If you could own all of Central Park, would you do it?" I ask.

He smiles slowly, not sure what to make of me. "How could anyone own the park?" he says. "Like, legally own it? Does that mean no one else could go there?"

I shrug and say, "Forget it."

I move toward him, running my hands down his chest. His kisses are sweet and eager and he's more like a puppy than like Patrick Bateman. When I open my eyes I see his are closed, delicate blond lashes catching the moonlight. I try to heed Lee's advice and stroke his hair, and he strokes mine, and I can see his pulse in his throat and it's too much, not something I am supposed to see. I lead him to a bench, where he puts down the key and I straddle him under the gaze of the judgy statue, though he is still too gentle. I yank his shirt open so hard two buttons pop off, pattering on the cement.

"Hey," he says, a bit alarmed, but sort of into it too. I run my hands under his shirt and all I can hear are my hands on his body, no party, no cars, not even a man walking his dog.

"Hey yourself," I say.

I unbuckle his belt and dig my nails into his huge arms. But he's not so innocent; he has a condom in his wallet and he slides it on his thin long dick. I push my underwear to the side and guide him inside me, which is when I realize I'm only sort of wet, so I pull his cropped hair as best as I can and bite his neck and it begins to work and he starts getting rougher too. He gets this deranged gleam in his eye and squeezes my sides kind of unpleasantly, because not everybody is good at fucking this way, but I can't stop him except by slowing down myself. Now he's really on this gripping and grabbing and biting kick and he takes hold of my hair and my necklace, which breaks off into a million little pieces, beads flying into the night.

"What the fuck?" I say, easing off him and pushing him away. He's pissed as I fix my skirt and pick up the pieces, pretty stones I put in my pocket along with the chain, wishing I were the kind of girl who knows how to put a necklace back together.

He gets up and I imagine he's another statue in the park, somber and muscular and genteel, and he turns away before I understand what he is doing. He jerks off into a bush and moans a bit as the sad little spurts tumble out. He's not a statue anymore; he's a fountain. He buckles his pants, wipes his hands on his lap, and glares at me.

"Who the fuck do you think you are?" he says. "Really."

"I'm sorry," I say, gathering more beads. "I'm engaged to a man I love."

"Lee?" he says, looking back in the direction of his apartment. "Fuck, I thought—"

"You don't know him," I say. "His name is Matthew Mussolini."

He shakes his head and storms out of the park without tucking in his shirt or catching his breath or looking at me one last time. Which is a shame, because if he had done any of that, then he might have noticed that I'd swiped his key. I lock the gate before I leave, to be a good citizen, to keep out the riffraff.

It's three in the morning and I'm exhausted, but I can't bring myself to return to my apartment in Greenpoint. I consider my options. I can go downtown to Papa's old office, a short walk from the fallen towers, and I can stand in front of it, wondering what he would think of how my family turned out, of the direction the country is headed, and if he too would disapprove of the garish new skyline. I can go to the Freedom Tower and stare into the abyss. Or to Veselka, my brother's favorite twenty-four-hour diner, where he loves to embarrass me by speaking his surprisingly good Russian to the waiters. But the thought of seeing any of those places exhausts me. I buy a Gatorade at a deli and start walking to Penn Station.

A few months after Papa died, my friend Lily dragged me to get wasted at a sushi place in the West Village that didn't ask for IDs; then she forced me downtown to face the Goldman building. She furiously waved a bottle of Stella at the vacant building on the deserted street. "Fuck you, Goldman Sachs!" she had cried, tossing the bottle at the entrance, though it didn't break through the thick glass, and we ran away, cracking up. I was still too numb to work up that much anger or to really thank her.

But I am brimming with feelings by the time I make it to Chelsea. "Fuck you, Goldman Sachs!" I shout at a street of brownstones, tossing my Gatorade at a trash can. A couple turns back to scowl at me and then walks faster, as if I pose a threat.

I end up sitting on a stoop across the street from my fiancé Matthew Mussolini's dance studio, a silver building with tall glass windows, which Mama had once pointed out with her signature smirk. I have only spoken once or twice to Mama's friend Yuri, a handsome bald man with a mustache who told me I looked exactly like my mother back in high school, which no one had ever said to me before or since. Just one of the rooms of his partner's studio is illuminated, a bright rectangle two floors above the ground, surrounded by darkness.

A dark-haired woman flutters under the lights, moving gracefully for all the world to see her, or maybe for nobody to see her, she just loves to dance that much. I'm not even sure she's real; for all I know she's a dreamed-up tropical fish shimmying in a tank. My skull is throbbing, my brain wants to ooze out of my ears, and I wouldn't care if it did. I didn't ask to have a mind, or a body, or for any of this.

My phone rings and I think it's late for Mama to be calling, but I see it's Lee.

"Shifty's freaking out," he says. "He thinks you took his key. You did, didn't you?"

"I'm watching this dancer practicing. She's so fucking beautiful."

"Don't be a cunt, O. Bring back the key. I don't care about you and him. Please," he says.

"I wish you could see her," I tell him. "She's so free."

"Are you serious right now? There's nothing free about being a dancer, O. It's all a performance. I thought you knew better." He tells me again to come back, his voice so steady he could be reading from a book, and I wonder who is going to read me to sleep from now on, whose voice will soothe me so much it enters my dreams after I drift off and vibrates in my bones long after I wake up.

"I'm going to school in California next year. I already accepted," I say.

Lee laughs a sad, big-throated laugh; I can see it. "They can still call you out there, you know," he tells me.

"Well," I say. "They need me." I hang up before he has anything to say about that. My phone tells me I have ten minutes to catch the 5:14 to Jersey. I know that's where I need to be.

I stand up and scatter the beads from my pocket at the door of the studio, like birdseed. Maybe they will be of use to somebody. The plaque tells me the studio doesn't belong to Matthew Mussolini after all but to another man. I've been at the wrong place this whole time.

I get off the train as the sun drifts up, bathing the sky in hot-pink light. The walk home's not long. The buildings close to the station are little brick boxes just inches apart, but the houses are larger and pastel-colored as I get farther away, passing streets renamed after local soldiers who died in Iraq. An old couple sits on their porch, with mugs of coffee steaming before them like tiny cauldrons, and they give me comradely nods though I must look like shit. I stumble toward my family's house, my underwear sticking to my ass. I sneak into the house through the back, walk through the kitchen brimming with serving dishes and elaborate bouquets awaiting the party guests, and creep up the stairs.

My brother is in bed, staring into the void of his computer, surrounded by a half-empty Coke, a bag of Cheetos, my tattered copy of *The Bell Jar,* French flash cards, and *The Romanovs: The Final Chapter,* so he's still winding down, nocturnal creature that he is. He lifts a hand and gives me a lazy smile.

"You changed your mind," he says.

"I tend to do that."

He studies me and frowns. "What happened to the necklace?"

I put a hand to my neck and say, "I left it at home."

I am officially no longer drunk, just delirious, and my brother's bed is not my old bed from high school but a crib, and the Coke is a baby bottle, and Mama and Papa and a preteen me are peering down at him as he sleeps.

"Such a pinched face," Mama says with a frown. "He looks a bit like Yeltsin."

"Nonsense," Papa says, putting an arm around both of us. "He is perfect."

"More like a drowned rat," I say, but Papa sighs so I add, "but he's no Yeltsin."

"Shame on you, Oksana Banka. The child is perfect," Papa says, shaking his head at Mama and me. "Treacherous women, you just don't see it."

Misha is staring at me and I know I need to tell him I am leaving in a few months, that I won't be able to come home as often, that he won't be able to visit me in the city anymore but that he can always call and I will answer. That he has to call, in fact.

"You are perfect," I tell him.

He rolls his eyes. "And you are drunk. I'm ready to sleep."

"Same," I say, and he doesn't kick me out, so I join him under the covers, the sun already slinking in through the blinds. I say, "Remember the last time Papa took us to the city? To Central Park? That was such a good day."

"I don't remember the park," he says. "I remember he

let me have so much ice cream I got sick and puked all over his shoes. He was so mad."

"Now, that I don't remember," I say, laughing a little.

"Maybe I dreamed it, then."

I move closer to my brother and smooth down his hair. His bed is perfectly warm. I reach into my pocket and say, "I got you something." I turn the key over in my hand. It really is beautiful, shiny and silver and ancient.

My brother holds the key up in the thin dusty light.

"What does it open?" he says.

THE YALTA CONFERENCE

Anatoly Petrovich arrived in Yalta to try to bed my grandmother a fortnight into our trip. I was already going insane by that point, realizing that my plan to take a break from the mess I'd left behind in California was a bust, feeling more annoyed by my grandmother than usual because I was lovesick. I had only been living on the West Coast for a year and had already managed to screw up my romantic life more than I ever had back in New York. So when Baba's suitor appeared and began to distract her from annoying me, I felt myself relaxing slightly, thinking the remaining half of my trip might be more bearable.

He joined us on our hotel's veranda, where we drank Georgian wine and watched the sun go down. As we opened our second bottle, a troupe of girls with daisy garlands in their hair walked past.

"Oh! Youth," said Anatoly Petrovich. "It makes the soul dance."

"What nonsense," my grandmother said. "One day,

those children will be old and ugly, just like you and me. That goes for you too, Oksana," she told me.

"Thanks for looking out for me," I said.

"You are neither old nor ugly, my duckling," Anatoly Petrovich said, squeezing Baba's hand. He lowered his voice and hovered his mouth near her ear. "Come on, Sveta, one night with me and you won't regret it."

"Who are you to know what I won't regret?" my grandmother said.

"Don't be that way, my rabbit. . . ."

"Get out of here, you old toad. Before I regret talking to you at all," she said.

Anatoly Petrovich bowed and kissed her hand and then mine. "It has been a treat to see you again," he told me. "You're all grown up. You look just like your father."

"That's what people tell me," I said.

"Only a little," Baba said, tilting her head to study me. "Her nose is much bigger. And her father's eyes were as blue as the sea. Her eyes are the color of storm clouds, just like mine. . . ."

I hadn't seen Anatoly Petrovich since I was a kid, but he had known my father well. He had been the director of the Kiev children's choir when Papa was a member. Anatoly Petrovich had fallen for my grandmother the moment they'd locked eyes when she'd brought a nine-year-old Papa to the choir audition. A few years later, Anatoly Petrovich was transferred to the more prestigious Moscow choir, but once my grandfather died shortly after that, he took the train from Moscow to Kiev to see my grandmother year after year, though she never gave in to him. Their semi-romance had cooled after Baba moved to America with us but had picked up when she'd retired in Kiev. I had the sense they were platonic because Baba didn't reveal intimate details about their time together to me like she did about the others. Still, they acted like lovebirds.

Her suitor walked away with perfect posture, head held high. With his white whiskers and formidable belly, he looked like an elegant walrus. He was staying at the Oreanda Hotel, which was named for the region of Yalta visited by the lovers in Chekhov's story "The Lady with the Dog." I had already visited the picturesque namesake town for research purposes. The tricky little story about two ordinary married people who meet on an embankment on summer vacation and fall in love in spite of themselves was the reason I had come to Yalta, courtesy of my PhD program.

Baba and I were staying at the thousand-room industrial monstrosity, the Hotel Yalta. It looked like a corporate office and the sheets smelled like ammonia, but Baba refused to stay anywhere else. As we climbed into our twin beds, I saw she was exhausted, that all the toughness she had put on for her suitor had melted away. I tried giving her a look to show I'd never forgotten the adventure of sharing a room with her when I was a kid, that I'd forgiven her rude comments, and that I too was confused over matters of the heart.

"Don't make that face," she said as she turned off the lights. "It's unattractive."

"Consider yourselves 'underground men,'" Dr. Vainberg had said, rubbing his hands together. "Or 'women,'" he added, winking at me and the other girl there, a mousy thing named Marnie.

I was at the orientation for first-year PhD students in the crypt-like basement belonging to the Slavic Studies Department of UC Davis. As the chair droned on, I tried to hide my despair and studied the cobwebs all over the room to calm down. I'd moved to Davis because I wanted to be as far away as possible from New York, but I was already bored out of my mind in the too-hot cow town, realizing that if a place was two hours from the ocean, then it could be anywhere at all. I hadn't exactly pictured myself on a beach with a strawberry daiquiri in hand, ardently discussing *Quiet Flows the Don* with spectacled versions of Fabio, but I still wanted it to feel more different—beyond the palm trees and bikers—or maybe I just wanted it to make me different. I must have failed to hide my feelings, because a guy across the table smiled at me.

My new classmates and I escaped the underground lair for the farmers' market. After we ordered beers, the guy who'd seen me sulking introduced himself. His name was Roman.

"Are you all right?" he said.

"I think I've made a huge mistake," I answered, sipping my beer.

"I don't think so," he said. "It's not too late to switch to wine."

He had the slightly tired face of a man in his mid-thirties, with a firm jaw, light wavy hair, and a trimmed beard. He wore sandals that revealed big feet with neat toenails. There was a bit of underground-lair cobweb on his big toe, and I wanted to touch it. I was surprised by the deep blue of his eyes and didn't know how I had missed them earlier. It was the color of the ocean I had been dreaming about. Eyes that made me want to tell him everything, which is what I found myself doing.

I told him I'd left my job at the literary agency in Manhattan when I realized it was the worst place in the world to work if you actually liked to read. I told him I'd loved reading since I'd moved to America when I was seven and my father read to me in Russian every night so I wouldn't forget my native tongue. I told him it didn't feel like anyone in the program actually liked literature, that they only cared about Marxism and deconstructionism and other isms that seemed to exist only to ruin reading, and the creepy chair didn't put me at ease. I expected him to think I was crazy for rambling, but he reacted with a calm that steadied me.

"Don't let Vainberg scare you. He's not so bad," he said.

"I don't want to be an underground woman. I don't even like Dostoevsky. He's fucking insane," I said. Now I was just complaining because it felt good.

"He seems perfectly rational to me," he said. When I made a face, he laughed. It was nice to see his stern face break into a smile. It felt like something I had earned. He said, "I may be a bit biased because I named my dog after him. Fedya."

"That's a little intense," I said.

"I'm a little intense," he said.

We watched a clown juggling oranges for a crowd of extremely blond children. Marnie the Mouse brought over a sliced watermelon.

Roman bit into his slice like a boy, the juice dripping down his big hands, his chin, his torn jeans, with a joy that delighted me and made me wish I could do a single thing without overthinking it. He got shy after he finished eating and wiped his chin, watching me watching him. I was sure the others could feel the wild thing between us, but they just chatted about their new seminars. I knew almost nothing about this man except his name and the name of his dog, but I knew we had to be together. Later, I would tell him it was love at first bite.

"I think you should give Dostoevsky another chance," he said. "And you should give the program another chance too. It's a little early to be drawing conclusions, don't you think?"

"Sometimes you know right away," I said.

The lovebirds and I took the ferry to the Swallow's Nest a few days after Anatoly Petrovich arrived. He had his arm around Baba as our rickety boat chugged through the sea. The water was a dumb, ordinary color, a blue-crayon blue, and it was pretty enough in the sunshine, but it didn't move me. The happy pair were reminiscing about the first time they'd seen each other, or, rather, Anatoly Petrovich was reminiscing while Baba drank cognac from a plastic cup.

"You should have seen your grandmother when we first met," he told me, stroking the air. "She came toward me holding your father's hand. There were dandelion seeds in her hair. As I reached over to brush them off, we were hit by a jolt of static electricity. . . ."

"What dandelion seeds, you old fool?" Baba said. "I was so busy with work and family that I was hardly outside long enough to spot a dandelion back then, let alone have time to get covered in the seeds of the idiot flower.

It was dust, no doubt. I had been cleaning the house all morning."

"Do not be contrary. You felt it too."

"I felt my back aching. My feet also," she said, but she gave him a coy smile.

The Swallow's Nest, it turned out, was a Disney-looking castle perched on the edge of a cliff. It was supposed to be the symbol of the entire Crimean peninsula, but it wasn't that impressive. It had just one short tower, a few spires, and an observation deck. Anatoly Petrovich informed me that it was built for a German businessman in 1912, which did not pique my interest. It looked even more precarious as we got off the boat and onto solid ground. At the harbor, we passed a battalion of merchants peddling trinkets. Some of them had hawks on their shoulders. I shrieked when one of the birds jumped on my arm and dug its claws into my skin.

"Take your picture, miss?" his owner asked.

"Get it off me!" I shrieked. Baba and her boyfriend laughed.

The owner took it away, leaving me shaken.

"Relax, Oksana," Baba said. "You are too sensitive."

I argued that my reaction was appropriate, but she and Anatoly Petrovich walked ahead holding hands, not moved by the fact that I wasn't following. Fuck the Swallow's Nest, I decided. It could crumble into the sea at any minute, and I didn't want to be inside when it did. Besides, it was built after Chekhov's death and was useless for my research; I needed to see the author's house, not this cartoonish building.

I surveyed the trinkets for sale, hoping to find something to give Roman if he would accept it when I returned to California. There were miniature versions of the Swallow's Nest, magnets from Livadia, and paintings of the Foros Church, but there was nothing even vaguely literary, nothing that would make his heart leap. I thought of ways to make Roman laugh the next time we spoke. "You wouldn't believe it," I'd say. "The sexual tension was so thick you could cut it with a cane."

When the lovers returned from the castle, Anatoly Petrovich loped ahead of Baba, gathering wildflowers into a bouquet. From the way he moved, you wouldn't guess he was seventy-seven, a few years older than my grandmother. I couldn't help but be charmed by this man, just as Papa had been. They'd stayed in touch until Papa died, calling each other on their birthdays. "Old Tolik, that rascal!" Papa would say when their conversations were through, shaking his head as he hung up the phone, still a schoolboy with a crush on his teacher.

On the boat ride home, I waited for Anatoly Petrovich to step away to smoke so I could be alone with Baba.

I said, "Why can't you just be with him?"

"It's complicated," she said, sniffing her bouquet.

"It doesn't seem complicated to me."

"That's because you don't know anything. Anything at all," she said. "You were scared of a bird that can't even fly."

Roman had taken me out to dinner a few nights after our first conversation. And then to another dinner. And another. He was nine years older, and his parents had moved to Palo Alto from Leningrad when they were teenagers. I had never met a West Coast—or a second-generation—

Russian American Jew before, and everything seemed easier for him. Even when he spoke of how his parents and older sister were doctors who were baffled by his previous career in publishing and by his decision to study literature, he didn't seem tortured about it. He lived in Sacramento, one train stop away. He was a real man compared to the idiots I'd dated in New York, married corporate losers or failed musicians whose hookup tactics included sharing a cab home and saying "Mind if I come up to piss real quick?" when it pulled up at my place.

I knew he liked me, but he wouldn't make a move. After our fourth dinner, I decided enough was enough.

I said, "You can only eat so much."

He laughed and said, "I can't get enough of you." As he said it, a waitress hovered over us and pivoted away. He turned toward her and said, "I was talking to my pasta," but she was gone, and I laughed until his face became somber and he turned off his phone.

"It's not a great idea for us to be together," I said. I considered listing all the reasons. There were only six people in our cohort. If it didn't work out, it would mean years of awkwardness, walking into underground-lair cobwebs to avoid each other. Also, he was my only friend in the state. My other classmates didn't even get my jokes.

"Of course it's not a great idea," he said.

When he came over and finally fucked me that evening, I felt utterly consumed, so beside myself I could barely do more than lie there and howl. It felt criminally good. I saw that I had not been alive until that moment. I had been living a false life, a life the world saw that meant nothing, when inside I had just been waiting for Roman to find me, and he had been waiting for me too.

When he collapsed next to me, I waited for him to echo my feelings with one of his careful phrases. When he didn't, I searched for a way to tell him what he had done to me.

What came out was, "That was like the grand opening of my vagina."

He laughed, and I made a silent vow to leave the poetic language to the masters I studied. Still, I hoped he'd say something poetic in return.

He gave me a look that frightened me as he dressed. He said, "I need to walk my dog." I followed him to the door, wishing I could say more and wanting more from him all the same.

"I think I'm in love with you," he said.

"You don't think with your heart," I said, and he gave me a smile, which seemed sad for some reason, and walked to his car at a fast clip. He drove off without turning on his lights.

Baba and I were alone on the beach a week into her suitor's visit. I still had not found the right gift for Roman. I had been good about only turning on my phone once a day, on the off chance I would hear from him. Baba indulged in one of her romance novels while I reread "The Lady with the Dog" in Russian at a snail's pace. She kept trying to get me to go in the water, but I refused. It was crawling with jellyfish. I'd never seen so many in my life, and that included every summer I spent at the beach in Florida and later the Jersey Shore, watching my parents drink beers and canoodle. Lately, though, the only time

I went to the beach was in the Hamptons with Mama, my brother, and my stepfather, Sergei, who had a summer home with a private beach that made me long for the crowded mess of the Shore, jellyfish and all.

"Don't be such a spoilsport," Baba said, nodding at the water once more. "A few jellyfish never hurt anybody."

"That's not exactly true."

"Fine, fine," she said, frowning at me. "Tell me—how are your studies?"

"Challenging."

Baba had been a biologist for thirty years and wouldn't be able to understand my reservations about my murky career path. But I didn't plan to tell her I might quit, because I didn't know what I would do next. Maybe I would write poetry again, or try my hand at a novel. Maybe I would get a marketing gig in Silicon Valley. Maybe I would audition to be a clown at the farmers' market. Or I would leave the country altogether and join my friend Lily at her meditation temple on a remote Korean island. It all seemed equally possible. A subject change was in order.

"Listen to this," I said, holding up my book. I was at the part of the story where middle-aged Gurov feels overwhelmed by passion when his mistress, Anna, returns to her provincial town after what he thought was just another summer fling. Back in Moscow with his wife and daughter, he can only think of Anna. I read, "*She did not visit him in dreams but followed him about everywhere like a shadow and haunted him.*"

"That old windbag," Baba said, shaking her head. "He

needs to cut to the chase. Listen to *this*," she said, sitting up. *"He sucked on her ripe, pulsating breasts like a hungry child. Oh! The sweetness!"*

We had captured the attention of a nearby family, but she didn't care. I tried to hush her.

"No offense, but aren't you too smart for those books?" I said.

"I've read the classics. Who needs to read about suffering at my age? I need look no further than my own life. Look at me running around with Tolik like some hormonal teenager. . . ."

"I think it's sweet. I just don't get it. All these years— why didn't you marry him?"

"Oh, there was some talk about it after your grandfather died. But then Tolik had a heart attack, then Alla got sick, and then the Soviet Union collapsed and I left with your family; you know how it is. And now," she said, "it is beyond too late, though the rascal keeps coming back. Sure, we could have a few good years together, and then what? I don't want to spend my dying days cleaning a bedpan. This isn't like your mother finding Sergei—she is a smart woman and they have many years of companionship ahead of them."

I tried not to roll my eyes at the thought of my mother's husband, whom I had been trying to accept. "But you and Anatoly Petrovich love each other," I said.

"No," she said. "Your grandfather and I loved each other, forty years ago. It's too much of an effort to work up the love muscles after that. But this man, I have known him for too long for it to be—as casual as I would like it to be at my age."

Baba almost never mentioned her dead husband, and I

was stunned. By then I knew that when she said her husband had "died of being a Soviet male," it meant that
he'd drunk himself to death, though Mama assured me
that they had a great love in spite of that hiccup. I wanted
to know so much more, but now was not the time. I
needed to refocus her efforts on Anatoly Petrovich.

"You're thinking too much," I said. "There's something to be said for living in the moment. . . ."

"And that's just what we're doing here, my darling,
isn't it?" she said. Now she was the one desperate to
change the subject. She ran a hand over my tattered book
and said, "Don't worry, my dear. We'll go to Chekhov's
house soon."

"I'd love that," I said, as if this mattered at all.

It occurred to me that all of the things I used to think
mattered—running four miles every other day, calling
my mother and brother at least once a week, reading
books I loved, maybe even my research—didn't mean a
single thing once Roman had repeated my full name back
to me.

In the middle of our second semester, Roman told me he
was married. We had taken a weekend trip to Berkeley to
escape the liquid-hot boredom of Davis and had spent
our last morning there walking down Telegraph, passing
by the psychedelic pipes and handmade dream catchers
and disheveled undergrads. Roman had gone to undergrad there, and I told him I wished I'd gone to a place
like Cal instead of Duke, where people cared more about
what you wore than what you read.

He came to a halt in front of a bookstore called Randy's. Books were stacked up outside, and FINAL SALE signs were plastered to the windows of the tired, unremarkable building. He looked like someone dear to him had just gotten hit by a bus.

"You know how much time I spent in there?" he said. "This is where I learned to love books."

"I'm sorry."

"You don't get it."

He was quiet over lunch, at a restaurant where we ordered fifteen-dollar sandwiches in a cave with tattoo-smattered waiters. I knew I wouldn't understand what the store meant to him and that it was better to leave it alone. As I watched him staring out the window, it was hard to imagine that this was the person I'd felt closest to in the world just that morning, the man who had gone down on me for so long that afterward, once I recovered, he said, "I guess I am an underground man after all," making me laugh and laugh as I smacked him with a pillow.

But there were tears in his eyes now. I wanted to fix him so we could go back to having fun.

I said, "One day we can open our own bookstore. After we become insanely rich as Slavic studies professors . . ." I could see this wasn't working.

"You do know I'm married, right?" he said, rather sternly. I stared at him, waiting for an explanation. "I thought you knew," he said.

I held my coffee to steady my hands. How had I not seen it? He wasn't affectionate in public, though neither was I. He didn't call me his girlfriend, though I'd never asked him to. He never stayed the night, but he said it was because of his dog. He lived in Sacramento, after all, and who knew what he did there—he had never invited me over. Maybe I did suspect that something was wrong, but I'd chosen to ignore it. I was a poor grad student. I only wanted to use the facts that would strengthen my argument.

He said, "I thought you knew because of that time at dinner. You said it wasn't a great idea for us to be together—"

"Because we're in the same tiny fucking program!" I said. "Your dog. Is he even real?"

"Of course he's real," he said defensively, as if he had a leg to stand on.

He told me a story I had heard a million times before from the married men I'd slept with in New York. "We were together for so long that I couldn't imagine being without her," one said, slipping his ring back on as he left the shitty apartment I shared with four other girls. "She was the only person I had ever been with, and I love her, even if we have nothing in common anymore," another whispered as he said goodbye to me in front of my downtown office. "Our families love each other. We have the same friends. I can't disentangle myself," one man had told me as he drove me away from the city to his cabin.

But those men meant nothing to me. Roman was the only one who mattered, though he told the same story. As he talked, I watched his lips, trying to understand. He said she was like family to him, that he absolutely adored her parents and did not want to let them down, but I didn't know these parents I would never meet and didn't care.

The only part of his story that interested me was that his wife was a large-animal vet—he said she was never around, like that would make me feel better. I only felt worse, picturing her as a focused, useful person saving the lives of beloved horses while I sat in a seminar, hungover, debating whether there was historical evidence that Catherine the Great rode her horses to achieve orgasm.

He said, "I'd been fooling myself into thinking everything was fine, until I met you."

"Let me guess. You never got a parking ticket before you met me. You're not a bad person."

He looked away. "I never said I was a saint. This is different. I think you know that. Since the day we met, I knew you were important. I knew you weren't just some—"

"Just some slut," I said, rising from my seat. "Maybe I am."

I stormed away. I hated his wife for having him at night, and then I felt sorry for her for not fully having him. Then I felt sorry for myself for being the other woman the one time it mattered, and then I hated myself and thought this was retribution for all the times I didn't give a fuck who I hurt. I made it all the way to the Berkeley campus before I realized I needed a ride home. I walked all the way back to where I had left him, and he was still waiting for me there.

Anatoly Petrovich approached me on the beach three days before Baba and I planned to leave. I was writing Roman's name in the sand with a stick. Baba was passed out under her umbrella with a hint of a smile on her face, her bare-chested-man–covered romance novel splayed open on her stomach. Her suitor was growing desperate. Even his dignified mustache was wilting in the heat. He put a hand on his heart and grimaced and I worried he was having a heart attack, but he was just emphasizing his amorous intentions.

"I need your help," he said.

"Do you love my grandmother?"

"Very much."

"Then I'll do whatever it takes."

His plan was to cover our room in rose petals and chocolate, light some candles, and leave a letter on her bed that would make her swoon. But I needed to butter her up before the romantic nonsense.

When she woke up, I followed her into the sea and pretended the jellyfish weren't there. I got stung on my calf and acted as if nothing had happened; I just kept treading water. When we returned to shore, I asked her to read me more choice passages from her novel and agreed that they were very evocative. By the time we packed up, she was in a good mood. Still, I knew Baba needed more than chocolate and a good day at the beach to change her mind, though I was charmed by Anatoly Petrovich's simplicity.

"What a lovely day. A lovely day with my granddaughter," she said. "I can't believe I lived to be so lucky. . . ." Then she went off on a tangent about how the Nazis had burned the buildings to the left and right of hers during the war, that only two other families in her apartment had survived intact, that it was amazing she was alive at all.

"It was a great day, Baba. I'm lucky to have you," I said. I stopped her on the way to our room. "You know,

Papa loved Anatoly Petrovich. He called him his second father."

"I know that, child."

"One time, just after your final visit, he mentioned you two. . . ."

"Oh?"

"He said he was happy you were doing so well on your own, but he wished you would just be with Anatoly Petrovich already, because it was obvious how much you loved each other."

"He really said that?" she said.

I nodded, letting her soak in my lie. Of course, Papa *could* have said something like that, or thought it, at least.

She composed herself again, and I led her to our room. When she opened the door, she gasped at the candles, the flowers, and the chocolate, and put a hand on her heart. I had not let her suitor down. She read his letter and her eyes filled with tears. She said, "I'm afraid you're on your own tonight, my dear. Can you keep yourself entertained?" I told her I was a grad student and was used to spending many hours alone, but she was already heading for the shower.

I woke up from a short nap to find Baba facing the mirror, trying to put her necklace on. Her hands were shaking. I rose from bed and stood behind her and helped her to clasp it, admiring her image: her rosy cheeks, her silver dress and bright-red hair. We didn't really look like each other, so I was surprised to find two matching pairs of big eyes staring back at us.

"Gray eyes aren't so bad after all, are they?" she said.

I laughed. "Blue eyes or gray, you don't look a day over fifty."

"You little liar," she said, pinching my side. "How I love you."

I escorted her to meet her suitor and she kissed me on the cheek. I watched as she walked toward the embankment outside the Oreanda. Jellyfish bites ran up and down the backs of her legs, garish swollen stings. Anatoly Petrovich emerged from the hotel, took her arm, and turned her in the other direction, toward the vast sea. I saw that they had no idea what they were doing, no more than I did. I ran my hand over the sting on my leg and no longer minded the pain. And then I turned away from my grandmother and her soon-to-be lover and decided to go for one more dip in the sea.

I had tried to stay away from Roman after he told me he was married. The academic year was nearly over, and I walked around town peering into all the bright, clean restaurants filled with bright, clean people, thinking it unfathomable that anyone had ever felt despair in any of these places. The edgiest person in town was the guy who ate fire outside the froYo shop on Thursday nights. I kept thinking of jokes I'd tell Roman. "If we're together we could open a coffee shop called Grounds for Divorce," I would say. I ran almost every morning, before it got too hot, until I reached the farms north of town, where I would finally stop to watch the cows chewing grass. I spent too much time skyping Baba, who tried to convince me to visit her in Yalta. "This is my last summer there, child," she kept repeating. "I'm getting old."

I visited Dr. Vainberg's lair to see if there were opportunities to study abroad or transfer or finish the remaining five years of my degree remotely. The best he could do was offer me the summer-travel grant money that Marnie the Mouse had freed up when she'd dropped out. I jotted down some nonsense about going to Yalta to study how Chekhov's impending death affected his perspective on the lovers in "The Lady with the Dog." It was a feeble idea; it was common for writers to become obsessed with death in their later years, as Tolstoy had with *Ivan Ilyich*.

Vainy loved my pitch. He took my hands in his and said, "You must return to us. You're the last underground woman. And your teaching evaluations were above average. . . ."

I promised to stay and asked him for Roman's address, saying he needed me to drop off some books. Then I took the train to Sacramento.

Sac was even hotter than Davis. My shoulders were singed as soon as I stepped out of the train, and I wished I had brought some sort of cover-up. I wasn't good at sneaking around. I wasn't even wearing sunglasses. I found Roman's cute yellow house and stared at it from a bench a block away. I didn't know how long I'd been sitting there when I heard Roman's voice.

"You came here," he said. "That means you still care."

He wore a gray T-shirt and jeans and had a tiny white dog at his side. He didn't seem mad that I had invaded his space, only surprised.

"*That's* Fedya?" I said. "I thought he would be big."

"Hey," he said, crouching down and covering the dog's pointy ears. "Don't say that about my man. He'll get a complex. He considers himself quite large for his breed. . . ."

I watched him petting his runty pet and understood that spending two weeks away from him had not changed a thing. My feelings were stronger than ever. I couldn't say why. He was handsome, but I had been with men who were better-looking. And I had been with other men who loved books. I had been with other men who were good in bed. I had been with other men who'd appreciated my sense of humor. Even if I had never found all these qualities in one person, I knew this was too simple, that there was no explaining away how I felt. I just loved him.

"It's nice to meet you, Fedya," I said, and the dog growled at me.

Roman laughed. "He's very protective." We stared at each other while the dog tugged on his leash.

"Let's go somewhere and talk," he said. He entered his house to drop off his dog and left me on the sidewalk. I was dying to follow him but also relieved that he did not invite me in. I didn't think my heart could take it, seeing photographs of them together, the furniture they sat on, the drab contents in their fridge, the contours of a life that did not include me.

We got in his car and drove to the edge of another park. He said, "Don't worry—Julia's at work." Then he swallowed, realizing he had said her name. I wanted to unlearn it.

"I've missed you like crazy," I said.

"I've missed you too."

That was when I stopped being innocent in the matter. I straddled him and ran my hands through his hair.

"The problem is, I can't stop thinking about fucking you," I said.

"There's more to it than that."

"Not this second," I said, and he laughed as I unbuckled his belt and started fucking him, hard, to remind him how amazing I was. I couldn't look in his eyes. It was all too much. When it was over, I felt disgusting and I collapsed in the passenger seat, panting like his gross dog. I had not conveyed the proper message.

"I want you to be with me," I said. "I want you to leave your wife." I wasn't planning to say it. Until that moment, I wasn't even certain it was what I wanted, but once the words came out, I knew it had to happen.

"I've been thinking about it," he said, which surprised and scared and excited me.

"You have?"

"Of course I have. But it's complicated. It's not like I don't care about her. We have a history. I just . . . I need to know you're sure about me, Oksana." He looked down at his hands.

"Why wouldn't I be sure?" I said, slipping my underwear back on. I didn't notice how awful he looked until then. There was a heaviness under his eyes. His usually neat beard was bushy and uneven.

"Don't take this the wrong way," he said, meeting my gaze. "But you hated college. You hated your job in New York. You said you hated our program the day we met. I just want to make sure—that you really love me. That you're sure about us."

Of course I was sure! What did he think I was doing in Sacramento? But his list didn't help. I felt my soul unraveling. Why should I trust myself? What if I was breaking up the marriage of two nice people—just because of a feeling?

"How can I prove how I feel?" I said.

"I don't know."

I looked at my purse, as if there were an answer inside it. Like there was something I could give him to prove how I felt.

"I'm going to Yalta for a month," I said. "Maybe being away from you will help me think clearly. We can talk when I get back. Or never talk again, I don't know."

I could see how crushed he was that I was leaving and how happy he was that I was coming back.

"I'll see you in a month, then," he said.

"Unless I fall in love with a Crimean stud and never return."

"I hate you sometimes."

"No," I said. "You don't." Then I added, "I'll get you a souvenir, all right?" This got him to smile.

We kissed one more time and I got out of the car. I turned around at the end of the block and saw him lower his head on the steering wheel.

Back home, I realized I could stalk his wife on Facebook now that I knew her name. Roman didn't have an account, but she was easy to find. She had short hair and thick arms and I wished she were prettier so it didn't mean that something deeper connected them. I clicked through her pictures, watching her age in reverse, until she wasn't posing with injured cats and was just a Berkeley undergrad looking at Roman with sad eyes, as if she had already lost him. I hadn't realized that they had gone to school together, that they had fallen in love there, and then I understood what Roman was crying about that day on the street when he saw the gutted bookstore.

I ate dinner in the hotel restaurant, ordering two bowls of borscht with pampushki, one after the other. I was moved by my grandmother and Anatoly Petrovich's love and wondered what changes this turn of events would bring. I didn't want to give myself full credit, but I knew my story about Papa had helped. I wanted to call Roman, to tell him all about it.

The waiter cleared my second bowl and said, "I hope you enjoyed your meal."

I considered how much of our lives we wasted by exchanging foolish banter. How was I supposed to answer? "My soup was delicious, but my heart is ripped to shreds because I'm in love with a married man, because every breath I take only makes me think of him, makes me think not of his presence but of his absence, of how every wave that crashes on the shore, every drop of wine I drink, every spoonful of fucking borscht I eat, means absolutely nothing because the man I need more than the air I breathe isn't here"?

I had not given the man the answer he needed. "My soup was delicious," I said. "But my heart . . . craves a third bowl."

"Very well."

After dinner, I returned to the room and put ice over the sting on my leg. I picked up Chekhov's story again. I skipped all the way to the end, to the part after Gurov tracks Anna down and the lovers realize they cannot live without each other and have to figure out the rest. Chekhov wrote, *And it was clear to both of them that they had still a long, long road before them, and that the most complicated and difficult part of it was only just beginning.*

I threw the book across the room and tried not to

think of myself. I should have been glad that at least my grandmother was grasping at a bit of joy; she certainly deserved it. But my life was still my life, and I curled up in a ball, wanting Roman.

I ate Anatoly Petrovich's chocolate, iced my leg again, and masturbated to a random passage in Baba's romance novel, but nothing worked. I picked up my phone and dialed. It rang twice.

"Oksana?" Roman said. "Is it really you?"

"It's me."

"I've missed you like crazy. I'm so glad you called— you got my email?"

"What email?"

"So you called on your own," he said, his voice weak. "Listen—I'm ready to leave my wife."

"I'm ready too," I said. "I know you doubted how sure I am, Roma, but I'm absolutely sure, do you understand? I'm sure because I know what it's like not to be sure, because I've spent my entire life not being sure about anything until I met you."

"I can't stop thinking about you," he said. "I think I'm going mad."

"I know. It's awful."

"I didn't even ask you. How's Yalta?" I could hear relief and giddiness flooding his voice.

I outlined the situation. "You know, just hanging out with two horny geriatrics," I said. He laughed, so I kept going. "The sexual tension is so thick you could cut it with a cane." But he didn't laugh again, a sign I was trying too hard.

"It's lonely here," I said.

"Here too. . . ." he said, and he began to cry.

"I know you'll miss her," I said. "I know this won't be easy."

"Of course I'm going to miss her. But that's not it. I didn't really think about it until this moment, but this means she's going to take Fedya. Of course she's going to take Fedya . . ." he said, crying more than I had ever heard a man cry, angry, jagged, childish sounds that made me wonder if I knew him at all. And all this over a dog! Had he ever cried this hard over me?

"We can always get another dog."

"What are you talking about?" he said, sounding horrified, as if I had suggested he drown the poor runt. "I would never, ever do that. Do you understand?"

"Not really." I looked out at the sea and saw how stupid our argument was, how much he meant to me. I thought of more dumb jokes I could make. "I guess you could call this our Yalta Conference," I could say. "I'm sorry. I didn't mean that. I got you a souvenir," I added pointlessly, though of course I hadn't yet. When he didn't respond, I said, "I wish you knew how much I love you."

"I have some idea."

"I'm scared, Roma."

"Me too. All right, then. Give me a few days. I'll call you when the dust settles."

I couldn't sleep. I kept sweating and tossing and turning and imagining Roman telling his wife everything. I wanted to know what she'd said, whether she'd already known about me or if she'd tried to change his mind, and if it worked. I kept checking my phone and my email—though it cost a fortune—but I heard nothing beyond his original email, which only said, *I miss you*. Worst of all, a song that had come on in his car when we'd driven to

Berkeley, Thin Lizzy's "Cowboy Song," kept playing over and over in my head, and it was ridiculous and did not echo the hysterical and life-altering things I was feeling, and yet as I sweated and worried and wondered and stepped out on the balcony to stare at the murky sea, it became a dirge.

Roman was right. Dostoevsky was perfectly rational. I was overheating and insane and I would have tried to fight somebody if I hadn't been alone. How was I supposed to know what to do now or after the dust had settled? How?

When I opened my eyes, sunlight flooded the room and Baba was fussing around in the bathroom. I'd expected her to be giddy, but she only looked tired, as if she hadn't slept all night. That could have been a good thing, of course.

"You're finally up," she said as she secured a sun hat to her head. "Good. Today we visit Chekhov's house."

"Is Anatoly Petrovich coming?"

"No," she said sharply. "He's staying behind."

I knew not to ask further questions. Maybe they'd had a fight, maybe he'd begged her to move to Moscow and she wasn't ready. Maybe she was ready but was waiting to tell him so.

I checked my phone, but Roman had not called. I pictured him down on his knees before his average-looking wife. I left my phone in the hotel.

We took the bus to Chekhov's house, a charming white building surrounded by a beautiful garden I could not have cared less about. I tuned out after the guide told us that the White Dacha had been built in 1898, six years before the author's death. I was struck by a porcelain figurine of a dog, on the mantel over the fireplace. I wondered if it had inspired Chekhov's story, if he'd acquired it after he wrote the story, or if it was just a decorative touch of the tourist bureau. I considered pointing it out to Baba, but she was distracted, scowling and fanning herself. The house was stuffy and I was relieved when the guide led us to the garden.

"He planted everything himself," the guide said. "The cherry and peach and cypress trees . . . A hundred years later, the garden is still flourishing. Isn't it something? He was a master gardener. I'll leave you to explore the grounds," she said.

Baba and I explored the gardens, which really were a wonder. I waited for her to say something, but she didn't.

"Chekhov was a doctor and a writer, and he was also this amazing gardener?" I said finally. "I'm just trying to find a single thing I'm good at. It doesn't seem fair."

"Who said anything about fair?"

I followed her to the edge of the garden. The sea sparkled in the distance. I wished Roman was standing behind me, so I could lean back and put my head under his chin, so we could take it in together.

"What's the matter?" I said. "I thought you realized you should follow your heart."

"Follow my heart, and look where it takes me," she muttered. "You know what he told me in the morning? He's sick again, Oksana. He'll be dead by the end of the summer."

"I'm so sorry."

"I should have known better. Your grandmother is a fool, just as naïve as her granddaughter. . . ."

"What did I do?"

"You didn't do a thing," she said, shaking her head. "I know I'm hard on you, my dear, but it's because I want to toughen you up. When you get that lost look on your face, you really do look like your father. He had that look when we got to America and he thought he would still be a physics hero—it was as if he didn't know the Cold War was over, that no one needed him anymore. And you! You expect life to be this incredible romp, and then you get crushed when the smallest thing goes wrong. Life will throw you things harder than you've ever imagined, and how will you deal with them when you're afraid of a jellyfish or a dumb bird?"

"I'm not afraid of everything," I said. "I'm in love with a married man. He's leaving his wife for me."

Her eyes flared up. "You're still young, why get involved in such a mess? If I were you, I would run in the other direction."

"But you're not me. You don't feel what I feel."

"What are feelings?" she said, swatting away the air. "Dandelion seeds in the wind."

I left her to visit the gift shop. I would get Roman a souvenir, just like I'd promised. I had to show him how serious I was, to let him feel my beating heart. The trinkets did not inspire me and I knew what I had to do. I made sure no one was around and snuck back into the living room. The dog figurine was waiting for me there. I hoped it would set the right tone for Roman, a souvenir from the time when we decided to be together as well as a gesture toward our future, the only new little dog he might accept from me. I stuffed the figurine in my purse. It seemed like a minor offense, considering all the mistakes I had made.

Baba spent the rest of the day in bed, and the next morning. I stayed in bed too, turning on my phone every fifteen minutes to see if Roman had called. Anatoly Petrovich was leaving that evening, but my grandmother had already said goodbye and did not want to see him again. I told her I was going for a walk and asked if she needed anything.

"Only peace," she said.

I left, knowing I could not help her with that. The day was cruelly gorgeous, and the promenade was full of happy people. I found Anatoly Petrovich on the embankment in front of his hotel, watching the water. He looked defeated, wearing a thin coat he didn't need. I approached him slowly, not wanting to startle him.

"I'm sorry," I said.

"What can you do?" he said, shrugging. I knew I should have felt sorry for him, but his defeated tone annoyed me.

"All these years, you've kept on pestering my poor grandmother. Even now. Why haven't you been able to leave her alone?"

He turned away. "If you only saw her as I first saw her," he began. "Strutting into the auditorium holding your father's hand. Her red hair bathed in light like she was on fire. There was nothing in her hair, child. But I just had to touch her, because I knew I would die if I didn't." He turned back to me and clasped my hands. "I want to thank you for the other night. Your grandmother and I made sweet, sweet love. I will never forget it."

"I wouldn't have done it if I knew the situation," I said, trying not to picture my grandmother in the throes of passion.

I thought of what Chekhov wrote about this very sea when he had come to Yalta with sickness in his lungs, knowing death was around the corner. When Gurov and Anna are first falling for each other, they share a quiet moment staring out at the water. Chekhov described the sea before us, writing my favorite lines in all of literature, gorgeous and somber words that comforted me in dark times by reminding me of my cosmic insignificance, words that might comfort Baba's suitor since I could not produce my own. Words I tried to quote carefully in Russian.

I said, *The monotonous hollow sound of the sea rising up from below spoke of the peace, of the eternal sleep awaiting us.*

Anatoly Petrovich stared at me, his mouth quivering.

"What lies," he said, putting his head in his hands. "I'm not ready to die."

I felt sorry for him, for my grandmother, for everyone who failed to love or be loved. I reached into my purse and handed him the porcelain dog.

"What is it?"

"It's from my grandmother. A parting gift from Chekhov's home."

"You are a wonderful young woman," he said. "I cannot thank you enough."

The waves crashed meanly on the shore. Anatoly

Petrovich played with the figurine, turning it over and over in his hands. I didn't know how I could replace it. I would have to find another way to show Roman how much I loved him, if he gave me the chance. I didn't know what would happen to us. I didn't know when he would call or what he would tell me. I didn't know a thing. I didn't know if this was just the beginning or if we had already reached the end.

PHOTOGRAPH

"Guess what I picked up this morning?" Jim says, rising from his exercise ball at the head of the table. His bald head is shining, radiating excitement, though our morning meeting has already gone on far too long. I look at the other editors for signs that we are actually supposed to guess, but no one does. "Voilà," he says, producing a gray case from his shirt pocket. "Google Glass! One of the first hundred beta pairs in Silicon Valley. Lucky me, right?"

Jim looks like a tool with the square glasses planted on his round face. He founded Howtopia, with its empowering slogan of HACK YOUR OWN LIFE TODAY!, a top-100–ranked company in the United States, but he still manages to be a tragic figure. He is middle-aged and shaped like a garden gnome and wears ill-fitting T-shirts and jean shorts, his wife left him for her yoga instructor and fled to Hawaii without looking back years ago, and his teen daughter, Abigail, thinks he's a joke—she's been interning at Howtopia all summer.

Fiona whistles when she puts the glasses on and Jim tells her to scroll here, blink there, look over here, madly barking instructions.

"Pretty sweet," she says. She's my closest work friend, though she's desperate to escape, using her popular travel blog to try to get a gig out of the country; our third musketeer, Gilly, quit last month, leaving behind, on top of the fridge, a family of paper cranes she made for an article. The glasses cycle through the other eight members of the editing team, most of whom are, like me, marginally employable creative types who like working from home every day except Wednesday, when we have to schlep all the way out to the Howtopia House from the more affordable crevasses of the Bay. All of them, I am disappointed to note, are impressed by Jim's new toy. Even Josh, a permahigh long-haired poet, nods like he's watching the world burn.

Abigail is mesmerized by the glasses and gives her father a rare smile. This is her last week with us; soon she'll study photography at an arts college in New York. She is as polished as her father is frumpy, sporting black jeans and tank tops and professional-level makeup at all times. She's a decade younger than me, but, like my sixteen-year-old brother, who would kill to be leaving for college already, she knows more than I ever will.

"Not bad," she says, and her father beams, delighted to please her for once.

"Such a crisp image, right? I didn't think it would be so crisp," he says.

I can't get the fucking thing to work. Jim hovers over me and barks more adamantly, but all the blinking and clicking doesn't do anything. I'm stuck on a picture of a field of poppies.

"It must not be my day," I say.

"It's all right, Oksana," Jim says, quickly plucking them off my face, like I've contaminated them. "Maybe it doesn't recognize your face shape. I'll customize it for you later."

"It's no big deal," I say.

Jim walks past the fuzzy beanbag chairs and fake Pollocks and dim IKEA lamps and up the stairs with his new big-boy toy, and once he's gone a silence falls over the room and everyone stares at me warily, as if I am tainted. No one moves either, as if they expect an explanation. The best I can do is a story. A story featuring my poor dead father—who is never far from my mind after my two-hour hell-on-earth commute to Palo Alto from East Oakland.

"One time in high school," I begin, "I convinced my parents to take me to this fortune-teller down the Shore. But her crystal ball didn't work on me. She couldn't see anything. It really freaked my dad out—it was like I didn't exist. But I'm still here, right?"

"Unfortunately for us," Fiona says, elbowing me.

"You would die without me," I say.

"Only a little," she says with a wink.

"Lovebirds," says Josh.

"I just hope you got your money back," Abigail tells me before going up the stairs.

The editors put in their earbuds and return to their private musical worlds and article lists, the Apple logos on their silver laptops glowing like the fruit of a zombie garden in the dark house canopied by palms. I put my own earbuds in and play *The White Album* and plop down on the zebra couch with the pink pillows that say YOU ARE A UNICORN!—which is what Jim always calls the versatile writers of the editing team. If I had unicorns working for me, I'd give them more than thirty an hour without benefits.

Though I do make significantly more than my fiancé, who is home working on his dissertation on serfdom in 1800's Russian literature. After I quit our PhD program over two years ago, I was pumped to write articles read by thousands a day instead of by one overworked professor, but the articles in the queue were mostly about twerking and making out instead of life's big problems, as societally useless as exploring ekphrasis in *The Idiot*. Though I embellish my How-to hours to write fiction, I've been too drained to make progress. I've decided to leave this job if I don't get a fucking raise, which is why I've scheduled a meeting with Jim at the end of the day.

I finish "How to Be a Mime," text Roman about our save-the-dates, and move to the upstairs lounge, where Abigail is taking photos for Josh's "How to Make a Paper Boat" article. The five steps of the paper boat are lined up in a row, starting with a flat piece of paper and ending with a crisp paper vessel. I settle at the teal worktable, which still holds a matchstick model of Versailles that Gilly and I helped Fiona make for an article. The palace is huge but not so impressive, just a few tan rectangles and a gate, though I am told the inside is where the extravagance lies. Beside it is a stack of alpaca hats a techie who works in the house next door brought back from Peru, alms for the poor editors. I already took four home.

Abigail tilts her camera to show me the finished paper-boat series.

"Not bad," I say.

She rolls her eyes. "Not exactly inspiring. Four more days and I can take pictures of whatever I want."

"You'll miss it here, at least a little bit."

"We'll see about that."

"You'll miss your dad."

"No chance," she says. "In New York I'll actually find people I have something in common with. Everyone in Shallow Alto is so fucking vanilla. I'm talking to my new roommate today—she's a painter."

"Good for you," I say.

After she uploads the photos, she takes actual photos of finished items out of her bag and tapes them to the walls: among them, a flower crown made by yours truly, a friendship bracelet made by Fiona, a pumpkin with a cat carving made by Gilly, and a horse hand puppet made by Josh. This is kind of sweet, Abigail's concession that her time here has not sucked.

"Photos were as modern as my dad would go," I say. "TV hurt his eyes. He never had a pager or cellphone. I can't imagine what he'd think of Howtopia—Google Glass would make his head explode. When I was a kid, he loved sitting down with his photo albums, pointing at grim sepia-toned Russians and explaining how each one had died in the war, repeating, 'No future without history!' I was bored out of my mind then, but now I'm glad he kept a record of it all."

"Your dad and I would have gotten along," she says.

"I have a million albums at home. My dad's always post-
ing family photos on Facebook—it's mortifying. Do you
make albums too?"

"Sometimes," I say, though this isn't exactly true. She
gives me a look that says she doesn't believe me, and I
don't try to convince her otherwise.

I write "How to Be a Stenographer" next. And by
"write" I mean look up twenty articles on the subject,
cite them, add bullshit of my own, write a bunch of steps
and sub-steps with detailed examples, and request art-
work from people in the Philippines who get paid a dollar
a day. Then I log the hour it took me to write the article
plus an extra thirty minutes, which I devote to looking at
wedding dresses and centerpieces on Pinterest and ending an email fight with Mama, who keeps trying to add
more random Russians to our guest list though we've
only got three months until the wedding. I keep telling
her that the farm we booked in Davis won't be the fancy
Russian community's idea of a good time anyway, but
she won't be deterred. I should be nicer since she and my
stepdad are paying for so much of it, but she doesn't make
it easy.

Jim struts in, looking potbellied and proud, even more
sweaty than usual because he is fresh from the tread desk,
dumb glasses clipped to his T-shirt collar.

He grins at me and nods at his daughter. "My little
jet-setter," he says. "Just yesterday she fell off the monkey
bars and got a concussion. And now—"

"Dad," she says, rolling her eyes. "Please."

Upon closer inspection, Jim seems less jolly than
usual, his face a bit worn, no doubt upset about giving up
his only child to the clutches of the East Coast. I hope

this means he will be more vulnerable, instead of firmer, when I ask for a raise. Maybe I'll even try the I'm-the-loyal-daughter-who-isn't-leaving-you angle, though that may be a bit cruel. I have already asked about every six months since I started working here and have only gotten a five-dollar raise and an occasional bonus in response, so he knows what's coming.

"End of the day, right, Oksana? I have to run to Mountain View for a bit," he says. He says it instead of saying he's visiting Google, the way some say they "went to school in Cambridge" instead of just fucking saying they went to Harvard. He reaches over to stroke Abigail's hair, but she flinches.

"Seriously," she says. "Come on." If her dad wasn't there, I would smack her.

"So sensitive," he says, holding up his hands, but he's still smiling, proud of his darling. He spots her photos on the wall and gives her a thumbs-up, adding, "Very cool," but she just shrugs. He puts the Google Glasses back on and his face glows. He taps the side of his toy and says, "Soon enough, everybody will be walking around in these things. I just know it."

"Ready for your big chat with Jimbo?" Fiona says. We have taken our fifteen-dollar lunch allowance from Jim and are at our usual spot, a French bistro called La Bou-lange, which we boycotted for about three weeks when we found out it was owned by Starbucks. We sit in the sunshine and pick at our Niçoise salads while Fiona swipes through her phone.

"I guess I'm ready?" I say. "If he says no again, I'll just

look for another job. But what am I supposed to do? What if anything that isn't writing fiction crushes my soul?"

"Girl," Fiona says. "This is your time. You've been here forever. Plus you can pull all that 'I'm getting married and need money' shit. Meanwhile, I can't even get a date." She holds up her phone to show me a shirtless man grinning on a rock. "What about this one?"

"Such a crisp image," I say, and she kicks me under the table. "He's cute. Why not?"

She sighs, spitting an olive pit into her napkin. "I don't know why I bother, honestly."

"But you have so many options." I don't bother pointing out that she is a stunner, all legs and luscious red hair that falls to her waist.

"That's the problem. They have so many options too. If a guy met me in a bar before phones, he'd just ask me out, but now it's, like, should I ask her out or just message the sluts on OkCupid? You're lucky you found someone," she says. "How is Romey anyway?"

Fiona has been impressed by Roman since I convinced her to come out with us in Oakland, a long, sloppy night that ended with us drinking red wine on Lake Merritt while Roman recited Akhmatova's "Seaside Sonnet" and moved both himself and me to tears.

"Romey's great," I say. "Actually doing shit he loves."

I show her my phone, to which Roman has recently texted a picture of Tolstoy in the snow. The count is wearing a thick fur coat and hat and his brows are covered in flakes, looking boundless and severe.

"Now, there's a real man," Fiona says. "Is he single?"

"It's Tolstoy."

"So what? He looks like a boss. Not some pussy who would be like, 'Oh, this is getting too serious' if I tell him to go down on me more than once."

"The count is kind of conservative," I say. "But I'll ask him to pleasure you next week."

"About next week," she says, meeting my gaze. I don't like the look she gives me one bit. I know it's bad when she puts her phone away.

"No," I say, swallowing hard. I throw a napkin at her. "Seriously? *Et tu, Brute?*"

"I'm sorry," she says. "The British travel company made me an offer this morning. I'm leaving for Edinburgh next week. Pretty cool, right?"

"Of course it's cool. You dumb cunt," I say, giving her a hug. "I'll miss you like hell, but I'm happy for you."

"I'll miss you too," she says. "You're such a talented writer, Konnie. If Jim says no again, there are a million amazing places where you can work and finish your novel."

"Such as?"

She gives me a movie-star smile. "You can go anywhere you want. You're a unicorn, remember?"

My brain is numb and my back and wrists are aching by the time I have to meet Jim on the Howtopia House porch; I spent the last hour reading my friend Lily's travel blog and tinkering with my novel. Even if I'm just rewriting the scene where my grandmother's family eats their dog during World War II, just moving the words around rejuvenates my soul and gets me ready for Jim. When I open the front door, Abigail is standing with an arm around her dad, showing him something in her camera that's cracking him up. She pales, ashamed to be seen having so much fun with her father. When they both look up at me, I realize they have the same brown eyes. Jim chuckles as his daughter darts off to the backyard.

"Sorry to interrupt," I say.

"No problem. Look, Oksana, I know why you're here," Jim says, and I shake off the image of Abigail and jump into my spiel.

I deserve a raise. I am the only editor who has stuck it out for over two years. Two of my articles are in the top-ten most-visited. I've on-boarded half the team. I reach my crescendo with, "Plus, traffic on the entire site spiked ten percent after Gawker picked up my article 'How to Dry-Hump Safely'—"

"I have good news for you," he says. "Don't worry."

"You do?"

"Indeed," he says, smiling big, and for some reason I feel dread. "All summer I've been thinking of what to do with you. You've been such a rock here, and weddings are expensive, and don't even get me started on kids! And you've been such a good role model to Abigail. So hear me out," he says, opening his mouth and drumming on his lap. "Cellphones!" he declares.

"Cellphones?"

"It's happened. As of this week, over half the traffic to our site is coming from mobile users. Can you believe that? This is going to change how we write our articles, use our photos, everything. We'll have to write with mobile users in mind first."

"So we'll have to dumb everything down?"

"Exactly! And I can't think of a better person to put in

charge of it," he says. "You'll take half the team and will work on mobile-friendly articles. You can test the numbers yourself. I'm talking full-time status, just like you've wanted. Seventy K a year and benefits, how does that sound? Of course, you'd have to come in to the office every day. . . ."

This would mean Roman and I could leave our cramped apartment and move closer to the lake. We could spend money on our wedding and honeymoon and the restaurants in Piedmont without freaking out. Though I would barely make it home in time for dinner most weekdays, and if I did, I would be too exhausted to go out. I regard the palm trees on either side of us, beautiful trees that make the house so dark, and find that I can hardly breathe.

"Count me in," I say.

He smiles big and claps his hands. "Great, wonderful, I'll put everything in writing over the weekend." He shakes my hand. "Oh, one more thing."

"Yeah?"

He hands me the Google Glass. "I tinkered with it a bit. See if it works now."

I put the glasses on and blink and move my head around, and it does work. I blink through a series of generic landscapes. First, the field of poppies again. Then the jungle. The desert. Then the ocean, which is where I pause. Jim's right—it is surprisingly crisp.

"It's like you're really there," he says.

Bright foamy water fills the screen. It crashes on a nearly white beach, and the sky above is cloudless. Sunlight kisses the waves. There are no people walking along the water or swimming in it, no logs or seaweed on the shores; not a single grain of sand looks out of place. I have never felt further away from the ocean in my life.

"I'm so excited for you, Oksana. I see a long and rewarding career for you here," he says.

I stare into the nothing ocean and remember the beginning of Akhmatova's "Seaside Sonnet":

It will all live longer than me:
even the rickety bird boxes,
and the air that makes the crossing
in the spring from over the sea.

I hand back the glasses and wipe my eyes, and only then can I see the ocean a little bit. Jim looks puzzled but not defeated by my display of emotion. He gives me a nervous smile, puts the glasses on, and grins wildly. The daylight is fading but he seems not to care. He is an astounding man, really. He has lost his hair, half the editors, his wife, and soon he will lose his daughter, and yet in this moment he looks as if he has everything he has ever wanted and more.

"Just like you're really there," he says again, waving the glasses in the air. "Pretty amazing, right?"

Our trip down the Jersey Shore was the last my family took before Papa died on his commute. It had been his idea, actually. It was unlike him to plan a family adventure and I suspected it was because he wanted to test out his new BMW, but I was just happy to spend time with him, even if we only spent two days in Wildwood. It had been a great trip until the last afternoon, when I convinced my parents and brother to see the fortune-teller.

Her booth was at the edge of the boardwalk and smelled like incense and ocean water. We sat on velvet cushions and tried not to laugh at the woman with long white hair and bloodshot eyes. I faced her as she waved her hands before the crystal ball and closed her eyes, but apparently nothing happened. She tried again, frowning as she peered into the dormant orb, but it didn't swirl or crackle or get covered in mist.

"I can't see anything," she said, as if delivering a death sentence. "I'm sorry."

"Your equipment is broken," Papa said, and he stormed out and we followed him.

Mama thought it was all a joke, but Papa was melancholy as we hit the boardwalk.

He put a hand on my shoulder and said, "Poor future-less child." He held up a finger and said he would be right back, he just needed a moment.

Mama and Misha and I stood at the edge of the boardwalk and watched Papa take off his shoes, set them down, and walk toward the water. The beach was crowded with painfully tan people, garbage, crab skeletons, and seaweed, but nothing got in Papa's way. We were supposed to head home then. He would have to get up at five the next morning to commute to Wall Street, but he didn't care. He gazed at the horizon, and who knew what he saw—maybe visions of the flowing waters of the Dnieper, back when he was a young and happy childless scientist in Kiev, before he'd had to sacrifice everything for his family. Papa lifted up his hands.

Mama laughed. "Your father is such a romantic," she said. "Look at him standing before that filthy water! As if he expects to be lifted up into the heavens."

"Maybe he's thinking," said my brother. He was three.

"Maybe he thinks it's beautiful," I said.

"A philosopher and a poet," Mama said, shaking her head. "What did I do to deserve such children?" But she put her arms around us anyway. "Driving a nice car is not enough for your father. He wants to fly also," she said. "Pure foolishness."

Papa was wearing his work khakis and a button-down shirt, his uniform no matter what day it was, a constant reminder of how hard he worked. As he stepped into the water, I could see Mama calculating whether she had a fresh pair of clothes for him for the drive home.

My brother thought it was the funniest thing. He ran down to the water, and by the time he got there, Papa turned to him with a big smile, soaked from the chest down, and grabbed his waist and lifted him up for a little while. I wanted to run in there and join them too, and I should have, but I was sixteen and embarrassed and just wanted to go home already.

I can still see them there, framed by the boardwalk, reaching toward the ocean on one side and a jutting mass of sandy rocks on the other, white foam frothing near my father's waist while my brother squeals. They look tiny below the vast sky.

The other editors have all gone home and my computer is the lone soldier stationed at the table next to a bowl of colorful erasers a techie brought back from Japan; I take a handful. Fiona has left a note on Howtopia stationery on my keyboard. It had been previously folded and I see that it came from one of Gilly's paper cranes. *Tell Tolstoy to sext me.* On the other side, Josh has drawn a picture of Jim with his new glasses on. A knife protrudes from his bald head.

As I pack up, I spot Abigail scowling into her phone by the community garden, sitting in front of the kale I have been liberally helping myself to all summer. Seeing the light falling below the pastel-colored houses and orange fence and bright porch furniture, I wish I had spent more time out here, which goes to show that if you look hard enough, there is always something about a place that you will miss. I'll wait until Jim sends his daughter away to let him down.

From a distance, the girl doesn't look more cranky than usual, but up close I see she has been crying. Without makeup, she looks about ten.

"What happened?" I say.

"I don't know if I want to go to New York."

"You were dying to go hours ago. You've been dying to go all summer."

"I just got off the phone with my roommate. She says there are rats in our dorm—rats! And that her boyfriend is basically going to be 'crashing' with us for a while. I don't think we'll be friends either. She kept bragging about how she's already shown in galleries and everything. I don't know if I can keep up out there," she says, looking at the house. "I could have gone to Berkeley and stayed near my dad. What's he going to do without me?"

I see Jim on the porch, smiling into his new glasses like they contain a galaxy.

I see Papa walking toward the ocean. This time, though, he keeps going until he is under the water. A wave crashes over the spot where his head had been and then there is stillness.

"You can't spend your whole life worrying about your dad," I say.

"No," she says, sniffling a bit. She keeps staring at me, expecting more, but I'm done.

I rip out a few heads of kale and toss them into my tote. Then I give her a hug, wondering if I will ever see her again. I don't realize how small she is until I have my arms around her.

"Wait," she says, digging in her bag. "I have something for you."

She hands me an off-center picture of our Versailles model. In the corner, above a palace wall, I'm cracking up at something Fiona's saying; my eyes are closed and my hair is in my face and my hand's on my chest. I remember that day well, actually. It was the start of summer. Fiona, Gilly, Abigail, and I had ended up staying late because Versailles was taking forever, though we played Taylor Swift and danced around to get energized. I'm pretty sure I even remember what Fiona said to make me laugh, nodding at the palace: "Those poor fuckers. They thought they were at the height of luxury, but they still had to shit in chamber pots. They didn't know anything." Abigail had cracked up too, which is why the photo is crooked.

She shrugs when I thank her for the picture. "For your photo album," she says.

THE HIGH DIVE

"My heart will always be in San Francisco," Beverly says. "And the rest of my body too. When I go, Rick and Julia will throw my ashes in the Bay. We'll have a reception at the Hi Dive, my favorite bar in the world—have you been? It's right on the Embarcadero. No funeral for me—just a party. No people looking sour and wearing black, sneaking whiskey in the bathroom. Everyone will tell stories about me and laugh and dance and get hammered. I've already called to confirm that we can do it, though of course we haven't set a date. Doesn't that sound nice?"

Rick sighs. "If you don't shut the fuck up about the fucking Hi Dive, I'll blow my brains out and somebody else will have to scatter your ashes—and mine too."

"Now, that doesn't sound nice at all," Roman says.

Roman used to be married to Beverly and Rick's daughter, Julia, but he has been married to me for almost two years now. Once a month since he split with his wife, though, he has continued to visit his former in-laws at

their home in the Berkeley Hills, but until Beverly got
cancer I was never invited to come along, not that I've
exactly been clamoring to join him. Beverly is starting
chemo next week, which makes me feel silly for still being
wary of her and Rick's relationship with my husband, and
which also makes it matter less that they might know I
basically stole Roman from their daughter. The chemo
element should also make me less resentful that I have to
spend Sunday, my writing day, meeting these people, but
I can only do so much.

"I still think it's a nice idea," Beverly says, crossing her
arms and staring off at the backyard filled with bright
plants and hummingbird feeders and a pool rippling with
leaves. She is a beautiful woman in a faded sun hat; her
hair is wavy and golden and she looks forty though she's
over sixty, with the Bay Area glow of a person whose
blood is mostly kombucha and wheatgrass and whose
muscles are sinewy from decades of downward dog. She
has made an absurd amount of kale chips to go with
Rick's endless supply of expensive wine, and I've already
had two glasses of Napa chardonnay and about fifty kale
chips to avoid talking. The kale chips taste like nothing,
making me wonder why the woman couldn't just eat real
fucking chips since she knows she isn't going to live all
that long.

"We've walked by the Hi Dive. It seems like a nice
place," I say. We've passed the bar on the rare times we've
gotten Giants tickets from our lawyer friend, and with
the drunk fans sitting with buckets of Tecates by the
water, it hardly seems like a place to scatter your ashes,
though who am I to judge? I turn to Beverly and gear up

to say something that does not have to do with her impending death. I settle on, "I like your hat."

"Thank you," she says, touching it, as if to check that
it's really there. "This hat is older than my children. It's
my favorite gardening hat. I plan to wear it every day,
once my hair goes."

Rick snatches it off her head. "Stop it. I've always
hated that hat."

"It's a good hat. Very slimming," she says. "Not that
I'll need it, once—"

"Knock it off, Bev," he says, turning away from her.
"I've always loved your hair. Why do you want to hide
it?"

There are tears in his eyes but Beverly ignores him.
"It's my thinking cap," she says, victorious. Roman and I
have been holding hands under the table and I have forgotten whether it started because I was comforting him
or he was comforting me, but now we let go because our
display of vigorous love and health and relative youth in
the face of this couple's obvious pain is untoward, even
aggressive. I eat another kale chip and smile.

"You can think just fine without it," Rick says softly,
but he plops the hat back on her head and she rubs her
temples and hums while winking at him.

"When I think of you, I always think of you in that
hat," Roman says quietly.

"I'll take a picture for you before they turn me to
dust," Beverly says.

"Jesus," Rick says, shaking his head.

I take a sudden interest in their swimming pool, which
is more spectacular than anything Roman and I can ever

dream of affording; our Oakland apartment has no yard, just a tiny balcony with a basil plant on life support. Rick is a retired LinkedIn executive and Beverly is a retired elementary school art teacher and apparently an incredible painter, but they weren't retired long enough to enjoy it before Beverly found a lump in her breast and was told she had a year to live at most. The house is close to their daughter's in Orinda, and an afternoon's drive away from Folsom Prison, where their son has spent the last decade for dealing. Roman is another son to Beverly, who provides the laughter and encouragement he never got at home, with parents and a sister who are so serious that it seems impossible they are related, which is yet another reason why I never complained whenever he visited his ex-in-laws.

Rick squints at me like only I can save them all, as he takes a long sip of wine. "Please, Oksana, tell us about your goddamn job. I heard you love it," he says at last.

"It's the first job I've ever loved," I say.

This is no lie. I was lucky enough to get a gig teaching English at a private high school in the Oakland Hills two years ago. My only complaint is that I have even less time to work on my novel than I did when I worked at my dumb start-up writing job. I do wake up at five every morning to get an hour of work in, but I don't mention this, or the fact that I have been covertly researching MFA programs, though I don't know if I have the courage to apply. Instead, I tell a story about how amazed I was when I was teaching *Oedipus* to my freshmen and realized the dramatic irony was lost on them, that they did not already know that his wife and mother were one and the same.

"They shrieked like hell," I say. "You should have seen them. I had to draw a family tree and everything."

"I guess high school is where they learn all that stuff," Beverly notes.

"Exactly," I say. "And I'm the one who teaches it to them. I feel so unqualified."

"Who's qualified?" Roman says.

They laugh and I wonder if what Roman tells me is true, that they don't suspect he and I were having an affair before he divorced Julia. They have been alarmingly nice to me. So nice, in fact, that I have the sense that they are almost grateful Roman's with me instead of their daughter now; she remarried a fellow doctor and already has a kid and is pregnant with another.

Whereas I, at thirty, have been campaigning for kids since we got married, though Roman wants us to get on our feet first, which could take years—he's finishing his dissertation and there's no end in sight. My parents had me in their early twenties and I am already geriatric to have a child, by Soviet standards, though Roman likes to remind me that we live in Oakland, not Kiev. But having a gay brother doesn't help my fears of letting my poor dead father's genes flame out, though I try not to let that keep me up at night too often and to focus on being proud of my brother, who has just started his freshman year at Brown, for being who he is. Though I must admit that when I agreed to meet Beverly, I had the sick thought that seeing a dying person with me would encourage Roman to get going in the baby department, since life counters death, on to the next generation, we need to procreate to forget our impending doom, et cetera.

"I love my students," I continue. "But they're so sensi-

tive. They wear me out with their anxiety and questions.
I can't wait for summer so I can get back to work on my
novel." I realize it's only October—it's not the best sign
that I'm already thinking about summer.

"Good luck getting anything done over the summer,
though," Beverly says. "When I was teaching, anytime
summer rolled around, I always said I was going to paint,
but I was so zonked I could barely work. You know what
I did instead? Laundry. Cleaned the floors."

"Come on, Bev. You've still found time, and your
work is incredible," Roman says, and I try to picture him
jumping to defend my work like this but can't.

"Writing's not just a hobby for me," I say. I see from
Roman's face that I have majorly fucked up. I have completely forgotten myself. "Oh my God," I say. "I'm so
sorry. I didn't mean—I'm sorry, just, ever since I started
this job, I keep thinking I'm teaching all these books to
these eager kids who are eating them up, and I'm like,
why am I teaching literature instead of writing it? Am I
going to be doing this forever? You know? Fuck, I'm so
sorry."

There is no iciness to Beverly's smile when she puts a
hand on my arm. "Don't be sorry, darling. I don't think
of my painting as a hobby either."

"Of course not."

"To think, you could have been the one to write *Oedipus!*" Roman says, and Beverly and Rick laugh nervously.
Now we are the ones who have made them uncomfort-
able.

"That's not what I meant," I mutter, though I have no
ground to stand on.

"Oksana's very serious about her writing," Roman

notes, and he gives me a gaze that encompasses all of this—his resentment of me for pounding away at my keyboard every morning on something I care about while he struggles to analyze anti-Semitism in Dostoevsky and Gogol; his fear that he's never going to be a real professor and that he has wasted his thirties on his dissertation; and his belief that I care more about my silly novel about my dear boisterous grandmother's childhood during World War II than anything else, including him.

"You've got a tough woman on your hands," says Rick, not without approval. "What should I open next, another chardonnay or a chenin blanc?"

"I'll take the California wine over the French, you old snob," Roman says, but this barely gets a smile from Rick.

"Wonderful plan," Beverly says, nodding at me genially. I nod back, trying to communicate how deeply sorry I am.

I eat another kale chip and say, "Delicious. So much better than real chips."

"Thank you," she says. She is still gorgeous and not sick-seeming, and it's hard to imagine that she is going to die before the rest of us. She disappears to help her husband with the wine. Roman looks away from me. He is just as compact and wavy-haired and handsome as ever, even more handsome when he hates me, when his jaw is firm and I need to win him back.

"I'm sorry," I say. "I didn't mean—"

"A woman is dying in front of your eyes, and what do you think about? Your writing. Your dreams. You have time for your dreams, Oksana. You know who doesn't have time?"

"How many guesses do I get?"

This earns a smile. "Thank you for coming," he says, squeezing my hand. "I know you'd rather be writing."

"It's my pleasure."

"Shut up."

"I will," I say. "It'll go better if I do."

"They like you, Sana. I can tell. They argued in front of you. It's a promising sign."

"Very promising," I say. I watch a hummingbird drinking from its feeder. "This is a real fucking pleasure cruise, isn't it?" I say.

"I am having the time of my life."

"It kind of reminds me of that honeymoon we never took to Hawaii."

"I could do this kind of thing all day, every day," Roman says. "If only I knew more people who were on the brink of dying."

"I'll ask around," I say.

Then Beverly is back without Rick and with a desperate gleam in her eyes. She pulls her chair close to Roman's and clutches his hands.

"Listen," she says. "I meant what I said about the Hi Dive. I want to scatter my goddamn ashes in the water out there, and Rick and Julia will need your support. I need you to be strong for them, Roman."

"Of course I'll do it," he says, his voice heavy, and I feel sorry for him, for both of them. Beverly is probably a little bit in love with him, but this doesn't make me feel weird, and in fact, I can't blame her. Every year, he settles into himself more, the wrinkles around his eyes and the gray in his temples making him look sexier, more distinguished. Does he have affairs? It would serve me right, after all, but I'm pretty sure he doesn't. I get up and back away from them, because I'm not supposed to be there—not for this conversation, or at the house, or maybe not even with Roman. But my foot cracks a twig, and they stare at me like they have just remembered I exist.

"Sorry, sweetie," Beverly says. "You're invited too, of course."

I thank her and even consider laughing, because her invitation is so absurd, but luckily Rick returns.

"More wine?" he says, and we all gratefully accept.

As Roman tells an anecdote about a student who has a crush on him, his blue eyes twinkling with mischief, his hands moving wildly as he describes his tactics for discouraging the poor lovesick girl, I try to wrap my head around the fact that he will die one day. The two days a week he commutes to Davis, I hold my breath until he texts me that he's safe; whenever he flies to a conference, I am mad with anxiety until he lands; and every morning I watch his chest rise and fall to make sure he didn't go in his sleep. One day he will die, but I hope to go first; I don't know what I'll do if he dies before I do. There's yet another reason to pop out a few kids. Carrying on our genetic material, a buffer against loneliness, a desperate crack at immortality.

Another bottle of wine later, Beverly takes me inside, which is the last place I want to go; I had been relieved when they'd led us straight to the yard when we arrived. I had hoped to avoid exactly what I see right then, which are the walls plastered with photos of Julia and her brother in their younger years. Her brother is messy-haired and

handsome like Rick; Julia has short sandy hair and a
plump figure and possesses none of her mother's beauty,
but she looks like a nice person in all the pictures I have
ever seen of her. I had stopped obsessing over the twelve
years she'd spent with my husband long ago, and now she
looks about as threatening as a second cousin.

But Beverly doesn't linger on these pictures of her
progeny—she wants to show me her paintings. As I follow her up the stairs, I say, "I'm really sorry."

She pauses and gives me a look I can't read. "Why,
what for?"

"For what I said about writing not just being my
hobby."

She shakes her head. "It's okay, sweetie."

"It's not. I—I'm just really overwhelmed with this job
and I didn't mean to take it out on you, especially since—"

"Since I'm dying?" she says with a laugh.

"I didn't mean—"

"You are wise to be sensitive about your work," she
says, and I follow her up one more flight, to the attic, and
she opens up the room, which is filled with sunlight and
crowded with terrifying portraits. They really are incredible, though I am no expert. The strokes are thick and
not at all realistic, but wild, making everybody look tortured and holy. The only painter I have known is my
long-dead aunt Alla, but these blow her work out of the
water; Beverly is a real artist. I identify a younger Rick,
Julia and her brother as teenagers, and even the poor dog
Roman surrendered to Julia when he left her.

"Before Julia and Jack, I painted all the time. Now it
really is a hobby."

"This is amazing," I say.

"You think so? I think so," she says. "Don't get me wrong, I love my family, and Julia has been nothing but a joy, but my son has nearly killed me, and Rick has had his moments too. I spent forty years taking fucking care of everyone, driving to the fucking prison every week, and I've reached the end of the dock—and, hell, I love my family more than life itself, and I don't mean to be cocky, but in my darkest moments I wonder what it would have been like if I had spent the last forty years alone in a fucking room, making art. Without a single person depending on me. I could have been really good. See, that's the kind of nutty thing you can say when you're going to die."

"That doesn't sound nutty."

She shakes me off, slightly embarrassed, and wipes her face. She says, "I want you to have this." She hands me a portrait of Roman. I hate it. It is from well before we met, most likely from his college years, when he had just begun to date Julia. He's sitting somewhere green, probably the backyard, in fact, and this painting isn't wild and tortured like the rest but realistic, and he looks scrawny and insubstantial, just another college boy smoking too much weed, not the man I was ready to die for when we locked eyes at our PhD orientation, by the end of which I realized that I didn't want the PhD, that it was him I wanted. This boy is a stranger, but I take him in my hands.

"Thank you," I say. I keep looking at it, only because it seems better than looking at her.

She tosses her head back and laughs. "For a second there earlier, I thought you were saying sorry for fucking around with Roman while he was married to my daughter."

She is stony, free of her girlish giddiness. Washed out by the bright light, she could be a corpse. It's a relief I have never believed in God—I've never thought you could plunge into the afterlife and await a fate corresponding to your earthly actions. I have tried to love people, but I am selfish at heart, whether it means falling so madly in love with someone that I didn't care if he was married, or ignoring that someone years later to write a fucking book, yet another stab at immortality. If you weighed all the good and bad I have done, I don't know which side I would fall on, and I would take oblivion over a gamble between heaven and hell any day. Whatever the case may be, though, there is no sense in lying to the woman.

"I'm sorry for that too," I say. I look at the portrait of my husband as a near stranger again. "I really love him," I add pointlessly.

"So do I," she says, sighing. I wait for her to tell me her daughter is better off without him, that she knew they'd fallen out of love years before I came on the scene, that she knows Roman held on because of her and Rick more than anything else, that I did the poor woman a favor. But she just looks out the window, to see Roman and Rick laughing by the pool. "I hardly ever had time to swim in that thing. All it's good for is collecting leaves," she says. I follow her back to our men, more confused than ever. I think of my students and *Oedipus* and wonder if there is something so obvious about all this that I just can't fucking see.

The sun drifts below the horizon by the time Roman deems himself sober enough to drive and we say goodbye to Rick and Beverly with the portrait and a bottle of chenin blanc in tow. As they wave to us from the driveway, it's hard to believe my husband has driven here once a month for years, though I have never seen the place until now, or that we may never see the two of them together like this again.

As we veer down the hill, the lights begin to flicker on in the tasteful pastel houses with the tasteful water-saving lawns and the tasteful well-meaning people in them, marking the fact that we are all another day closer to the grave. I study Roman's face, trying to gauge if he's the kind of upset where he'll lock himself in our tiny office and read Raymond Chandler with our cat on his lap or if he'd rather watch *Bar Rescue* while holding my hand and pounding Rick's wine. I know I belong in a ring of hell for selfish people, because even then I hope he's the first kind of upset so I can squirrel away a few hours on my novel before bedtime.

We manage to snag a parking spot not too far from our apartment but we don't get out of the car right away. Roman puts his head on the steering wheel, and when he lifts it his eyes are wet. He turns to me and says, "You're right. I've been such an idiot. What, I want to put off kids because I need to finish my fucking dissertation? Make more money? Live in a bigger apartment? God, none of that means a thing. Let's do this, Oksana. I'm game if you are. Let's start a fucking family." He gestures at the empty street and adds, "I mean, what else is there?"

It takes me a moment to realize that his question is not rhetorical. I turn to him in the sudden darkness and tell him I don't know.

MOTHERLAND

As Mama and my brother and I wait for our driver outside the airport, I try to imagine where my grandmother's atheist Soviet soul has gone. I am slightly delirious from the twelve-hour flight to Kiev, most of which I spent staring at the seat in front of me, willing myself not to puke and waiting for Baba to pop up and declare, "Surprise! I'm not dead in the least, you fools!" I decide she is in the swaying poplar trees by the highway, scowling down on us.

"Oksana," I say aloud in my best Baba voice, "you come all the way to your ancestral home and don't even think to comb your hair? And Misha—foolish boy, why are you dressed like a vagabond? Tanya, why do you wear no makeup at all; don't you know the features tend to melt down the face with age? You are not a product of the first freshness, my dear."

"The more you go on, the less funny you are," Mama says. She looks cold and beautiful, streaks of white dancing through her dark hair.

"Do you guys think the Maidan is still fucked up?"

my brother asks, ignoring us. He is a junior at Brown, a Slavic studies and anthropology double major who does not believe there have been nearly enough revolutions. The Maidan is a huge plaza in the center of the city that was ravaged by bloodshed, fire, and smoke after protesters fighting to keep Ukraine close to the European Union instead of Russia set up camp there. But all the chaos ended four years ago, so I don't know what my brother expects to find.

"Dearest God I don't believe in," Mama says, shaking her head at us. "What have I done in a past life I don't believe in to raise such children? A comedian and a revolutionary! Groucho Marx and Karl Marx, I don't know which is worse. Where did I go wrong? Tell me, did I not give them enough to eat, put clothes on their back, offer the occasional encouragement. . . ."

Mama is unmoored and husbandless too, having left my stepdad at home, while my almost-professor husband is interviewing in Tallahassee. My stepdad promised never to set foot in Kiev after he left, and though I have come to accept his and Mama's quiet love, his absence is a relief. He and my brother are constantly feuding, and it would only complicate things.

When the van pulls around, Mama tells my brother to help the driver load our luggage.

Misha rolls his eyes. "Long live the patriarchy," he says, pumping a fist in the air. "You're both capable of carrying your own luggage, but you think only a man can do it. What can I do that you can't? I've worked out, like, twice in my life."

I smack the back of his bushy idiot head. "Save it for your professors."

"Your mother is tired and your sister is expecting," says Mama. My pregnancy has made her nervous, conjuring her own pregnancy struggles, and she hardly lets me lift a finger.

My brother regards me as if he had forgotten this until now. "Right," he says, and he finishes loading the bags, though the driver does most of the work.

We are silent as we speed past the birch trees and highrises on the outskirts of the city. Normally Misha would scandalize Mama with stories of his college co-op antics and she would act horrified while being secretly amused, but they are not in the mood to clown around, though that is all I can think to do so I don't dissolve. It seems impossible that three days ago Baba's brother, Boris, called to tell us that her heart gave out in her sleep.

Baba had seemed fine when I'd skyped her the other week to tell her I was twelve weeks pregnant. Her hair was still dyed a fiery red and she wore a face full of makeup and complained about her latest suitor. I sported a sweatsuit and had been devoting my energy to being pregnant and finishing my novel by the end of my final semester at the Iowa Writers' Workshop. Baba regarded me as if she smelled something burning, so I braced myself for a thorough critique of my appearance.

"Imagine," she said. "A great-grandchild of mine born in Iowa. Ridiculous!"

"We'll speak Russian to the baby," I told her.

This made her cackle. "You—and Roman? What nonsense. You will send the child to Kiev every summer to visit his great-grandmother. There is no other way to do it, don't you see?"

The Mother Motherland, a monstrous steel statue of a woman lifting a gleaming sword and shield to the sky, looms before us on the opposite bank of the Dnieper River, which means we have almost arrived at Baba's. Misha and I have visited her several times since she returned to Kiev—though we haven't seen it since the revolution—while Mama only returned with us once a while back, though she had been the first of our family to return years before Baba, to bury her own mother. She had spent most of her return visit with us escaping Baba to see her cousin Marina. My grandmother was offended by her lack of attention and referred to Mama as Sappho. "Why is your mother spending so much time with that woman?" she had cried. "Those two have wandered off to the island of Lesbos!" Mama and I still laugh about it, though it stopped being so funny after my brother came out to me.

The driver drops us off in front of Baba's building. Instead of her boisterous brother, I see a leather-jacketed man standing near the entrance, sending smoke rings into the air. His hair and beard are as dark and lustrous as his jacket and he looks like he can lift up a car with one hand. We lock eyes as the last of the smoke rings dissolves over his head, and I wonder if I've finally fallen asleep. I don't realize he's here for us until he approaches.

"Valentin," he says, shaking Mama's hand first, then mine and Misha's. He's one of my grandmother's protégés from the Toastmasters Club—whenever she mentioned him, I pictured a younger boy, not a full-grown man. "I am sorry to meet under these circumstances," he says. "Your grandmother changed my life."

"For the better, I hope," I say in my battered Russian, and when he laughs I feel as if I have finally swallowed something that has been trapped in my throat for days.

"Enough," Mama tells me.

My brother looks up at the building. "It hasn't changed," he says.

I say, "Why would it?" We follow Valentin into the elevator, past the concierge, an old lady in a tiny booth watching a soap—we barely fit. He tells us that Baba's brother is up there, entertaining the guests. "He got caught up in a fit of singing," he explains. We smile politely and shrug and he turns to me. "Are you a singer, Oksana?" he asks as the elevator finally releases us.

"Not even in the shower," I tell him.

My brother has our father's rich voice, though he doesn't like to show it off. But Mama and I can't carry a tune to save our lives. I always wished I was a singer, not a writer—it would suit me better, being good at something I could show off to a crowd, basking in flagrant adoration instead of squirreling myself away with my sad novel, never knowing if I was any good.

The apartment hits me with its smell of Baba's lilac perfume and cigarettes. I hear Boris belting out the last notes of "Katiushka" before everyone bursts into applause. He is standing in my grandmother's living room, which is crammed with at least two dozen people, half of whom I have never seen before, who hover over endless bottles of vodka and overflowing bowls of salat Olivier and pickled vegetables and herring. Two of my aunt Alla's paintings hang in the room: her three-headed self-portrait and a whimsical painting of her father in a field with a fan of scythes floating behind him like the tail of a peacock.

"Tanya! Oksana! Misha!" Boris cries, bounding over to squeeze us all, coating my cheeks with sloppy kisses. He is a vain, stocky man with dyed black hair who stands with his chest puffed out like a bouncer. He looks my mother up and down and whistles. "Tanya—you haven't aged a day."

"It's good to see you, Borya," she says, batting him away. He is four years younger than Baba and an old flirt, a lifelong bachelor. Baba always said he had a cheerful disposition because he was just a baby when their father was purged and too young to remember World War II. Mama doesn't care much for Boris; she finds him frivolous.

Boris drags us around and introduces or reintroduces us to distant cousins and Baba's friends from her university and literary journal and Toastmasters, and I can't keep them straight, still feeling drugged from the flight and even foggier after meeting Valentin. The only friend of Baba's I remember well is Anatoly Petrovich, who died months after we met in Yalta. Mama gloms on to Cousin Marina fast and they are already in the corner, conspiring like criminals. Boris whispers rather provocatively to two of Baba's younger lady friends. It takes my brother about five seconds to find people his age—Marina's daughter, a Goth teen also named Oksana, among them—and he's already holding court, gesturing madly, speaking a much cleaner Russian than mine. Though he is American born, he has studied the language and history of our country, while I care more for the blue of the Dnieper River, savor the way white fatty *salo* melts in my mouth, and feel desperate longing whenever my husband and I overhear someone on the street speaking our first language.

Valentin pays my grandmother a moving tribute—he is a businessman who had little meaning in his life after his wife left him, until Baba met him at a wedding and roped him into joining the Toastmasters. After enough people speak, I realize it is my turn. Mama is exempt because she's not Baba's blood, and my brother is considered too young and too American.

I raise my glass and ramble about how I can't believe Baba's gone, while I scramble for a way to define her. "She could laugh at anything," I say. I describe the tiny cicada-infested matchbox of a room Baba and I had to share back in Gainesville, Florida, my family's first home in America. I say that when she was feeling particularly spirited before bedtime, she would ruffle my hair, flick off the light, and say, "Another day closer to oblivion, here we go!" Her sporting declaration terrified me at first, but after a while I didn't mind it. I appreciated that she never sugarcoated anything with me or treated me like a child. "In fact," I say, "she made oblivion sound kind of fun."

This elicits a few nervous laughs and I drink my splash of wine in one gulp, because when you are toasting the dead, you don't clink glasses, something I learned half a lifetime ago, after Papa died. But I have much more to learn, apparently. Mama yanks me aside as I am filling my plate with all the pickled vegetables I can find.

I expect her to tell me that I have been overexerting myself and that it's time to rest, but she criticizes me for something else entirely. "You used the wrong word for 'dead' in your speech," she tells me. I'd said *pogibla* instead of *umerla,* which I'd thought meant the same thing, but apparently *pogibla* does not just mean "passed away" but "died under tragic circumstances," which is not the case.

"Of course Russians would have a word just for that," I say.

Mama nods, not without pride. "A rich language," she says.

I end up on the balcony with Valentin as the guests trickle out, facing a row of new apartments and an abandoned factory with bullet-riddled walls and shattered windows. He offers me a cigarette and I am tempted but remember my baby, though I don't mention it. Nor do I mention the nagging nausea that never leads to actual puking, my sore-as-fuck breasts, the fatigue pushing down on me that is even worse thanks to jet lag. This man is all dark-ness, simmering before me like a stack of hot coals, noth-ing like my Roma, who is sinewy and blue eyed and light haired. My dear husband, who is on a campus interview this very moment in the hopes of securing a better life for our growing family. I start rambling, not about my hus-band but about how much colder it is in Iowa, and Valen-tin's lips curl into a smile.

"What?" I say.

"Nothing," he answers. "I just like hearing you talk, Oksanka Amerikanka."

He is flirting but my accent is shit, my vocabulary no better than a seven-year-old's. My husband's is even worse because he's second gen—on the rare times he has to speak Russian to interact with relatives, he sounds like a five-year-old girl we call Romana, his alter ego. Still, we are determined to speak only Russian to our child, to pass down the dregs of our heritage even if Baba had thought it was impossible.

I am self-conscious now, watching Valentin watching my lips, and I try to think of the least sexy thing I can say.

"What kind of a businessman are you?"

He shrugs the question away. "Import-export," he says with a fatalistic nod. "And you, I know, are a writer. What are you writing about?"

I sigh, but it's easier to go on than I expected. I tell him I'm working on a novel based on the period Baba and her family spent in Kiev under Nazi occupation, dark years filled with heartbreak and intrigue, something I've been writing for over five years now, asking Baba about it during our Skype chats without telling her why. And now I stare out at the foggy, car-filled city and find it hard to imagine that most of its buildings and citizens were destroyed during the war, while my grandmother lived to tell about it. This is the first time I have told someone who isn't my husband what my novel is about, but there's no reason to keep the secret anymore.

"I wanted to show her a draft when I finished," I say. "I'm almost done. It was supposed to be a surprise." I don't bother wiping my face.

"I assure you it would have made no difference. She was proud of you anyway," he says.

"She was?" I picture her scowling at me over Skype.

"She was always bragging about you—more than ever when you began your prestigious writing program. Anytime you sent her a story, she would make all the Toastmasters read it. In fact, I have something to show you in that regard."

"You do?"

I follow him to Baba's bedroom, where Mama insisted I sleep. Being alone with him in a room with a bed in it— even if it's the bed where my grandmother died, red sheets to match her hair—makes me the slightest bit excited, perhaps heralding the return of the sex drive I have been awaiting since I started my second trimester two weeks ago. He smells like a hint of sweat from a long day, a scent that mingles with my grandmother's perfume. I have never cheated on Roman—I have never crossed the line, but I have tiptoed on it with my eyes closed a few times, and if a breeze had hit me I might have toppled like Lenin's statue during the revolution four years ago. We stare at each other and I forget why we're there until he opens a desk drawer, scans it, and hands me a notebook.

"She had a surprise for you too," he says. He puts a hand on my shoulder, tips his head, and says he will come by tomorrow.

It takes me a minute to understand what I'm reading— the words, which I have to whisper aloud because that's the only way I read Russian, are strangely familiar. Baba had translated my poems and stories into Russian, and who knows what for. Though she had taken quite a bit of poetic license, it amused me to see. In my poem about Baba and Boris and me getting drunk on the shores of the Dnieper on my first return to Kiev, she had cut out the last three lines, about me puking in the river, ending the poem with an image of the sun setting over the city.

Seeing what Baba has done to my poem reminds me of an anecdote Mama loved, one of many featuring a Jewish couple named Sara and Abram. Sara tells her friend, "You know, everybody loves Pavarotti, but I've heard the man in action and find him to be quite overrated. He rasps, he quavers, he bellows, he sings completely out of tune!" Her friend asks, "Oh, you have heard Pavarotti sing?" "No, no," Sara says. "But Abram did, and he sang it over for me."

I climb into Baba's deathbed after Mama and my brother fall asleep in the living room. Her bedroom has orange wallpaper, a small desk, and a dresser piled with Baba's necklaces and makeup. On the walls, there is a photo of Misha and me, one of Papa, and Papa's sister's painting of the Dnieper River that Baba had hung up in our Florida bedroom long ago. A stack of romance novels sits on her nightstand, a bookmark sticking halfway out of the one on top.

I imagine Baba falling asleep in this bed just days before, never to wake up. Did she feel the void eating her up? Somebody must have changed the sheets, though the bed still smells like Baba. Swaddled by my grandmother's scent, I am a kid in Florida again, staring at the dark ceiling as if this night is my last on earth. The edges of the world slip away from me.

I miss Roma. He never made the journey to the ancestral home with me, though he had met Baba when she flew out to California for our wedding. She liked him the moment he gave her his coat on a not-cold evening; he instantly liked her when she looked him up and down and said, "He's a bit too handsome, in my opinion, but otherwise he'll do."

I never asked her what she meant: A bit too handsome for me? A bit too handsome in general? I add this to the list of things I will never know. I call my husband.

"Oksana," he says, picking up after one ring, and I feel a warmth rush over me.

"I'm here," I say.

"How is it? How are you?"

"Depressing. Weird. I miss you."

"The baby?"

"Hanging in."

"I wish I could be there with you."

"Me too," I say, though we don't mean the same thing right then. If he were beside me, I wouldn't want him to hold me and hear me wail about my grandmother. I would want him to fuck my brains out. I am desperate to feel alive again. Though since I got pregnant, during the few times I've actually felt like fucking, he's stopped being fun in bed and has been all gentle, saying things like, "I don't want to scare the little girl," leading me to say, "Or boy. And go harder." Roma wants a little girl who will love her father madly, and I want a boy to spoil, like my brother. In fact, he doesn't want a boy to the point where he wouldn't come inside me from behind when we were trying to conceive because he claimed it would raise our chances of having one.

"How was the interview?" I say.

He sighs. "I think it went well, but there's just no saying. They'll call in a few days." I am grateful he doesn't say he wishes I was back home to calm his nerves. "Tallahassee is kind of a dump," he says. "I don't know if we can live there."

"We can live anywhere," I say. "But let's not get ahead of ourselves. You need to rest up for tomorrow. They'll love you in Colorado too. Everybody does."

"Even you?" he says, trying to be playful, but I can feel

the edge to his voice. He knows how I can be, even pregnant and grieving, because he can be that way too.

"Especially me. Though I hope they don't love you quite as much as I do," I say.

"I can't make any promises," he says. "Take care of yourself, all right?"

I flick off the lights and get under the deathbed covers and stare at the ceiling and hope my almost-child is resting better than I will. Though I've always wanted kids, since I got pregnant all I can think about is what I'm giving my boy life for—just to bumble around for a bunch of decades at best, get his heart broken, send me and my husband to our graves, and then return to dust himself, with maybe a few transcendent nights in between, moments when he feels infinite and like he's never going to die? This doesn't strike me as a very nice thing to do to somebody who didn't ask for it, not at all.

"Good night, little one," I say, resting a hand on my stomach. "Another day closer to existence, here you go."

Boris returns the next morning to help go through Baba's things—lipstick on his collar, shameless man that he is—though we insist we only want a few photos. He keeps trying to push memorabilia from Baba's travels on us, along with her fur coats and my late aunt's paintings, but I don't have any use for those things. I hope to get through it all as quickly as possible and check out the Maidan with my brother and Valentin, who called earlier, offering to take us around. But there is no end in sight with the boxes.

I spot an image of a teenaged, suited Papa with closely cropped hair, shaking Brezhnev's hand onstage to accept a Math Olympics gold medal. Brezhnev's eyes are closed. In another box, there's a stack from Papa's choir days, where the boys are stern and lined up in rows with starched shirts and obedient expressions, Anatoly Petrovich grimacing in the center. Then there's a photo of Baba at about the age I am now, looking unabashedly happy in a tall grassy field with Papa in his underwear, holding a sickle. I had only ever seen the version of this photo containing Papa and his father; I had never considered that Baba must have taken the picture and had been right there all along.

Boris puts an arm around my brother and begs him to sing at my grandmother's funeral reception. "You simply must," he says. "It's not a question."

"It is a question, and the answer is no," my brother says, impressing me by his facility with the language.

"But your grandmother said you have a beautiful voice, like your father."

"He does," Mama insists, but she's only half there, sifting, sifting.

"What am I supposed to sing?" Misha says.

"Your grandmother's favorite Soviet songs. Don't worry, there are a number of us singing, you won't be alone," he says. Then he brings in another box tower and begins singing.

> Dark is the night, only bullets whistle over the steppe,
> Only the wind hums in the wires, the stars flicker dimly

In the dark night, my love, I know you are not sleeping,
Near our child's crib, you secretly wipe away a tear

"Dark Is the Night" is a World War II ballad meant to
tug at my brother's heartstrings—the lonely soldier missing his beloved—but it does no good. When I first heard
it, I had latched on to the beloved part and thought it was
a love song, until Papa told me otherwise. Hearing this
old song in my native land makes me feel relieved to finally be home again but also devastated, because I won't
ever have a reason to return now. But my brother is un-
moved when the song is over.

"My Russian isn't even that good," he says.

"Good enough for singing," says Boris. "Your grandmother wanted this—she made this plan years ago. She
wanted no sadness, lots of drink, and for you to be up
there."

My brother shakes his head. "I'm not really a per-
former."

"You will rise to the challenge," says Boris. Then he
changes tactics. He pats my brother on the back and says,
"Handsome boy. Do you have a girlfriend?"

"No girlfriend," my brother says.

Boris chuckles. "That's the right spirit, boy. Better to
play the field, handsome boy like you. I was handsome
once, believe it or not, and I still play the field!"

My brother is not amused. "I won't sing," he says.

Mama does not look up and continues sifting through
the photos. Misha's sexuality is a subject she and I have
never broached, though I'm pretty sure she wouldn't be
happy about it. She might at least suspect it, given that he

wears my scarves and hangs out mostly with girls, but I don't know how many of those cultural markers are identifiable to a Soviet woman.

I'm suddenly pissed off at the injustice of it all, Mama showing us her old wedding photos and Boris joking about girlfriends while Misha has to pretend he's straight. I want to strangle Boris, though he doesn't even know what he's done.

When he leaves, Mama shakes her head and says, "Silly man."

"What makes him so silly? Would he be less silly if he settled down and had a few kids?" I say, and I am surprised by my own sharpness.

"Maybe so, but that's not why I can't stand the man," Mama says. "He always took such advantage of your grandmother. She paid for his dinners, his whores, his gambling debts."

"I thought they were great friends," my brother says.

"She thought so too. She had a big heart. A big, foolish heart. She couldn't resist her baby brother," Mama says. "And neither can you, Oksana." She tousles Misha's hair and says, "But your brother does not use his powers for evil."

My brother rolls his eyes and pulls away. "As far as you know," he says, and a mischievous smile flickers on his face. He has been given permission to scandalize Mama, and he has been holding back for too long: He tells her about making hummus laced with molly for everyone in his co-op, a birthday party featuring a piñata filled with whip-its, a festival where everyone got naked and threw condiments at each other, and a polyamorous roommate who has five different girlfriends who all claim to love him and one another.

"An education," Mama declares, shaking her head, but he has made her smile. As long as my brother doesn't mention fucking dudes, they are as thick as thieves, much closer than she and I can ever be. She pinches his cheek and adds, "I did not say you use your powers for good either, little fool. Only silliness."

I am surprised to find icons on Valentin's dashboard, but I shouldn't be. Though Baba was an atheist to the bitter end, many people got religious after the Soviet Union collapsed, desperate for something new to believe in. Valentin has snipped off the seatbelts in his car for what he says are cosmetic purposes and drives about 150 miles an hour, blasting techno; I guess his icons will save us in the event of an accident.

The square looks just as it did before the revolution, free of tires or tents or sandbags or burning wood. Just people shopping and getting off the Metro and staring into the abyss of their phones. I imagine Baba's soul shining through the spire at the center of the square. "It looks like you have finally made an effort with your looks!" she would tell me. "But that does not mean you have to be a whore, my darling."

The only difference I see is the memorial to the hundred who died fighting for Ukraine's independence, their photographs stacked up in neat rows like tombstones, surrounded by flowers, candles, and religious ephemera. My brother is visibly disappointed by how orderly the Maidan looks; he was hoping for more remnants of the bloody revolution.

"It looks fine," he says, surly boy.

"We were able to rebuild quickly. Thank God," Valentin says rather sternly, and I can't blame him for not indulging us American rubberneckers. He lights a cigarette.

"Where do you stand?" my brother asks him, and I want to shut him up. The last thing I need is a political discussion, but off they go, and I hope I am not asked for my opinion. Almost everything I know about Euromaidan comes from one Netflix documentary, and I don't like to talk politics. I'm just heartbroken that the Russians have taken Crimea, because of my fond memories of the summer I spent in Yalta with Baba.

I watch Misha and Valentin zip back and forth and realize my brother is flirting. Misha is convinced half of our male family friends are closeted, but this time, in this place, it's a dangerous assumption, and I hope he doesn't take it too far. Valentin tells my brother he's for Ukraine, the Russians are pigs, and Misha—who would rather die than be on the side he's expected to be on—says the Ukrainians are no angels either.

Valentin laughs. "Who among us is an angel?"

He does not wait for an answer, just puts out his cigarette and turns slightly away. He excuses himself shortly afterward, when his phone buzzes.

My brother cracks up and digs his fingers into my forearms, narrowing his eyes in an imitation of a smoldering gaze. "Who among us is an angel?" he says.

I push him away. "Incorrigible boy."

"There's a chance he wants me, Sana," he says. "Don't deny it."

I try to distract him instead of discouraging him. "Incorrigible boy," I say again, and add, "yet I hope to have a boy just like you. Next month we'll know if it's a boy or a girl."

My brother is unimpressed. "But when do you find out if it's gay or straight?" he says, and I smack him, hard, and he cackles.

Then I gaze out on the square, the bleak sunlight softening the gray buildings surrounding it. "Baba cursed the Russians when they came," I say. "But mostly because the fighting kept her from strolling outside."

Misha has tears in his eyes, and I didn't mean to do that to him. I am relieved to see our guide returning to us. We had promised Mama to pick up food and booze for the next round of friends and relatives, so we head to a store a few blocks away. Valentin smokes again and I reach out to dissolve his perfect rings. Once I have him to myself—Misha banters with the meat-counter lady—I grab his arm.

"Tell me—why did she translate my stories?"

He laughs. "She was always trying to get them into her journal. They kept getting turned down. The editors said, 'We suspect the original author may have some talent, but we can't say the same about the translator.'"

I laugh too. "What a waste of time. I can't believe she did all that without telling me."

"I don't think she saw it as a waste of time."

I grab a few thick Russian yogurts just for myself, treats that had always waited for me in Baba's fridge, even though they aren't quite sour or sweet enough to appeal to me in my current state. After we check out, I put three bags in each hand, but my brother grabs them before I can protest and says, "You shouldn't." So much for the patriarchy. Valentin watches the exchange and then appraises me. He holds my gaze and nods at me slowly but repeatedly, like he is deeply agreeing with something profound I am saying, but I haven't said anything he could be saying "yes" to.

Mama and Misha and I bundle up and step out to explore the city on our free day. I have never visited Kiev in winter and am used to the flood of green over the hills and the slopes and the riverbanks instead of the sad scraggly trees and flat gray sky. We cross the Dnieper to the left bank, where I grew up, and regard the *Mother Motherland* statue once more. She is terrifying and hypnotic, dwarfing the ancient gold-domed churches below her.

"Symbol of oppression," my brother says.

"Soviet nostalgia," I say.

Mama shakes her head, displeased with our observations. "Eyesore," she declares.

Sifting through the rubble of her youth, Mama leads us to a bridge a few blocks from her high school, keeping a hand on my back as if I'm planning on taking a spill at any moment.

"This is where your father and I locked eyes," she tells us. I have heard versions of the story before. "He loved to cut school and smoke under this bridge. When I walked by one time after class, he gave me this—manly look. He had a reputation for being a bit of a rogue, you see. But against my better judgment, I was smitten."

"This bridge?" Misha says.

It's a nothing bridge, just some wooden planks hanging over a dirt path surrounded by trees and brambles. I picture a young, rascally Papa smoking under it, tufts of brown hair falling into his eyes. A Papa not much younger than Misha.

"Your father was so brooding, so handsome. You should have seen him . . ." Mama says.

"Gross," says my brother.

"Little simpleton, it was a beautiful thing," Mama says. She squeezes my arm to imply I know what she means. If only she knew what I have been thinking. My parents' courtship was indeed a beautiful thing, even if it is sad to think of it now. Though what dominates my mind is not their long-ago love but yesterday's outing—Valentin in the driver's seat next to me, his jaw firm as he navigated us through the city, the edges of our hands touching near the gearshift.

"A beautiful thing," Mama says again as we turn away from the bridge.

"Sorry if that was depressing," my brother tells her.

"Silly children," she says. "It was a happy memory. Besides, how can I be sad when I have you two? It was all worth it, don't you see? Oh, dear Oksana, you are going to love being a mother, I just know it," she tells me. Then she looks at my brother, and looks away.

That evening Mama and Misha have dinner with her cousin and Goth Oksana—"Off to the island of Lesbos," Mama says with a wry smile—and after Valentin and I stroll down the bank of the Dnieper, we end up at his place. He lives on the top floor of what Roman and I call a doucheplex, a shiny apartment with shiny counters and floor-to-ceiling windows, which looks like it was built yesterday. Valentin asks if I'd like some wine, to call my bluff, but I say yes, and he drives in the corkscrew and watches me and waits and I do nothing, so he pours the wine and extends a glass in my direction and I take a big hearty sip.

"Why didn't you tell me you were pregnant?" he says.

"I didn't?" I say. I put down the glass. "I thought I mentioned it."

He gives me the smile you smile at a liar. "It wouldn't have scared me off."

"I am going to love being a mother," I tell him.

"I don't doubt it for a second."

I run a hand down his arm and lose my footing, feel myself dipping into the abyss. Why the fuck not? He's hot, he's here, and I might even like him a little bit. I'm tiptoeing over a telephone wire and the night is dark, the wind and bullets hum and whistle past my ears, and I look down and trip, trip, trip, as if I am the lonely soldier of "Dark Is the Night." All it takes for me to tumble isn't a declaration of love or the feeling that this man is clutching my heart but having this sexy near-stranger stroke my face as he says, "I want you" in my native language. Nobody has ever said this to me in Russian, and it stabs my soul.

He kisses me against his douche counter—his tongue is smoky and warm—and whirls me to his bed and he's on top of me, lifting up my dress, looking up like he's waiting for me to tell him to stop while knowing I won't. I arch my back and let him go down on me and think about the baby in there, wondering if he is confused and if he can see a little foreign tongue darting toward him, a less poetic stabbing, but, fuck, I feel like all the bloated stale air that has been coursing through my body for months has finally been let out, and it doesn't take me long to come. Valentin is serious when he emerges and wipes his mouth like he is at a business dinner.

I won't fuck him, but I return the favor—eyes closed after I am reminded of what it's like to face the dick of a man you don't love—and amazingly I come again when he comes in my mouth, and then I smooth down my dress and feel like it is all a fair exchange. I freshen up in the bathroom and study myself in the mirror. I put a hand on my slightly swollen belly, thinking I love my baby more than ever, because now we have a secret. In the moment I pictured the child cringing at the sight of Valentin's trespassing tongue, I became 100 percent sure he was a boy. I just know it. A baby boy like my brother. I will love him until I die.

Then I rush to puke in the toilet, the release I have been waiting for for months now, and it feels fucking fantastic.

Valentin drops me off—those damn icons stare me down the whole way home and I stare right back—and I am relieved the apartment is quiet and dark.

But there's a light coming from the kitchen. My brother is sitting at the tiny table, staring into the blinding light of his laptop. There is no avoiding him. He stands to face me, the computer glowing behind him.

"What is the matter with you?" he says. "I mean, really. Don't you get that you're supposed to be the fucking normal one around here?"

"Straight isn't normal," I say. "And since when are you

so into monogamy? What happened to all your free-love polyamorous bullshit?"

He ignores my questions, which are beside the point. He takes a step away from me as his screen goes black, retreating into the darkness. With his bushy hair and thick brows, he looks like a grown man; more specifically, he looks like my father. He is my father. How much fucking wine did I have? He is Papa shortly before his death, tired and coming home late from work, so late that I am already getting ready for bed, so late that the only reason he may see for living is Mama and my brother and, of course, me.

"I don't get you," my father says. "You're finally finishing your stupid book. You're finally having a stupid baby. What else do you want?"

I back away from my father, toward my deathbed. I laugh at the enormity of all the other things I want and settle on just one.

"I wish I could sing," I tell him.

Baba was cremated, but we still go to the cemetery to pay our respects. She gets to have it both ways, her ashes in an urn and a tombstone next to her long-dead husband and daughter. We stand before the plot with her portrait etched on the tombstone, one from her younger days, when everyone was alive and she was hip and wore tortoiseshell glasses. The cemetery is bleak and endless, crammed with statues and portraits of the deceased. Vines crawl over the untended graves, but Baba has kept our family plots in top shape. She must have been there recently, because there are bouquets of roses on her husband's and daughter's graves. Baba had leaned her daughter's painting of Kiev's Mariinsky Park against her tombstone. She preferred the earlier, simpler paintings of Kiev to Aunt Alla's later experimental work, and I couldn't help but agree.

"I've changed my mind," I say. "I'll take home Aunt Alla's painting of the Dnieper."

"That's wonderful, my darling," says Mama, squeezing my hand. "Kiev has always been close to your soul too. Your grandmother would have loved for you to have it."

I didn't want the painting because of the river. I wanted it because I wanted to remember the way Baba would stare off at it before bed when we shared a room in Florida. But there was no explaining that.

Something occurs to me then. "Mama," I say, "don't you want to visit your own mother's . . ."

She shakes her head. "What for, dear child? She's not there, don't you see?" She looks away, but I don't let go. My brother has wandered off, inspecting the nearby graves.

"Who was Yaroslava? Someone from the war?" I say.

"Pardon?"

"Your mother. She always called me 'darling Yaroslava.' I thought it was someone she knew when she was a kid in the war."

Mama laughs heartily. "Why did you think that, silly? No, no, Yaroslava was the washerwoman in our building when I was growing up. She had the most generous cleavage!"

The discussion is closed before I have a chance to decide whether I'm glad I asked.

A handful of Baba's mourners begin to trickle into the cemetery—there will be a livelier crowd at the reception.

Valentin is present, though unchanged toward me, as if
we had simply completed a business transaction, import-
export.

Boris holds Baba's ashes and gives a short speech, and
then he turns to my brother and me. "Though Kiev was
Sveta's home, America treated her well," he says. "She
loved her years in Florida and said her days at the beach
with her family were some of her happiest. To that end,
she'd like her ashes to be scattered in the Florida ocean,
though she specified that she'd like them to be on the Atlantic side, not the Gulf, so the waves will carry her away."

I realize this is my cue to take the urn and I do, so
stunned I don't even worry about dropping it.

I tell Valentin I will see him later. Maybe the line I
have been tiptoeing on is not the telephone wire from
"Dark Is the Night" but the state of Florida; I am Baba's
granddaughter, after all, and if I were tiptoeing across the
long state, I would prefer to fall to the Atlantic side over
the Gulf too.

As the van takes Mama and Misha and me back to
Baba's, my brother turns toward the window with his
arms crossed.

"I won't sing," he says again.

Mama's eyes are fluttering shut; she has had more than
she can take—and she knows what I have done, though
she will never mention it—so I am an unlikely person to
give him a pep talk. I don't have the leverage to tell him
to make this small concession for his family.

"If you sing, I'll take Baba's ashes to Florida myself," I
say. "Seems like a pretty good deal, don't you think?"

"What makes you think I don't want to take her ashes
to Florida?"

I shrug and say, "All right, then." But I'm weirdly pissed he wants to go, not because that was my gambling chip, but because I don't want him to encroach.

I don't realize Mama has been listening until the van drops us off back at the apartment. "You think you two will truly go to Florida? With the baby on the way?" she says. "You don't have to let your grandmother boss you around anymore, you know. Dearest God I don't believe in," she adds, "what have I done to deserve such sentimental children?" She goes inside, and my brother and I remain standing under the awning, facing a row of poplars.

"Don't sing for Baba," I tell him. "She's not here."

"I know, I know," he says, rolling his eyes. "Do it for the living, right?"

"No, no," I say. "Do it for yourself. You don't want to regret it later."

We tilt our heads and stare at the tall, funny-looking leafless trees I am convinced contain part of my grandmother's soul, something I refuse to dismiss, even if I don't believe in an afterlife. My brother squints at the trees and I imagine what he sees. *Tyrannical bastions. Sad attempt to counteract climate change. Row of cocks.* I put an arm around him.

"So fucking pretty," he says.

I call Roman before the reception and he has good news: Right after he finished his interview in Boulder, he received an offer from Florida State. He told the University of Colorado about the offer and by the time he got off the plane in Iowa, he had an offer from them too. Hearing him say my name and discuss these normal matters makes me want to stab myself a little bit for what I've done. I eat my creamy strawberry yogurt instead.

"Can you believe it?" he says. He sucks in his breath, awaiting my verdict.

"Which one do you want more?"

"I don't know," he says, and he runs through the pros and cons again, ending with the fact that Florida was kind of a dump.

"I've never been to Colorado," I say.

He laughs. "I knew you would say that."

"But I have fond memories of Florida . . ." I say. I consider mentioning Baba's ashes, but I suppose that shouldn't be a deciding factor, or even a selling point. "I guess it doesn't really matter," I say.

"Not as long as we're together."

"I love you," I say. "You decide." Then I add, "I can't believe it. Our kid will grow up in Florida or Colorado."

"She'll still be a Russian girl at heart," he says, switching to Russian. He almost never uses his Romana voice when it's just us, and it makes me choke up. He has a deep, commanding voice in English, but he sounds like a little bitch in Russian and we both know it.

I see how absurd it is to think that he and I can pass our language down to our child. Why should we bother—how can I expect to teach a child to live with a Russian soul when I don't even know all the words for dying? Us teaching someone Russian is as bad as Abram singing Pavarotti to Sara.

"I guess you're right," I tell him in our first tongue. "I guess he will be."

"A Russian girl at heart," he says again.

The reception is at a restaurant a few blocks from Baba's, a place where I had attended her seventieth-birthday celebration. That evening, she had worn a glittery silver pantsuit and danced the night away, dragging her friends and relatives and me onto the dance floor. She had even tried to set me up with one or two of her Toastmasters, but they didn't hold a candle to Valentin. "My Oksana is a writer," she had said, whipping me around, sloshing cognac on my dress. "Coming all the way from America to see her grandmother! Tell them about your stories, dear girl!"

I've changed into a more vibrant blue number Baba would have approved of because it shows a bit of my now-impressive cleavage—I left her urn in her living room and patted the top before we left like she'd been a good, good girl. I walk to the restaurant with difficulty, because Mama said the shoes I had planned to wear were too casual even for a pregnant woman; my swollen feet were too small for Baba's heels, but I squeezed into them anyway. The hall is crammed with chilled appetizers and guests speaking in hushed tones and a table near the bar with a picture of Baba—on a Florida beach, wearing a visor—in which she is positively smirking, getting one over on all of us.

Behind the table, there's the small stage where the men will perform. Uncle Boris has cornered my brother and is gesturing wildly, but I do not rescue the poor boy. Instead, I listen to about a dozen people I have never met or only vaguely recognize praising my grandmother and finally manage to escape outside with Mama, who has suddenly decided to take up smoking.

"What's this?" I say.

She says, "Your grandmother did it right. She started to slow down and decided that was it, she wouldn't be a burden to others. If I smoke a bit, drink even more, walk a little less, you'll be lucky to find yourself in the same situation one day. I refuse to go out like my own poor mother. I promise you won't be schlepping to the nursing home to see me drooling in diapers, no sir." I consider mentioning that hopefully Sergei will be by her side but don't bother. The women in our families have always outlived the men.

"That is extremely comforting," I say.

"As it should be, little idiot." I start to tell her we're moving to Colorado or Florida over the summer, but she is distracted. "Your grandmother was a clown, but she had a big heart," Mama says. "Even that Sappho business—she was just hurt because I was not spending more time with her."

"She could have phrased it a bit differently," I say, but I don't disagree.

"Yes, well, she had her way of doing things." Mama looks around to make sure we are alone. "Imagine if she had lived to learn the truth about your brother," she says. "She would have gotten a kick out of it, I think."

I watch her cigarette smoke drifting into the sky so I don't fall over.

"You mean—"

"Your mother is not blind."

"You should talk to him."

"Oh, he will talk to me eventually. . . ." A fog has settled over the street and I can't see a thing. Mama looks toward the hall, where the voices grow louder, more reckless with drink and memory. She says, "I could have given you more love, but it wasn't easy, not when we were all under one roof. The two of you in the house, draining my energy, laughing everything off and doing whatever the hell you wanted while I was trying not to blow my brains out! It was too much for me. You were like two drops of water; it was unbearable."

"Me and Misha?"

"No, no, silly one. You and your brother are not alike—he's a sensitive creature. You and your grandmother. It was awful—the two of you are exactly the same, don't you see?"

"I do," I say, though I haven't considered it until now.

"Two stubborn comedians," she declares. "Desperate for love."

I have more questions for her, but then my brother steps out and shakes his head at us for avoiding the festivities. He takes a drag of our mother's cigarette before extinguishing it with his shoe. In his dark suit and combed-back hair, the dear little idiot looks wildly grown up, even a bit tired of living already. He doesn't care to stand with Mama and me and contemplate the cold foggy street of our former home; he's fussing with his suit, though it fits him perfectly. Then he clears his throat, preparing to sing, and nods at the restaurant. Come on, let's go, he says as he guides us to the door, come inside already, come on, everything's about to start.

ACKNOWLEDGMENTS

I must have done something really extraordinary in a past life to deserve knowing so many incredible people in this one.

First, my teachers. My high school teachers Carolyn Green and Bohdanna Vitvitsky showed me what books could do. My college professors Christina Askounis, Faulkner Fox, and Melissa Malouf made me think pursuing a career as a writer was not completely insane. At UC Davis, Pam Houston, Lucy Corin, Lynn Freed, and Yiyun Li took my fresh-out-of-undergrad work seriously well before anyone should have, and continued to help me years after I left their orbit. At the Iowa Writers' Workshop, Paul Harding, Ethan Canin, Charlie D'Ambrosio, and Sam Chang challenged me with good cheer. Sam also convinced me to drop everything and move across the country to Iowa City, which changed my life forever and made this book possible.

Oksana would be helpless without my classmates at Iowa. Claire Lombardo read far too many of my pages outside of class and encouraged me to keep going. Jason Hinojosa asked hard questions. Mack Basham read my prose with a poet's eye. Regina Porter made one statement—about Oksana being like her grandmother—that made me see my book in a new light. Lindsay Stern helped me put Oksana in the right hands and was a stellar friend, reader, and human being.

Other shout-outs: To John Lescroart, for your generous funding and belief that I was capable of writing a novel years before the fact. To Jan Zenisek, Deb West, and Connie Brothers for everything you do for the Workshop. To Amanda Kallis, for those glamorous author photos. To Adam Eaglin, who advised me every step of the way when I tried to introduce Oksana to the publishing world. To friends who have given insightful feedback on my earlier work and made my life so much richer: David Owen, Ashley Clarke, Richard Siegler, Noah McGee, and Megan Cummins.

My agent, Henry Dunow, has kept me afloat with his jokes and keen eye, and found my book a warm home at Spiegel & Grau. My editor, Cindy Spiegel, asked questions that made Oksana and her family come alive. Janet Wygal made sense of Oksana's trajectory, and Mengfei Chen was always there to answer my questions.

Many thanks to the editors who took chances on Oksana chapters early on: Emily Nemens at *The Southern Review*, Nyuol Lueth Tong at *McSweeney's*, Olivia Clare and Adam Clay at *Mississippi Review*, and Caitlin Horrocks at *The Kenyon Review Online*.

My family has been supportive far past the point of reason. Thank you, Mama, Papa, and Andrew, for your endless encouragement and cultural fact-checking—I'm pretty sure our happy family is not like any of the others. My grandmother Svetlana Yelchits believed in me while always giving her honest opinion, and I wish I could have heard her criticize this book. Wherever you are, Baba, I hope the cognac meets your high standards.

No words can express the love and gratitude I feel toward my husband, Danny. You make me feel like this is still just the beginning, in the best possible way.

ABOUT THE AUTHOR

MARIA KUZNETSOVA was born in Kiev, Ukraine, and moved to the United States as a child. She is a graduate of the Iowa Writers' Workshop, and *Oksana, Behave!* is her first novel.

mariakuznetsova.net
Twitter: @mashawrites